PENGUIN BOOKS

THE LOVE SECRETS OF DON JUAN

'Funny, sad, desperate . . . a great read. I whizzed through this novel. Horrifying, fascinating, psychologically compelling and very well-told' *Scotsman*

'Unnerving, thought-provoking, provocative' *Good Housekeeping*

'Compelling, very readable' *Sunday Telegraph*

'Angry, funny, invigorating. All-too-believable . . . to be relished' *Literary Review*

'An uncomfortably acute insight into contemporary life and a blackly funny howl of despair' *Metro*

'The jolliest book I've read in a long time. Lott delivers depth with lightness . . . packed with witty apercus that make you either pause and laugh, pause and consider your own life, or both. A book for every bedroom' *Spectator*

'Rather brave. Lott is very good at depicting male friendship' *Sunday Times*

'Scorching . . . wise and well-written' *Daily Telegraph*

'Readable, funny and humane , well-paced and well-observed. A war report from the battle of the sexes' *Times Literary Supplement*

D1385923

'It hits every emotional button of English urban male middle age by way of jolting flashbacks to teens, twenties and thirties. Laced with a devastatingly overarching irony' *The Times*

'Smile-a-page, comic, twinge-a-page, cringe-a-page, throw-yourself-under-the-next-train-a-page' *Sunday Herald*

'Meticulously honest and self-ridiculing. Lott deals dextrously with the maudlin melancholia of male mid-life crises and maps the terrain of damaged, sceptical loners and lovers with courage and clarity' *Uncut*

ABOUT THE AUTHOR

Tim Lott was born in Southall, Middlesex in 1956. He attended Greenford Grammar School and Harlow Technical College, after which he joined the local newspaper. He subsequently worked as a pop music journalist, a publisher and an entrepreneur. In 1983 he attended the London School of Economics as a mature student and achieved a degree in history and politics, after which he worked as a magazine editor and a TV producer before turning to writing. He is author of *The Scent of Dried Roses*, which was awarded the 1996 J. R. Ackerley Prize for Autobiography, *White City Blue*, winner of the 1999 Whitbread First Novel Award, and a second novel, *Rumours of a Hurricane*, which was shortlisted for the Whitbread novel of the year. All are published by Penguin. He is divorced, has three daughters and lives in north-west London.

tim lott

the love secrets of don juan

PENGUIN BOOKS

PENGUIN BOOKS

Published by the Penguin Group
Penguin Books Ltd, 80 Strand, London WC2R 0RL, England
Penguin Putnam Inc., 375 Hudson Street, New York, New York 10014, USA
Penguin Books Australia Ltd, 250 Camberwell Road, Camberwell, Victoria 3124, Australia
Penguin Books Canada Ltd, 10 Alcorn Avenue, Toronto, Ontario, Canada M4V 3B2
Penguin Books India (P) Ltd, 11 Community Centre, Panchsheel Park, New Delhi – 110 017, India
Penguin Books (NZ) Ltd, Cnr Rosedale and Airborne Roads, Albany, Auckland, New Zealand
Penguin Books (South Africa) (Pty) Ltd, 24 Sturdee Avenue, Rosebank 2196, South Africa

Penguin Books Ltd, Registered Offices: 80 Strand, London WC2R 0RL, England

www.penguin.com

Published by Viking 2003
Published in Penguin Books 2004
1

Copyright © Tim Lott, 2003
All rights reserved

The moral right of the author has been asserted

Typeset by Rowland Phototypesetting Ltd, Bury St Edmunds, Suffolk
Printed in England by Clays Ltd, St Ives plc

Except in the United States of America, this book is sold subject
to the condition that it shall not, by way of trade or otherwise, be lent,
re-sold, hired out, or otherwise circulated without the publisher's
prior consent in any form of binding or cover other than that in
which it is published and without a similar condition including this
condition being imposed on the subsequent purchaser

For Rachael

1

This is how it feels to be me.

Imagine yourself standing on the wrong side of a high brick wall erected across a pitted, unmaintained highway. Now imagine that highway is your life. It's raining. You don't have a ladder. And it's getting dark.

This is what being me has come down to. Who put me here? They did, of course.

Here – to wrench myself from the figurative into the literal – being this small bedsit in Acton, West London, lacking enough space to put up my six-year-old daughter for an overnight stay. Without enough money to buy her a trip to the cinema. Without enough stuffing in me to want her here anyway, since to see her father like this, so bitterly shrunken, cannot be a good thing. And I want good things for her. Not bad things – bad things like me.

They put me here. Bad things like me. When was this person conceived? This martyred, myopic, self-pitying shadow. Thinking the kind of thing they would think. Saying the kind of thing they would say.

Them. They. Me. I. How coy. And I have always

ventured to be straightforward. So allow me to be frank. Women put me here, capital 'W'.

Allow me to be still more frank. They didn't put me here by themselves. I helped. Bad choices, lack of courage, a wilful inability to see straight, selfishness, insensitivity.

Call me Spike. It's been my nickname since I was thirteen years old, although of course I wasn't aware of its Freudian implications then. Am I angry? I'm not angry. Not any more. I've been angry. God knows I have, angry enough to get myself the old Uzi sub, shin up that water tower and start popping away. Take that, honey. How's that for a big kiss, Toots? *Blam*. But I'm not angry, not any more. I'm just old. Old and sad, and I want the battle to end. I want us all to be friends. I want us to understand one another.

I'm old and sad and I'm surprisingly naïve.

My name is Daniel 'Spike' Savage, and I am a man.

(Pause for shouts, handclaps, 'Way to go Spike, thanks for sharing with the group.')

Middle-aged, although it shocks me to say as much. Sometimes nowadays I feel much older. I've been separated from my wife, Beth, for more than a year, so I'm single now in an impure way. My daughter, Poppy, has curly hair, almond-shaped eyes and a birthmark the shape of a frog on her elbow. I love her. Except that the word love feels too small for the emotion.

All the words ever, together, feel too small.

Professionally I'm successful-ish, but not so successful as I once was. I'm in advertising. I weave dreams around everyday objects. I blow things up to larger than their actual size.

Not so successful as I once was. That's putting it mildly. Once I worked for BMW, Gap, Levi's. Now my main account is for a low-budget chain of supermarkets, and a particularly foul-smelling brand of dog food, and toilet paper, the hard sort that they barely make any more. Imagine having to come up with a slogan for that.

What went wrong with my career? I stopped believing in it. It's like marriage. Once you stop believing in the product you're dead.

I've got a good family – my mum and dad, Iris and Derek, are still alive, albeit in a semi-retired sort of way, and my (also-divorced) older brother, Sam, is very much alive in an up-yours-I've-got-my-own-problems way. We get along as well as any family does. I like them, on the whole. Or, at least, I don't actively *dis*like them. Or, at least, not all the time.

Here on the westernmost drift of central London, the dull double-glazed terraces face out towards the lusher suburbia of Chiswick and Ealing. I used to live in Hammersmith, and before that Shepherd's Bush, so I'm gradually being edged outwards, by some impersonal historical force, towards the final oblivion that is Pitshanger, or beyond that, beyond West Ealing, to the town I grew up in: Hanwell. I can imagine myself sometimes in twenty, perhaps ten, years' time, sitting in some overlit café called the Coffee Pot, or the Copper Kettle, in a shopping mall, eating baked beans and smelling of packet soup, trying to engage reluctant strangers in violently inconsequential chat. If I am still writing advertisements then, it will be for chatlines and local Indian restaurants.

What else? Oh, yes, I'm lonely, and sometimes I'm desperate and want to die. But it passes.

Everything passes. Even the belief that everything passes, passes.

So next week, I'm going out on a date – in the hope that the collapse of my belief in the future will pass. I'm aware that you're meant to feel great about yourself before you start dating. I know that you only find someone when you're not looking, when you don't care. But that's unrealistic. Everybody cares. Nobody feels great about themselves. The thing is to learn to pretend. To learn to lie.

A date – with a woman. A *woman* and *me*. After all I've been through with them. After all the seconds, minutes, weeks, months and years of my life I've squandered, all the mental space that's been taken up, all the pain and chaos that's been generated.

There's an installation I once saw where the artist filled up a garden shed with junk, blew it up with explosives, photographed it, then re-created the whole thing as a static object – detritus flying everywhere but held still in space. That's where I'm at. At the still edges of a never-ending explosion. And still I try to turn back towards the unstable centre. As if seeking movement, entropy. Why do it? What's the point? Perhaps, at the very centre of the centre, there's stillness.

I am soon to be divorced, and I am going out on a date next week, and I'm no longer angry but old and sad, and above all wanting to learn, wanting to get it right, because I like this woman, I really do, even though she's – after all is said and done – a woman. But I can't afford to mess up again.

So before I embark on this relationship, I'm going to do what I should have done before I embarked on all my other relationships. I'm going to sit down and think about miracle product A: *women*. I'm going to sit down and think about miracle product B: *me*. I'm going to sit down and think of the chemistry that happens when products A and B combine, or collide, falling meteors burning on the edges of cold, black space. I'm going to use all my memory, all my accumulated history, all my resources, sorely depleted though they nowadays are.

This *thinking* may seem an extraordinarily obvious thing to do, and it may seem surprising that it hasn't occurred to me before. I've been getting some therapy lately, as middle-aged men do, and I have been told that I am an *extrovert*. This doesn't mean that I like to juggle walnuts or play practical jokes or burst into song at parties. It means that I, and I quote Terence, my therapist, 'construct my significant meaning structures out of exterior rather than interior events'. The interior world is much less real to me than the tangible, exterior world.

I think I've got that right. I wrote it down on the back of a sandwich wrapper, which was all I had at hand during the consultation, and I couldn't quite read it afterwards. It's not dysfunctional: half the world is like me. It's just a way of dealing with stuff. I'm not good at 'searching within'. My inner eye is myopic. I am practical. I see things primarily in terms of external appearances. I'm the sort of person who is inclined to say things like 'You think too much', or 'Why don't you just get on with it?', or 'If you can do something about it, do it. If you can't, forget about it.' It's all black and white to someone like me. Or it has been. But now, in almost-divorced middle age, as the world has unstoppably presented itself in myriad tones of grey, I can't sustain it. Reluctantly, haltingly, my thoughts have been turning inward. I have to say what I find there is . . . quite interesting. I won't put it any stronger than that. Interesting, and disturbing.

Thus, in the spirit of introversion, I'm going to do a

thing, a very conventionally male thing. I'm going to try to work it out, add it up. I'm going to gather the evidence, sift and sort it, analyse it and try to reach firm conclusions that can be extrapolated into real life. Then I'm going to try to apply that knowledge to a relevant situation, i.e., this forth-coming and aforesaid date with a woman and any sub-sequent relationship that may emerge from it.

Terence suggested this. He said it might be helpful to write these things down, everything that I was learning as I went along, this soul-mining. I've decided to take his advice.

I've got a flip-chart in my flat. A big white pad of paper on a frame that stands on splayed steel legs. I use it some-times to practise making pitches to clients. I work out the pros and cons, I give them the analyses, the way we target our markets, the possibilities for qualitative and quantitative research, I give the creative and demographic solutions to the problem of how to sell their lame, low-quality, half-baked products.

I've decided to use that flip-chart to solve my identity or, if you prefer, to refine my brand statement. I'm going to use it to note down the research findings as I uncover them. It might seem pointless, since I'm only making the presen-tation to myself, since I'm the client and the agency simul-taneously, the pitcher and the pitchee. But one of the things I have discovered about changing the way you are is that you have to ritualize, you have to externalize, to help stop your resolutions dissipating like mist.

A presentation is a kind of prayer.

By writing it all down, by codifying and structuring, recording the lessons as they occur to me, these ideas and lessons will become more real, I will be better able to apply them in real life. The flip-chart is the answer. If it can sell hard toilet paper to even harder-nosed businessmen, it can certainly sell me some painful truths.

This is my fond hope, although reason and experience tell me it is futile, because the psychology of this new woman, of any new woman, will be unique and special to her, and even if it isn't she'll out-think me and turn me inside out, and if she doesn't, then I probably won't fall in love with her.

So who's saying it's women who are irrational? Certainly not me. And definitely not yet.

Anyway, I'm going to have a crack at it. I'm going to work this out. What's wrong with women. What's wrong with men. What's wrong with me. What's *wrong*.

I take out a big black marker-pen and go up to the flip-chart. A white page. A *tabula rasa*, a pristine symbol of possibility. First I need a heading. A strap-line. A product statement. Since this is, clearly, an absurd exercise, I need an absurd title. Something self-deprecatory, something that will hide the truth that this is a deadly serious enterprise on which what's left of my whole ragged future might hang.

I bother and pester at the dragging heels of my imagination, until a few possibilities kick themselves up. *Love Lessons*? Too alliterative, too cheap and hackneyed. *Things I Must Learn In Order Not To Fuck Up Any More*? Accurate, but won't leave any spare room on the paper. *One Hundred Nightmare Things About Women*? Good, but how do I know there are only a hundred? *Women: A User's Guide*? But who's using whom?

In the end, I go for irony, the Esperanto of the modern copywriter. Self-defensive, self-mocking, never quite serious so never quite challengeable.

In thick black strokes, at the top of the clean white page, I write in simple capital letters:

THE LOVE SECRETS OF DON JUAN

Two starting places. With what is axiomatic – the war of the worlds: Mars *vs* Venus; Titania *vs* Oberon; anima *vs* animus. And with where it all began – in the beginning. In the pre-dawn of the de-evolution of the love life of Daniel 'Spike' Savage.

I must have been out with something in the order of – I can't remember. Twenty-five women? To make the calculation first requires the asking of a vexed question: what does it mean to 'go out' with a woman?

It would be bound to include some sort of sexual liaison, even if, in the earliest years, that liaison amounted to no more than a kiss. It would certainly require some sort of unwritten contract the first clause of which stipulated not 'going out' with another woman contemporaneously. It would involve some kind of duration – the standard measure, I believe, is three dates during a period amounting to no more than a month. It would involve a considerable number of other, more subtle criteria – like what *is* the full text of that unwritten contract? For now, though, I want to stick to the ingredients at their most basic – some sexual contact, some unwritten contract, a duration of three dates.

The strict application of these criteria cuts the number to, maybe, seventeen. Seventeen in, what, thirty years? Not so many, really, given the huge quantity of women out there – half the population, according to the more pessimistic estimates. Even seventeen's too many – far too many for my purposes. How many of those women have I actually had relationships with that were serious enough potentially to learn anything from? Probably four. One of those four I married. All of them I loved in one way or another (and there are so many ways). So I'm going to concentrate on those few, that eroded, half-forgotten, virtually spectral quartet. If I can work out what went wrong with them, what I learned during my nights and days and months and years with them, perhaps next time I'll be able to solve the riddle of the Sphinx. Only it's harder than any riddle the Sphinx could devise. Because the Sphinx not only knew the answer, she knew what the riddle *was*. Women know neither. They only know, like men, that there *is* a riddle, and the man they're with has to solve it for him to be worthy of their love.

I must start my investigation not with opinion but with facts, with empirical research. I must start at the promised beginning of the history of my relationships with women. From the first one, when I was thirteen years old, to the last one, which hasn't happened yet. Or, perhaps – as Terence suggests – I should really start at the very, very beginning, with my *real* first, unconsummated, sexual relationship.

I should start with my love affair with my mother.

My mother's name, as already recorded, is Iris. *Iris*. It's really not the stuff of Oedipal myth. I can't imagine myself butchering Derek then throwing Iris passionately down on the continental quilt, my shins picking up fabric burns from the thrusts against the nylon valance. I don't really buy it, and I don't think Terence does either. But obviously she was the first woman I had a relationship of any kind with. I held her breast in my mouth, and, I surmise, sucked it, although when I look at her today – etiolated, authentically mumsy,

fond of ladies' fours at golf and addicted to daytime television – it is entirely impossible for me to grasp this.

Iris, the primary erotic love object. Funnily enough I can
see, when looking at old photographs, that she was an attractive woman before boredom, childbirth, time, gravity and
Derek flattened, hollowed and dried her out. She was
buxom, with long curly blonde hair, when she was raising
me. Terence once asked me if I had ever fallen in love with a
brunette, and the shock realization dawned that I hadn't
even been out on a *date* with one. So much for choice. Gusts
of circumstance propel us both without and within. As
Terence always reminds me, the past never dies.

But it does not always rule everything. Perhaps it goes
thus far, the influence of Iris: the setting of the physical tone,
the initial calibration of the rules of attraction.

I apologize for the crudity of insight. I'm new to this sort
of thing – to introspection. I am greatly tempted to just tear
all this up, throw it in the bin and go out on that date with
Juliet – Juliet Fry – without further consideration or
reflection. But I'm going to get as much homework done as I
possibly can before that first assignation, next Wednesday,
eight p.m., at Harry's Pub, Hammersmith.

Juliet has brown hair, and I think that's progress. Surely
it's some proof that this self-scrutiny is paying off. She's *not
blonde*. Juliet's hair isn't even curly, it's absolutely straight,
Japanese straight. Yet there it is. I'm attracted. And not
entirely out of desperation, although that does, clearly, play
a part. She's got something – although I always say that
before I go out with a new woman. But will it be the right
thing?

What is the 'something' this time? With Helen, my first
love, it was simply her hair – curly, yellow, long, Iris-like,

etc. With Kelly, it was her air of calm and her other-worldly aura. With Natasha, it was her vibrancy, her sexual and animal energy. With Beth, it was –

It was her hair.

This introspection can be thoroughly depressing. It exposes the myth of progress, and we need our myths, as anyone in my profession can confirm. I can see now why I've avoided introspection all these years. It shows you things that the extrovert will always identify as best buried, denied, cast out. Take those emotions, the extrovert says, take that pain, that rage, that loneliness and . . . swallow. Eat up your dinner like a good boy.

Eat up your dinner like a good boy. That's what Iris used to say to me. Funny that I should remember it at this particular moment. It was the most important thing that transformed me from naughty to good in Iris's eyes. Eating up my dinner. Even if I hated it, which, given Iris's rudimentary, half-cocked and usually indigestible cookery, I invariably did. So I ate. I swallowed. I stuffed it down. I wanted to please my mother.

Have I already, after a mere fifteen minutes of introspection, stumbled on a vital piece of evidence in the study of the spiritual, romantic and professional discombobulation of Daniel 'Spike' Savage?

It *was* desperately important to me to please Iris, to gain her approval. Unconditional love was not what my mother did – not then, not now. I suspect it's not what any parent does, as a matter of fact: it's a comforting illusion, but some mothers were a tad more unconditional than Iris. If you didn't do what Iris wanted, the way she wanted it done, you were demoted to non-person.

My mother never smacked me. Compared with what my

mother *did* do, a smack would have been a blessing. A smack would have been a knickerbocker glory and a chocolate Flake. When my mother suspected me of any wrongdoing or disobedience an icy sheet would descend between us. If I pushed it too far – and what is too far, where is that border when you're four years old? – I was exiled to Siberia. And the tundra melts slowly in Siberia, if ever, if at all. She would not speak to you, would not touch you. Iris would just look at you . . . Iris would just look at *me* – let's get the language correct. One thing you learn about language as an advertising copywriter is that words are power. Iris would just look at me as if I was something that had crawled out of the dustbin. At times like that I would long for a smack, so that things could be over. But they wouldn't be over.

They're still not over.

I rang Iris the other day. I do from time to time, ever the dutiful, ever the hopeful son.

Hello, Mum.

Hello.

There it was, in that one word: Siberia. What was it I had done? I still don't know. Iris isn't quite ready to part with that knowledge yet. In a week, maybe two, the hints will become large enough, her purposes will be rendered transparent enough, to be positively identified. In the meantime, she knows that her power lies in keeping me in the dark. It works. Silent outrage is her diet, her food of the gods, her ambrosia. That's one nightmare thing about women: the way they love their anger, the way Iris clutched it to her as if it were a hungry child. Like the hungry child I . . .

Stop. Rewind. Play. Pause.

Suddenly I remember why I have hitherto understood introspection to be hollow. As you look inwards you see what appears to be light somewhere in the dark coils and spiralling smoke of your so-called self. You approach – and then, before you know it, you are blinded. The light blinds you, yet you are drawn to it, you become addicted to it, you are addicted to making sense, except you aren't making sense: you are simply making shadow puppets against the blinding light. You are hallucinating behind your eyes. So hold on. Check. Pull back.

And yet . . . there *may* be a clue here about me and women. I was desperate to gain my mother's approval. It was withheld. *Ergo*, I may be overly desperate to gain any putative mate's approval. First, it's probably the reason I fall in love too quickly – the anxiety to heal the unhealable. Second, the result of the inevitable failure of my unconscious search for unconditional love is always bitterness and resentment. Bitterness and resentment, which should rightly be aimed at Yiewsley, where my mother lives now, tundra-struck. But instead the poor woman that I happen to be sharing a bed with at any given time gets it in the back of the neck. My rage. My disappointment. My shame. Cue break-up of relationship. Cue more disappointment, shame and rage. Repeat cycle. Stand well back.

Or not. I think I'll let that one ferment. I'll bear it in mind. In the meantime I need to turn my mind back to Juliet. Can I be her Romeo? Perhaps not the best analogy, paradigms of self-destruction that those lovers were.

I first met Juliet at this wild party. There were women everywhere, and I had my pick. There was just something in the air that night. I felt lit up with male sexuality, power, allure. It was extraordinary. I saw her watching me, and decided that she was the one.

I simply walked up to her, and I took her, took her like

13

that – like snapping my fingers. Led her, with barely a word spoken, into the empty bedroom where the coats were, and although she gasped and weakly, unconvincingly, pushed me away, I knew that she wanted to be overwhelmed, and that's what I did: I overwhelmed her with the sheer force of my primitive, unassailable will. Later she said it was what she'd always hoped for but had long since given up dreaming about. Ever since that night, she's been hounding me for a date, and I've decided to cave in. What can stand in the face of that kind of intensity of desire from a woman?

None of this is true.

I didn't meet Juliet at a party. I didn't meet Juliet, full stop. I've never seen her – not in person. Even though I really like her, and I think she's great, and I know what she looks like because she emailed me a photo, I've never come face to face with her.

I contacted her through the personal columns.

Sorry, but I'm not going to apologize for it. Even though I feel sorry, I'm not going to say it. Even though I've just said sorry, I don't feel it. I'm confused. But I won't be – not after I've weighed all the evidence and come to some conclusions, however long it takes.

It was me who was advertising and Juliet answered. I thought, I'm going to be good at this. This is my ideal medium. I'm an advertising copywriter, after all. If I can sell hard toilet paper, I can certainly sell *me*.

It took me only thirty minutes to come up with this minor classic.

> Stop. Don't read this yet. Look at the other ads.
> *Then* read this.
>> Those people are everything you fear. They like

walks in the country, they are sensitive, they go to
salsa lessons, they are lost and they are lonely.

You are not like that. Neither am I.

I am 39, tall, good-looking, divorced, creative,
love literature, passion, conversation, *ER* and *Big
Brother*. Box No. 706A.

The work of a professional. Clever and knowing, it is
intriguing, confident, mildly amusing, flatters the reader. It
even stands a certain amount of deconstruction and, in the
way of post-modernism, plays loose with the truth. It is
amused that you could even think there was such a thing. 'I
am 39.' Not strictly true, since I am forty-five. But in the
crude economics of the marketplace, thirty-nine does the
work it's supposed to. Why is everything in the shops
always £4.99, £9.99, even £19.99? Because reason and logic
are walk-on parts in the theatre of the mind, are the Rosen-
crantz and Guildenstern of mental activity. The leading
players are wishfulness and denial. All the buyer sees is that
the product is not five pounds, not ten pounds, not twenty
pounds. And that this particular product is not forty years
old. If the date works out, and leads to another and another,
and you tell her you lied, three years later in your cosy
Saturday-morning bed, it's good for a nostalgic, retrospec-
tive, self-mocking, rueful laugh.

I am not 'tall', only average, five ten. Why bother to lie
about this? Because you have to target your market. If you
scan the small ads placed by women – like I did – at least
sixty per cent of them mention height, and the super-
abundance of it, as a prime factor. I don't know why this is.
I am depressed by the prejudice contained within it. I feel
sorry for little guys. They must have a hell of a time in this

marketplace. Women don't date shortcakes. Snow White didn't marry any of the Seven Dwarfs. They worshipped her, she made them supper and a cup of tea. Then it was off to do the nasty with the handsome six-foot-plus prince. As in fable, so it is in life.

'Good-looking' is, again, stretching the truth, though I've always been OK. Simply one of those eighty per cent of people who are neither handsome nor hideous but border-line both at certain times, depending on the hour of the morning, depth of suntan and that week's fat-to-muscle ratio, and so on. Remembering our post-modern stance, since Juliet and I are probably going to end up talking about literature if only to display a certain degree of refinement to one another, context is everything. The reader will interpret. She'll know, as sure as Jacques Derrida likes Judy Garland, that anyone qualified to appear in the Gap catalogue is not going to be advertising in the personals. She'll make the necessary imaginative adjustment.

'Literature', true, 'passion' (code for 'sex'), true, '*ER*' and '*Big Brother*', of course not, they're pap, but women love them. Why? It's not relevant. It's an introvert's question. The point is, can I wing liking them for the span of a date or two? Certainly.

Notice there is no mention of living in a bedsit, the exist-ence of one much-loved but distraught and sometimes diffi-cult child, and the occasional desire to strafe the entire pre-menopausal female population from the back of a slowly moving armoured vehicle. The importance of editing – you pick up the trick in the ad business.

So there it is. I haven't lost the old touch yet, the touch that used to bring me in £150,000 p.a. and a very close brush with the D&AD awards on more than one occasion.

(D&AD awards are the ad industry's Oscars. It helps convince us that we're artists.)

It did the trick. They put their answers on voicemail nowadays and, for a mildly exorbitant fee, you can get to hear all the people who bought into your branding statement. In my case, market penetration was significant, given the reach and media spend. I got twenty-three messages.

Juliet's was the third. The first went something like this. 'Hi. Liked your message. Give me a call.' Certainly I'll give you a call. Why wouldn't I? You're the kind of no-hoper who spends their spare time going through the personal columns, and you've left me no details of yourself whatsoever to mitigate this fact. But since I advertised in the same column, I must share your self-hatred enough just to call up anyone who happens to respond in however cursory a fashion.

The second call was from a Glaswegian, who seemed nice, challenging and interesting, but every third syllable she uttered was unintelligible, so that was that. Also, I'm not too keen on the urban Scots I've been out with so far – clever and witty, but a little bit too sure they've got your number, a little bit too certain of their place in the moral universe. I think of them as *faux*-Jewish princesses, but lacking the neuroses and the sex drive. Anyway, in either case, I prefer people who have the dignity to be wrong once in a while.

What I would really like in the ideal world I do not inhabit is someone Irish, English (any skin colour, preferably London-born), or Mediterranean, preferably French-born (*love* the accent), who works in the field of something *real*, perhaps a doctor or a cook, or a – Christ, when you think about it there are so few real jobs left. Perhaps that's why there are so few real *people* left. Lawyer, maybe. Or a criminal. Teacher, sculptor, car mechanic, postwoman, dogcatcher – anything that involves really *doing* something.

The third call was from Juliet, and she sounded quite promising. She was about the right class (v.v. important: I'm middle class, a bit, but first-generation, and even then not quite – Derek was a cabinet-maker, Iris a housewife, I went to grammar school), had GSOH (good sense of humour for those of you popular enough never to have to have done this), had a proper job (a furniture-restorer – admirable, interesting, real), had no obvious verbal tics and didn't castigate me once for having an inappropriate opinion during the half an hour we spent on the phone. Described herself as thirty-five (like I'm thirty-nine), brunette, attractive (she was quite brazen about this: not 'My friends think I'm attractive', but 'I'm attractive' – that plain, that direct).

Anyway, whatever she looks like, we're going on a date – so I have to start learning. And thinking. And learning about thinking.

Which all starts with remembering.

2

Before moving on to my forthcoming date, I think it's time to consider the nature, impact and consequences of my first kiss. This is not including Iris, who did kiss me from time to time, in a motherly and, at times, affectionate manner. Despite her fondness for conjuring up Siberia, my mother was not evil or entirely dysfunctional.

My first proper kiss was proffered and gratefully accepted when I was thirteen years old. I can't remember much about being thirteen years old. I recall that, after the still fresh exile from the enchanted crucible of childhood, it seemed vaguely flat and stale, and also that the idea of sex had suddenly detonated itself in my mind, enchantment's dark mutation. Thus I spent a tremendous amount of my spare time masturbating, as consolation for my exile, and as the only remaining place of transcendence to which I possessed the co-ordinates. With what limited time was left after masturbation I either used to go to school, watch TV or listen to records. This was my life in its entirety.

What I need to think about right now, however, is – what did I think of girls at that age? Proto-women, nightmares waiting to be dreamed. At what point did they begin to transform from strange non-boys, negatives if you will, into positive, active forces, that both attracted and repelled at separate poles? It was somewhere around this age, certainly. Somewhere around the time of my first kiss.

The idea of putting your tongue into somebody else's mouth, when you consider it from the childhood perspective of innocence, is a distasteful one. I do remember that it was not something that appealed to me, although I considered that its execution was, sooner or later, going to prove necessary if I were to achieve the apparently desirable condition of manhood. On that particular day, the prospect was that it was to be sooner rather than later for it was Sharon Smith's birthday party, and I was on the guest list – to my considerable surprise.

Imagine, if you will, after the fashion of the time (this was around 1970) a schoolgirl, in schoolgirls' uniform, with big panda eyes, made bigger by the liberal application of kohl. Short skirt, Brutus shirt, hair feather-cut in the skinhead style. Penny loafers. Thirteen years old, but sexually knowing, in some vague, unspecified way that I was able to observe yet could not fully comprehend. Sharon, to the boys in our class, was known as a bit of a slag, which was the label we put on any girl who disturbed us and challenged us with their sexuality. It was not meant to imply that we thought she was a bad person, or that she spent her spare hours jumping in and out of bed with a variety of well-hung lovers. We respected her for being a bit of a slag. The other girls in the class were teacher's pets, drabs, drones, children. Sharon was exotic, powerful. We all felt favoured if we could capture her attention. The boys who made the 'slag' references most often were usually those who were of least significance to her – nerds, losers, freaks.

So I was extremely flattered by the invitation to her party. It happened like this.

Scene: school cloakroom. Time: spring term. *Dramatis personae*: me, Sharon and Sharon's best friend, the less comely Sally Shaw, who, plain, fat and ungainly, seemed to have nothing whatsoever in common with her glamorous best friend other than the coincidence of her initials. Partly because of their habit of preying on the helpless and the excluded, they came to be known among those who feared them as the SS.

I am wearing shorts and a thin sleeveless vest, since I have just finished a games lesson. Sharon and Sally are dressed in school uniform, maroon and black. Sharon's blouse is customized, tucked in at the waist to emphasize her developing breasts, skirt hitched several inches above the permitted length.

Hello, Danny.

'Lo, Sharon.

I blush, look at the floor. This is bad. Can't escape. Stand my ground. No choice.

Hello, Danny.

'Lo, Sally.

Silence.

Do you know one thing about you, Danny?

No, Sally.

You've got very nice legs. They're very shapely. Aren't they, Sharon?

Sharon nods.

Thank you.

Silence. I remember there was no giggling, which was unusual because, in those days, teenage girls seemed to

21

spend the time that I spent masturbating giggling. (Did girls masturbate at that age? The idea didn't enter my imagination at the time. They certainly giggled. Almost constantly. But not on this occasion.)

Sharon's having a party next week, Danny.

Are you, Sharon?

Yes, she is, says Sally. *It's her fourteenth birthday.*

Fourteen, eh?

Yes, says Sally. *Sharon is thinking of inviting you.*

And then . . . I don't know what came over me. I was quite a shy boy and certainly nervous in the presence of girls when I had no other boys to back me up and form an emotional phalanx. I was feeling intimidated and embarrassed. But it was irritating me that Sally kept speaking to me on Sharon's behalf. Also, I suspected I was being teased and that Sharon had no intention whatsoever of inviting me but was just indulging in a bit of casual break-time humiliation. I suddenly felt I'd had enough of it.

Well, Sharon had better get on with it, then, I blurted out. *I'm getting fed up with talking to her pet parrot.*

Sally immediately looked offended, but I was surprised when Sharon let out a short but very juicy laugh. Sally, whose face had soured into petulance, opened her mouth to speak, but before she could, Sharon did. I don't remember what her voice sounded like, only that it was quite soft and at odds with her rather rambunctious appearance.

Will you come to my party, Danny?

I replied, with all the indifference I could muster, *All right*. Then I shot a glance at the sour, furious face of Sally Shaw, turned, and walked out of the door.

Two days after my encounter with the SS, I opened my school desk and there was an envelope in it. At first I

22

thought it was a detention slip, since that was the only form
of correspondence I ever received within, or for that matter
without, the school walls. But the fact that the envelope was
pink and that there was a purple butterfly embossed on the
flap militated against this initial interpretation. Inside there
was a rectangular piece of card, a shop-bought invite decorated with balloons. The inscription within confirmed that I
was invited to Sharon's Party, at 4.00 p.m. on 15 April.

Four p.m. may seem, to an adult, a strange time for a
party, but at thirteen years old we were all caught in a
strange gloaming between childhood and adolescence.
Between the light and shade of the passing and the
approaching condition we reeled, unsteady, among the
moving shadows. Sometimes Sharon Smith was sexual,
adult, knowing, predatory. Sometimes she was just a kid, a
precocious little girl. Hence the party being at 4 p.m. – after
school, parents in attendance, fairy cakes and Pass the
Parcel. Or so I imagined.

As it turned out, the parents weren't in attendance.
Sharon Smith was unusual in being so manifestly sexualized
at such an early age, but it wasn't the only unusual thing
about her. Although to all intents and purposes she was a
skin girl, her parents were hippies, or at least what I thought
of as hippies. This meant little more than that her father
wore jeans instead of proper trousers, and that her mother
wore smocks and read hardback books – books that were
bought, not borrowed from the library. But in the world of
school, where the moment that a fact emerges it is taken and
immediately twisted into myth – to render an incomprehensible world manageable – Sharon Smith's family and Sharon
Smith were respectively a crazy chick, a groovy guy and
a spaced-out bovver girl. In the duller, empirical world,

Mr Smith was a social worker and Mrs Smith was a nursery-school teacher.

This much of the myth was true about the Smiths, though: they were liberal. They believed in letting their daughter find out about life in her own way. She was told she could smoke if she wished. She chose not to. She was told she could wear her skirt short and dress like a skinhead if she wished. That option she took. She was told she could drink wine. She tried it once, and it made her sick, so she never touched it again. Their liberalism, on the whole, worked. And on this occasion it was in evidence again. Mr and Mrs Smith had gone out and left the house to Sharon and her friends.

The moment I arrived, I realized that Sharon had a lot of friends, and most were female and several seemed to share something of her sexual precocity. I could see that Bridie McCoughlan was there, with her famously premature breasts separated by a silver crucifix and inadequately concealed beneath an oversized patchwork jacket with yoke collar. Selina Danby, two years older, was there, demure but with gorgeous bee-stung lips and a seductive velvet choker. There was another girl, in a pink dress, small, sharp-eyed, compact, watching everything. I didn't recognize her, but she glanced in my direction and I got the strange feeling that she recognized me. I avoided her gaze – too direct, too knowing, and yet somehow, I vaguely sensed, benevolent.

I stood there just inside the doorway with a present for Sharon. I felt nervous. I understood that this giving of a gift was a very tricky call. What was she going to be that day? Kid or adult? Should I give her a rubber ducky or a dildo? I didn't phrase the question in that fashion, but it was the conundrum at the heart of my anxieties. Get the present right, and who knew what would follow? Get the present wrong, ditto.

I got it right. I had seen the gift when I was walking in a shopping arcade in Hanwell town centre, a few streets from where I lived. It was a slightly more sophisticated version of a plastic gift that had been recently given away in a girls' comic – a small, gold-coloured hinged heart, which you could wear either open or closed. If it was open, it gave the appearance of being broken – and this signified that you were available. If it was closed, you were 'going steady'. It was a brilliantly economical and public statement of your romantic status. Girls loved them. Half the girls in the school wore one. But they were all plastic, all free gifts. This one wasn't real gold, but it was one up on plastic. Also it was very cheap. Five shillings, as I recall. I worried a bit that she would take it as a love token from me to her, but I guessed that the little-girl part of her would simply see it as an amusing and desirable toy.

So it proved. When she opened it, she squealed with delight, threw her arms around me, and kissed my cheek. I felt her breasts press against my chest. I felt the warm breeze of her breath against my carefully scrubbed neck. I had never been so close to a female contemporary before, and certainly not one wearing a skirt even more abbreviated than the one she customarily wore to school.

There were about thirty people at the party, which was taking place in a small, detached suburban house about half a mile from the school, overlooking a local recreation ground. Clearly I wasn't the only boy who had received a pink envelope with a purple butterfly on the flap. There were four from my class, none of them close friends of mine. Two, Len and Kim, were tough, mean-looking, dimwitted but, so far as I had made out from school, more or less harmless unless you were natural bully fodder, one of those kids whose hangdog body language and broken demeanour acts as bait to the predators of the schoolyard. Len claimed to have had sex with a girl from the local supermarket on several occasions, and Kim was reputed to believe him. It was probably this on which their friendship was based.

Keith Lonigan was there; he was someone I did speak to now and then. He was pleasant and good-looking but rather dull, and obsessed with football. Having exhausted all the possibilities of creating an all-time great English football team, then running out of conversation, I found myself unhooking from him and moving on to Damien Cooper, whom I was surprised to see there. Damien was uncool, bespectacled, had three big spots along the Pennine ridge of his outstanding nose and was ten or fifteen per cent overweight. I suspected he was there for the benefit of Sally Shaw: Sharon was way out of his league, just as I was convinced she was out of mine. The good thing about Damien was that he liked music.

Music divided much more along gender lines then. Girls didn't like what boys thought of as real music. Girls liked pop – all those manufactured goons who prompted them to wet themselves and wave lamé scarves. Boys liked either football or music, and their taste in music could be relatively sophisticated. I was into the Stooges, Blue Cheer, Iron Butterfly – a wide variety of weird and exotic American underground bands. Damien was more British-oriented – Groundhogs, Man, King Crimson and so forth – but there was enough common ground for meaningful discourse.

Him: *You heard the new 'Hogs album?*
Me: *No. Any good?*

Him: *It's all right. Not as good as the last one.*

Silence while two chocolate éclairs are thoughtfully eviscerated of whipped cream.

Me: *I got a Stooges' import last week.*

Him: *Yeh? What's it like?*

Me: *It's good. Not as good as the first one.*

Silence. The rumps of the éclairs are masticated.

And so on, until finally I noticed that the girl in pink was watching me. When I looked back, she held my gaze, so I dropped my eyes, then looked back to Damien for salvation. He was gone. I was alone, and the girl in pink was heading towards me. She was holding a Donald Duck beaker with clear liquid in it – lemonade, I presumed. Her features seemed to come into focus as she moved closer. I could see the intelligence there, and a directness that unnerved me. I shifted uncomfortably from one foot to the other, and looked away until her direct proximity made it impossible for me to look away any longer.

Don't you recognize me? she said. She was close enough now for me to smell what I took to be the residue of some sort of soap on her – something citric, lemon or lime. Her voice was pitched low, confident, but with a shadow of vulnerability somehow. She took a swig of her lemonade.

Should I? I said, my embarrassment making me rather more abrupt than I had intended.

The swimming club, she said. *I'm the belly-flopper.*

The belly-flopper? I stared at her now, desperate to contextualize her. She was pretty, I suddenly realized, in a highly accidental, unpremeditated fashion. Her Marmite-coloured hair was cut wrong, her makeup was inexpertly applied, and there were the remnants of a fish-paste roll around her rather pale, delicate lips. But her features were

27

symmetrical, small, finely turned, what my mother might
have characterized as 'perky', what my older self might have
referred to as 'gamine'. There was something I liked about
her immediately, which made me more, rather than less,
tense. Then, while I was still in the process of chewing, I let
out a honk of laughter, which sprayed a fine film of éclair
crumbs on to the upper left-hand side of her dress. *The
belly-flopper!*

I remembered now. On Saturday mornings, I attended a
swimming club for an hour at the local pool. A couple of
weeks ago, the lesson had been diving, and there was this
girl who had just not been able to get the knack of it. Every
time she got up on to the board, her face took on an expression of concentration and determination. She curved her
body, bent her legs, delicately pointed her arms into an
arrow. Then – flop. She would come off the board completely flat, and hit the surface of the water like a paving
stone, creating a tsunami that travelled to the shallow end.
All the other members of the club were convulsed with
laughter, including me – all the more so because she would
not give up. Time and again she climbed back on to the
board, time and again she came down in the same ungainly,
hopeless fashion, and time and again she had to face a
wailing wall of unfriendly laughter. But she kept at it, with
no appreciable success, until we all grew bored with laughing and ignored her. Among the other members of the
swimming club she had come to be known, after this, as
the belly-flopper, a name she seemed to accept with a shrug
of equanimity.

This girl in the pink dress standing in front of me, looking
quizzical, concerned and pin-sharp, was her. The belly-
flopper. I became aware that her eyes were searching my

face for signs of malice, even as she tried to brush away the crumbs I had sprayed over her dress with a small, olive-skinned hand. But I felt only genuine amusement and surprise.

I'm really sorry. I didn't mean to . . .

You didn't mean to laugh? Or you didn't mean to flob all over me?

Well. Both. I suppose.

She pushed her right hand through her hacked-about hair, which had fallen into her eyes, as if trying to see more clearly through the uneven fringe. Then, to my surprise, she let the hand fall, but instead of allowing it to drop to her side, held out the palm to me. Realizing that she expected me to shake it, my eyes darted around the room and I hoped that no one was watching. The gesture seemed ridiculous, but her face was completely serious. I grabbed the delicate fingers, feeling their surprising warmth, then tried to let go as promptly as I could. But she held on. I tugged – in vain. She was inverting my palm. Inspecting it closely.

You've got a very long life line.

Thank you.

Your love line is very faint. It's very crooked, too. Doesn't look good.

Can I have my hand back?

It's a very turbulent palm.

I pulled away my hand impatiently. That I was being flirted with never occurred to me. I just thought the girl in the pink dress was being weird. She seemed unfazed by my summary withdrawal, smiling and giving the faintest sugges-tion of a shrug. She took another swig from her glass. My throat suddenly felt dry.

Can I have some of that lemonade?

She raised an eyebrow. *It's not lemonade.*

Cream soda. Whatever. I'm parched.

It's vodka.

What?

Try a drop. She held out the drink towards my face.

Smelling the alcohol, I turned away. *No, thanks. I just wanted some lemonade.*

You haven't asked me my real name.

No.

It's Carol. Carol Moon.

Oh. Right.

It wouldn't be true to say that my social skills had deserted me, because I had never, at the age of thirteen, possessed any. But I had reached the age where I recognized their necessity. Before, as a child, I could be more or less exactly who I was without any need to modulate my behaviour and yet be accepted. I was new to this making-conversation thing, and found it a struggle. The thumbscrew of the silence that followed nevertheless propelled me into a half-hearted attempt at small-talk.

The belly-flopper, eh?

That's right.

Did you ever get the hang of it?

Not really. No.

It's quite tricky, isn't it?

Not really. I just haven't got the knack. I'm a bit gawky.

I suppose if you keep trying, sooner or later . . . and all that.

She waved her hand, clearly bored with this line of conversation. *What's your name, then?*

Danny Savage. I'm in the same class as Sharon.

Danny Savage. I've heard all about you.

The way she said this made me blush. All the time she'd been talking to me, she'd barely taken her eyes off my face, which I found disconcerting.

Really? I said.

You've got very sexy legs, from what I've been told.

She began to laugh, a sweet, loud hee-hawing sound that, in its stridency, contrasted sharply with her low, conspiratorial voice. I didn't know what to say.

Actually it's true, she continued, when her raucous laugh had finally run out of steam. *I've seen them at the pool. Quite well formed. Longer than you would expect.*

Thank you, I said, staring at the floor.

You're easily embarrassed.

Am I?

There you are. Blushing again. I like that.

*Well, you wouldn't like me going on about **your** legs, would you?* I said, defiantly, risking a look at her still intent face, which remained wreathed in a sort of questing smile.

I don't know. I don't think I'd mind, she said, brightly, then looked around her as if suddenly tired of the conversation.

Who was that boy you were talking to before I came over?

Who? Damien Cooper?

I suppose so. The fat kid with the big nose.

Yes. It was Damien.

What were you talking about?

Again, I felt discomfited. This talk somehow didn't seem small enough: there was a directness, a catch-all curiosity about Carol Moon that was unusual and required you somehow to think on your feet, as if behind the innocent question a more deadly one was lurking that would floor and expose you.

Oh, rock music, that sort of thing, I breathed, certain that such a thing would not interest a girl in the slightest.

Ooh, I love rock, Carol Moon gasped. *Have you heard Big Brother and the Holding Company? You know, with Janis Joplin? It's so — I don't know. The atmosphere. That voice. Perfect. Fucking perfect.*

I felt my blink rate increase as two extraordinary revelations presented themselves to me. That a girl would even have *heard* of Joplin, in Hanwell, in 1970, let alone love her, was staggering. And to follow that up with the F-word — at a time when girls still chose to sell themselves on niceness, on processed innocence! Suddenly I found the belly-flopper fascinating. But it was too late to do anything about it, because I felt a tug at my sleeve, and suddenly Carol Moon was erased from my mind: the sleeve-tugger was Sharon Smith.

Sorry to butt in. Nice dress, Carol. My mum's got one just like it.

Carol's face turned from curious to blithe, indifferent and weary. *Thanks, Sharon. I'm flattered. Do you like the spit on the buttons? It's Danny's.*

I blushed, but Sharon didn't seem to be taking any notice of what Carol was saying. She was leading me away, even as she dismissed Carol lackadaisically out of the corner of her mouth: *Mind if I borrow Danny for a moment? I want to show him something.*

I bet you do, I could just about hear Carol say, but the tug on my arm grew stronger and I was pulled into a corridor at the back of the house.

Off it was a box room. Inside there was nothing except a

pile of empty boxes and a bean-bag. I felt a wave of panic rise inside me. I spoke in an attempt to conceal my nerves.

She's nice, that Carol.

She's a stuck-up little tart. Don't waste your time on her. Thinks she knows it all. Likes to poke about inside people's heads. Nosy cow.

Sharon was inspecting her sharp little fingernails while darting glances at me in the half-light of the room. I was thrown even further off-balance by this sudden show of malice, which, even as I registered surprise, was cast aside and replaced by an odd, cat-eyed softness. She seemed to be expecting something, but I wasn't sure what. I struggled once more for something to say.

What . . . what . . . do you want to show me then?

At this, Sharon took a half-step towards me, and thrust out her chest slightly. *Do you see my brooch?* she said. I noticed then that she was holding it in her outstretched hand. It was still open, or broken, indicating availability. She seemed to want me to take it, so I did.

It looks nice, I said.

My heart is broken.

Oh.

Will you help me to mend it?

I'm not sure what you –

Then she kissed me.

Or she tried to kiss me. I wasn't sure what to do. Her face moved forward, her lips clearly aimed at mine. I retreated slightly, but not enough to prevent their scented advance. I smelt her breath: sweet, like honeycomb, or maybe something more infant – bubblegum, Frosties, Coco Pops. I supposed I ought to open my mouth, so I did. Her arm crept around my back, and she pulled me towards her. I felt her tongue enter my mouth. Many times I had imagined this moment, and many times I had thought I might be repulsed. This was my first discovery about sex: that things viewed in the cold light of day, and at a distance, feel entirely different when one is at the centre of them. Immediacy, the present, transforms everything in a crucible of surprise. Self-consciousness closes down. A secret inner topography must be navigated. Her tongue in my mouth felt wonderful.

I wasn't sure what to do. I felt it was not enough just to provide space for her probing soft tissue to limber up. I clearly needed to reciprocate. I began to experiment by moving my tongue around hers. Again, not at all repulsive. Lovely, in fact. More than lovely. If I had known the word 'sublime' at that age, I would have thought it. But 'lovely' was the most intense word I knew.

Then I surprised myself. I was so encouraged that this hitherto unsought experience had proved so rewarding that I decided I wanted to investigate others. I sensed somehow that the situation positively demanded bravura. So I put my hand up her skirt. Instead of pushing me away in disgust, she parted her legs and gasped.

Under her skirt were, as implied by the pale signposts of her thighs, her knickers. And inside her knickers was . . . Until that moment, I hadn't really had a clue. I just didn't know what to expect. In 1970 most of the world (excluding the infinitesimally small iceberg tip for whom the 1960s meant something other than the arrival of washing-machines and package holidays) was nothing like as sexualized as it is today. Eminem would have been locked up – seriously. And so would Madonna, Britney Spears and Robbie Williams. When I masturbated, I used pictures of nude classical sculptures from my ten-volume Arthur Mee's

Children's Encyclopaedia – it was that hard to get a look at a pair of exposed breasts. As for vaginas, they were off the imaginative map, in a region marked – in crimson children's crayon – Here There Be Monsters.

So, I was unsure about the nature of the female anatomy. The idea of a vagina was merely an unsubstantiated rumour, as far as I was concerned. There had been a long childhood period in which I tentatively believed that babies were born out of women's bottoms. Then it had become apparent to me that there was more to it than that – but I wasn't sure what. An additional hole of some kind? Some unimaginably subtle groove or inflection? Or not even that – an . . . area? I didn't know.

The first and primary thing that surprised me was that the exploration of this . . . object, or non-object, or absence, or whatever it was, was not an entirely neutral matter for the female. Sharon Smith seemed rather powerfully in favour of the idea of my putting my hand in close proximity to it, whatever it was. I hadn't expected that. She wriggled when my hand touched the cottony softness I knew from my own pubescent development – a coiled furze, a dry, downy meadow. She *bucked*. Then came the surprise.

It – whatever it was – was wet. But not simply wet. More than. Different from. It was like the interior of a mouth, yet much more so. I couldn't make it out, but this much I did know: moistness was definitely a feature, moistness and clinging warmth.

Further north, the prototypical kissing was developing greater complexity. We were switching positions, exploring possibilities. Until this moment I would have hypothesized that the possibilities were limited – in, out, to either side, up, down – but that's not how it felt. There was a wide blue white-star-studded cosmos of potentialities. Each shift of the tiniest part of a millimetre sounded fresh chords within an unbounded space. It was a sensual Tardis, far greater in its span of dimensions than one could possibly have imagined from simple logic.

Southerly it was likewise, only more so. I was beginning to recognize that, along with the moistness, there was shape, although not shape in the way I experienced the rest of the physical world. This shape changed under my touch, receded, advanced, throbbed, stretched and realigned itself in endlessly surprising and delightful formations. I found something, then lost it, then found it. Then found something new, then found something else more than new, something unthought-of.

At one point during this space-probe, this Venus-trawl, Sharon Smith let out a low, soft moan. It sounded like a *cat*, like a miaow. That was the first time I had ever heard a moan like that, and I knew right away that I wanted to hear it again many times in the future, from many women.

That moan evoked in me a startling range of feelings and thoughts. It made me feel excited. It made me feel successful. It made me feel important. It made me feel grown-up. Above all, it made me feel powerful. Her body was rising and falling, trembling and stilling itself, all to my touch. My finger was penetrating regions close, as I imagined it, and as it were, to her heart.

After a minute or two of fumbling and exploring, I made the crucial discovery. The moistness, the contours, the fleshy landscape, the downy softness were a portal. They were trailers, signposts. There was something else, something more important. Something, I can see now, that would dominate my adult life more than any other single thing.

There was a gap, hardly a gap, a *valve* more like, muscled, tight, pressured and counter-pressured. If you pushed at it – I discovered – it gave way, parted. Parted enough for your finger to enter – enough for the whole of what constituted *me* to enter. And inside there were lubricated walls, velvet muscle; here the moistness became a clasping wetness. Again, considered at a distance, it would have amounted to nothing much, so described. A wet place, almost sealed off, located in the triangulated zone between the thighs. But there, in the box room with Sharon Smith, I felt as if my whole thirteen-year-old self was entering it, as if *I* was concentrated in the tip of my finger, and discovering what she was like within.

Because that, even then, was what I was intuiting, that this place really *was* a portal to the interior of another human being, and not just in the physical sense but in every sense. That place was where you escaped yourself, where you shook free from the lead-weighted dense aloneness that finally possessed each of us when childhood was cast off like a burning rocket stage. That was how you continued flight and how you achieved some union in your exile. This I understood, right away. It shocked me. I loved it.

Sharon Smith miaowed, and pulled away, with a flick of her feather-cut hair. *That's enough*, she said.

That was that. Green switched through to red without any pause at amber. What was once so astonishingly open was as suddenly and unexpectedly closed. Sharon pulled away, adjusted her clothing. There was a fading blush on her cheek and her lips seemed faintly distended, but otherwise she had absolute mastery of herself, as if she had efficiently completed a necessary chore. I noticed the heart brooch still in my hand and, for want of anything else to do, I offered it back to her. To my surprise and slight disappointment, she shook her head. Then she was gone, back into the other room to join the rest of the throng. But before she went, she smiled. I'll always remember that smile. I think about that smile often. That smile said, *So now you know*.

I did know. I wanted to know more. But I wasn't going to find out from Sharon Smith.

If I had had any doubts about the future of our relationship after Sharon broke away from me in that room, a girl in a pink dress was waiting to give me a full bulletin when I emerged, tousled and alone, from that dark corridor. Carol Moon was eating a raw carrot, and darted a look in my direction. She left whoever she was talking to and planted herself on the square yard of thick, swirly carpet in front of me.

Hello there, she said, formally, as if expecting some explanation of what she can only have assumed to be my behaviour. I smoothed my hair, tried to calm my heart. I saw Sharon Smith on the other side of the room giggling loudly with Sally Shaw and throwing glances in my direction.

Hello, I said, aiming unsuccessfully for an equanimity in my voice that I was far from feeling.

Did the earth move? said Carol, munching carrot calmly. She had a glazed look, probably the result of the vodka. The Donald Duck beaker, now set on a side table, appeared to be empty.

What? I said, not understanding a word of what she had said.

If you were wondering what all that was about, I can tell you, if you like, said Carol, her tone neutral, the carrot disappearing in small, jagged shards through her slightly pursed lips.

What are you talking about? I said, trying to shake some clarity into my head, and feeling obscurely annoyed with the compact, shrewd-eyed girl in front of me.

That's what Sharon does. It's her hobby. You're just today's hobbyhorse.

After four minutes in the box room, I was in love with Sharon Smith and I wasn't going to hear her badmouthed, even though I had the sickening feeling that Carol Moon was right. It infuriated me. *Oh, be quiet, Belly-flopper*, I blurted out. *Be quiet.*

Ooooh, said Carol, teasingly, and slightly drunkenly. *Spiky, aren't you?*

I felt the heart brooch in my hand, and it seemed to burn there, seemed no longer to be a love token but an emblem of humiliation. In a single movement, and before she could protest, I reached out and affixed it, a broken heart, to the neck of Carol Moon's dress. *Why don't you have that?* I said nastily. *It suits you better.*

Carol Moon simply smiled pleasantly and said, *Very spiky.*

She looked down at the brooch, then walked back to the friend she had abandoned by the food table and began talking again, while I shot angry glances at an entirely and incomprehensibly indifferent Sharon Smith.

As Carol had pretty much predicted, that was the last time I got anywhere near Sharon. The following week she began what turned out to be a two-year relationship with a sixth-former called Thommo Briggs, who had a meat-packer's slab of a face and the inevitable 50cc motorbike. She might even have mentioned something to him about our little moment of frottage, because shortly afterwards he took me to one side near the school water-fountain and told me he would insert a cricket bat up the full extent of my colon if I so much as looked at her again.

Carol had been right, which made me dislike her almost as much as I now loathed Sharon Smith, who, by my pubescent lights, had led me on, then spurned me. I saw Carol from time to time at the swimming-pool, trying to do backstroke as unsuccessfully as she had tried to dive. The other club members still laughed at her, but I had forgotten to find her funny. As I examined her tight, almost skinny body struggling through the chlorinated water, I felt, through my own anger towards her, a vague, complementary sadness. A fish out of water.

That date with Juliet Fry is tonight. Iris and Sharon Smith are as far as I've got with my self-therapizing. It's not even the prologue for The Love Secrets of Don Juan. However, it's all I've got to go on. This is my sentimental education in its entirety.

   1. My mum was sometimes unkind. So I seek women's approval more than I should.
   2. The discovery of the contents of Sharon Smith's pants was my personal Copernican Revolution of 1970.
It's not really enough to turn round a lifetime of failure. I'm just going to have to do the work on the job. I'm going to have to wing it, keep things as simple as possible while I try to work it out.

Work what out? What's *it*?

Currently 'it' is about me trying to get it right with Juliet, whom I haven't yet met, and certainly haven't slept with –

indeed, sleeping with her is not my main intention. Achieving intimacy is my main intention. Not being alone is my main intention. Connecting is my main intention.

The date is in one and a half hours' time. I am getting ready. Which clothes to wear? A blue shirt, obviously. She will wear black. That's how it works. Each sex feels that these colours flatter them. Aftershave, yes, Egoïste or CK, though I tend to overdo it or underdo it. It's like getting your trousers the right length – more complicated than it looks.

Conversation. What topics will I rely on if things go flat? I'm not good at dates. There are certain kinds of men who are good at dates, and I'm not one of them. It's that talent for genuine fraudulence, for pumping yourself up to being more than yourself without actually being fake.

It is very clear to me that some role is required of me, that it isn't sufficient just to be myself. *Be yourself* – where did that insane idea come from? Just about every Hollywood movie ever made, I suppose, most specifically those starring Robin Williams. But what if you're hopeless? Should you be yourself then? Even if you're not it seems to me that the first rule of dating is *don't* be yourself under any circumstances. That comes later, when you're in a relationship. A date is market research. A date is above-the-line advertising.

I wish I'd had more time to introspect about my past relationships but I keep forgetting to do it: it doesn't come naturally to me to turn inward. Living, until now, has always been about being hurled around inside the spinning wall of the hurricane, never at the still eye. I keep getting lost in life. It throws me around, sucks me up and puts me down in the desert.

Should I have a drink before I go? Possibly. But one leads

to another, and it's hard to be charming and seductive when you're dribbling down your shirt. I think I'll stick to tea.

What should my strategy be? Who am I going to *be* for this date? This permeates everything: how I comb my hair, which trousers I choose, which aftershave I apply.

If I arrive early, I should be reading a book. If so, which one? She likes literature. What will she go for? Obviously a female author. Perhaps a female author with some sexual overtone – Anaïs Nin, perhaps, or Erica Jong even, very retro, an intellectual frisson. The cover's important – it speaks volumes about the reader.

How will I sit, as I wait for her to arrive? I *will* wait for her to arrive, as I have already decided to get there early. Cross-legged and louche, smoking a cigarette, or straight-backed, intent on the fourth chapter of Jeanette Winterson's *Sexing the Cherry* (because I think, on reflection, that's more contemporary, more impressive and, given the Sapphic overtones, not too overtly suggestive).

What will I be drinking? A pint of lager? Too common, too laddish. A glass of dry white wine? Poncy, not sexy. A girl drink. Something short and on the rocks? A Dashiell Hammett detective drink. Not bad, especially if I wear my forties-style double-breasted pinstripe.

Condoms. Of course it's pointless carrying them, as I'm not going to ask her to sleep with me on the first night. This convention persists, don't ask me why. Some residual sense that an early proposal indicates lack of respect on the part of the male party remains. I don't think that's true. I think a woman who's self-confident enough to go to bed with you on a first date commands respect. It's impressive, not slutty. Anyway, what I glean from the ads – I understand the world through ads, not newspapers or the radio, it's where the truth lies, believe me – has shown me that slutty is OK now, so long as it's on the woman's terms, whatever that means: how can you *voluntarily* have sex with someone on someone else's terms?

No, I'm not going to carry any condoms. Not because it's pointless, although it probably is. I'm not going to carry condoms for a purely superstitious reason: it's tempting fate. If I carry condoms, it will predetermine that sex will not happen. The gods punish hubris. And the truth is – call *me* a slut if you like – I'd like to have sex tonight.

It just seems better than the alternative.

Half an hour to go before my date with Juliet Fry. I'm rather proud of what I've been doing in the intervening hour.

I've been introspecting. Just sitting here in this chair, shirt partially buttoned, aftershave unchosen, pub pose unselected. This introspection has led me to a surprising conclusion, a radical, frightening and entirely novel course of action.

I've decided to take the high road, the Robin Williams road. I've decided to be myself after all. Not, obviously, that I'm sure who 'myself' is or what is involved in 'being' that person. But somehow the word 'trust' surfaced in my mind after I'd sat there for a sufficient amount of time. It's a word Terence is fond of, and it's not my strong suit, apparently. Not that I've decided to trust Juliet Fry – that would be ridiculous. I haven't got a clue who she is, even though I really, really like her, so trust would make no sense. The trust I'm talking about is more abstract. It's about trusting the moment.

'Trusting the moment'. I can't quite believe I'm talking

like this. It's so hard not to submit to the pressure to turn into a surrogate woman nowadays. Women, like therapists, are always using phrases like 'trusting your instincts' and 'using your inner eye' and 'being spontaneous'. Yet on the basis of one hour's introspection, I can sort of see what these ideas mean. They mean stop trying. Float. Let the water carry you.

I'm just getting ready to pick up the phone to call a cab when it rings. It's Martin.

Martin Gilfeather is my best friend – or my best male friend, at any rate. He's a lovely man in many ways, sincere, witty, kind, although he does have this very irritating characteristic, which is doubly irritating at this exact moment. Martin's terrifically successful with women. I don't know how he does it. If he knows, he's not letting on. Martin's not spectacularly good-looking, or rich, or unusually charming. Yet you put him in front of just about any member of the opposite sex, and something remarkable happens. The women come alive: they start to twinkle and glow. He can take his pick, more or less. I've asked him how he does it, and he just shrugs and looks embarrassed. Admittedly he rarely stays with one for very long, but I assume that's just because there are so many alternatives on offer. Despite lacking the biological clock, most men, like women, are finally pressed into a long-term relationship by collapsing choices, the unstoppable narrowing of options. However, this is showing depressingly little sign of happening to Martin. He represents the male fantasy of easy, perpetual freedom, of relaxed semi-detachment. I'm jealous of Martin.

His current girlfriend, Alice Fairfax, has lasted nearly two years, which is a record for him. I've met her on a few occasions, and she's not like most of her predecessors: she's less glamorous, more thoughtful, more substantial than his usual fare. He may even love her, but he hasn't mentioned it to me. He barely mentions her at all. Women are just women to Martin – that's one of the secrets of his success. His quasi-autism. This male distance, so derided by women, has an undeniable power. He doesn't need them, so they flock to him. That's *definitely* a nightmare thing about women: their perverse and unvarying appetite for indifference. The way they yearn for love – but only up to the exact point at which it's won. A declaration of love, once offered, can be traduced into a gesture of weakness. That can be dangerous. Women never quite forgive you for loving them. It's all to do with female self-hatred – or so Martin believes. This is a solid-gold Love Secret.

Martin understands this impulse towards self-hatred, and it suits him, and he gives them what they yearn for: unattainability, and the fantasy that *they*'ll be the woman to surmount it. But, then, if they did, if they got Martin, or men like Martin, to love them, the appeal would be lost. He'd be just another man.

Spike. Can you talk? I've got a situation. It's tricky. It's a mess.

It's a bit difficult at the moment. I'm about to –

This won't take a moment. I wanted to ask your advice about something. I'm in two minds, in a tizzy, in a turmoil.

I get the gist, the juice, the gen. Shoot, then. You've got five.

One of the nice things about Martin is that he has the humility to ask for advice. He's not one of those men who sees seeking help from other men as a display of subordinancy. I like to give him advice. So long as it's not about women.

It's about Alice.

45

*God in heaven, Martin. What are you asking **me** for?*

Why wouldn't I ask you? You're my best friend. You've been married and everything.

I have to be out of here in a few minutes. I'm going on a date. But I can tell you what I know about women, if you like. They're a –

*Yeh, I already **know** they're a nightmare. But I just wanted to ask . . . I just wanted to know . . .*

I check my watch. Cutting it fine.

Come on, Martin. What else is there to know? I'm going to be late. Can't we talk later?

I just wanted to know what you think of Alice.

Alice? What does it matter what I think of Alice? It's what you think of her that counts. Why is this suddenly so urgent?

I'm getting a bit of pressure. A touch of the old thumb-screws.

I know what kind of pressure Martin is talking about. Martin hates that kind of pressure.

Time to take 'the next step'.

Apparently.

Martin, I really do have to go.

Right. It's just . . . I'm not . . .

Martin is a terrible ditherer. Oddly, that's something else women like about him. He's hapless, or possibly helpless. Women want to mother him.

This is ridiculous, you asking me about women. I'm clueless. It's well known.

I don't think you're clueless.

You don't think I'm clueless? My marriage has broken up, I'm single, I'm depressed, I'm living in a bedsit full of unpacked plastic bags.

*That's not clueless. That's just life happening. You were married. That's **something**. Christ, this is the longest relationship I've had.*

All right, all right. Look, Martin, let me ask you this. It's incredibly obvious, but I'm going to ask you all the same. Do you love her?

Well. Um . . . I think she's a great girl. You know. She's got . . . I think . . . I mean, what do you think?

What do I think? I don't know. I hardly know Alice. She seems fine. She seems OK. Do you love her?

*Well, what's love? What does that **mean**?*

*Martin, I really have to go. I really **do**. I know you'll do the right thing. I'll give you a call tomorrow, OK?*

Oh. OK. It's just that . . . it's all a bit shaky at the moment. I don't want to make the wrong decision.

All decisions are wrong, Martin. And all decisions are right. It's just a question of how long a view you take.

Now I can hear Martin brightening up a bit.

*That's right. That's **true**. So in a sense it doesn't matter which –*

See you, Martin.

Oh. OK. See you, Spike. And . . . thanks.

Forget it.

I put down the phone, not having a clue what I'm being thanked for, other than giving Martin some spurious justification for what he was going to do anyway. But, then, I suppose that's all any of us ever wants.

I went out with Juliet Fry last night, and I was spontaneous, I was *me*. And you know what?

Fuck Robin Williams.

The evening started well enough. I was waiting there for

Juliet Fry to arrive. I brought the book that I actually *am* reading, Carl Hiaasen's *Sick Puppy*, a middlebrow smile-a-page entirely non-thought-provoking comedy thriller. This is me. I was wearing a pair of not-too-fresh jeans, a not-too-fresh jacket, and a polo-neck sweater that, although purchased from Agnès b, has seen better days. There was a small food stain on the front. This is me. I was drinking lager top, and eating a bag of Mini Cheddars. Crumbs were distributed around my unfettered waistline. This is me. No aftershave. Battered trainers. This is me. I had a three-pack of condoms in my pocket. This is me. I felt good being me. I felt so spontaneous I was ready to combust.

Then Juliet walked in, and she was absolutely beautiful.

It turned out that ex-Gap models did get lonely. I suddenly realized that being me was just about the worst idea I'd had all year. I nearly walked out of the pub there and then, Mini Cheddars, rubber johnnies, bulging gut and all.

She was dressed perfectly – she'd made a hell of an effort. Black ski-pants, tucked into expensive-looking boots. A little candy-pink turtleneck, cashmere by the look of it. A black patent-leather three-quarter-length coat. Mouth a scarlet slash. Hair cut short and Japanese style, as promised by the photograph. Everything as promised. Then she looked at me. And something terrible happened.

Her face fell.

It was infinitesimal: it was the smallest of flickers at the corners of her eyes. I think she only let it slip because there was the slightest possibility that it wasn't me, that although I was sitting alone in the pub and was, as promised, carrying a copy of that week's *Private Eye*, that coincidence might be operating, that she might have got it wrong. Then she realized, without any doubt, that I was me after all. She recovered herself, but I knew that the decision to be myself had been an act of idiocy. All my carefully groomed confidence flew out of the window. But it was too late. I was clocked. We each spoke over the other.

Hello, I'm . . .

Are you . . . ?

We exchanged awkward handshakes. I got up from where I had been sitting on the chair, spreadeagled, being the authentic me, and felt all the muscles in my shoulders tighten.

Then I knocked over my drink.

Such a moment might have relieved the tension. It might have resulted in a flurry of relieved laughter and amused apologies. But the gulf that had opened between us at the moment we shared the fatal knowledge that she was disappointed in her date simply widened. She had thought I was a balding, middle-aged slob. Now she thought I was a gauche, balding, middle-aged slob.

I wiped myself down with my copy of *Private Eye*, made my apologies, went and bought her a drink. She ordered a pint of bitter. Clearly, unlike me, she knew how to be herself without being ridiculous. We arranged ourselves at a safe distance from each other in the corner, and then we had a conversation of the very worst kind.

A good conversation is a living thing. It is an improvisation, a flowering, a game of pat-a-cake, a series of entertaining, spontaneous flourishes. That is the kind of conversation we had had on the phone. That is exactly the kind of conversation we were unable to muster on this occasion. We had the other kind, which occupies the other end of the spectrum. Conversation here was a dead thing, a big ugly stiff that smelt bad. A conversation, in other words, made purely out of convention.

I know people who have made an entire life out of conventional conversations, who have no problem with them whatsoever. There were quite a few in the advertising industry, but you find them everywhere. My mother and father, for example. It doesn't seem to worry these people that the words spoken achieve nothing in terms of intimacy, entertainment or just . . . being mutually *alive*, for God's sake. I think that, for these people, the point of conversation is something separate. It's conversation more as a fetish, or ritual, in which a series of prescribed moves are made to reassure the participants that life is much the same as it always has been and that things are in their place, and that since words are meant, socially, to be spoken between people then now they *have* been, so that's all right. It's conversation as hygiene, as symbolic washing-up, a doleful necessity.

That sort of conversation is purgatory to me, and it was clearly hell to Juliet Fry. But that was the kind of conversation we had. It was constructed entirely of cheap, ill-used materials, of cliché and unexamined thought. The subjects we unenterprisingly selected were as predictable as the sentiments duly generated.

We talked, initially, about how strange it was to be meeting under those circumstances, which it unquestionably was. Both of us claimed it was the first time we had tried such a thing. This part of the conversation was the most interesting, but it only lasted thirty seconds or so. After that, we were in trouble.

We went into stand-by mode. We were into that dead zone of a conversation, a discussion about the merits of the part of town in which we lived and, heaven forgive us, property prices. Then we inevitably extrapolated into the problems about living in London generally, and how difficult it was, and it was great, really, though, wasn't it? There was a brief foray into the arid regions of our family backgrounds – her father was a solicitor, her mother a teacher, she had two brothers whom she never saw – and then, before the hour was up, we were talking about which films we'd seen. You know you're in trouble when you're into that territory, especially after only an hour. She liked Russian, black and white, long; I liked American, colour, action, snappy. Films in which Robin Williams might appear.

After films I felt there was nowhere else to go. Then things took a turn for the worse.

I had been smoking like billy-o because the evening was so grisly, and cigarette advertising, some of which I had written, had convinced me over the years that the inhalation of tobacco smoke could convert any experience, however negative, into something positive, cool and rewarding. My nervousness meant I'd been putting away the cigarette packet in different jacket pockets on each occasion and, fatally this time, I had put it into my inside left pocket.

Nothing dangerous about an inside left pocket, except that when I pulled out the cigarettes, the condoms flipped out with them. Right on to Juliet Fry's immaculate black ski-pants. The condoms were the cheapest make. This is me.

There was a very long pause. I suppose, in some circumstances, an incident like that might have broken the ice, set us on the right path, smashed through some invisible barrier and left us clutching our sides with mirth at the sheer improbability and poor taste of it all. Again, this wasn't one of those circumstances. A woman at a table next to ours had seen what happened. She looked at Juliet Fry, and Juliet Fry looked back at her, and I saw the look, and it made me want to set fire to myself instead of to the cigarette, which I was desperately trying to get into my mouth with a shaking hand.

She picked up the condoms and handed them to me delicately. I didn't say anything, just accepted them as if she was offering me a peanut. Then she shook her head very slightly, got up and walked out of the pub without another word.

I decided, I *definitely* decided, that being me was not a good policy.

3

There is one question I need to answer before I can begin to make real progress on this stumbling, half-blind grail quest. It is painful, complicated, and to me, although I suspect not to most women, obscure. The question is this: why does Beth, my ex-wife-to-be, hate me?

Beth and I never had a particularly bad marriage: we didn't hit each other, we weren't unfaithful, we tried to make things good for one another. It just dawned on us both at about the same time that we were two wholly different kinds of people who had married for, if not all the wrong reasons, then the insufficiently right ones. We decided to separate, and that was an improvement, so we decided to get divorced.

We had an OK marriage. I quite like Beth, I bear her no ill-will. I just don't love her any more. It happens – everyone knows that. It's life. She says she doesn't love me either.

So why is she suddenly acting as if I am a monster? Why do I see in her eyes the hatred of the violated for her rapist? Why do I hear in her voice the contempt of the torturer for his victim?

An answer of sorts is beginning to occur to me, with the help of Terence and my skinny-dipping in the icy waters of introspection. It's amazing it never occurred to me before, really. I've been making a huge mistake all these years.

The mistake I made is in thinking that there were just the two of us in the marriage and just the two of us in the divorce. That, I see now, was an underestimation. It dawns on me that there were, in fact, dozens of us. That your relationship with the person you're with – or are separated from – is a room full of people, of shadows, of *doppelgängers*. It's not only your partner you have to deal with. It's those people they bring with them. It's the same for them with you. All your shadows have to get to know and understand each other. Have to acknowledge, above all, each other's multiple id-driven nature. Doing what I do for a living, I should have understood this.

To take an example. It must have occurred to most men at some time or other that women get furious for no apparent reason. Until now, I had assumed that this was because I was too stupid to realize what I'd done wrong. The idea that women are in some fundamental way more moral than men both pre- and post-dates feminism. I have always believed, and it is a belief they appear to share, that women have a complex ethical compass that can sniff out subtleties of good and bad behaviour far more effectively than men can.

There's still a part of me that believes this may be true. But a larger part now thinks there's another explanation for those incomprehensible furies. Which is that people, particularly women, have a profound and complicated relationship with the past. That when they look at you they don't only see *you*. They see their father and their brothers and their former boyfriends, and all the pains and rejections and humiliations they suffered but never confronted at the time. Then they load them on to you.

Terence would say that it's the same for both sexes but, for a therapist, Terence can be surprisingly naïve. If women are in any way different from men – and they are – it is because they tend to operate on a symbolic rather than a literal level. Thus their shadows are more powerful, more complex. Everything stands in for everything else. That can be good – it can be great, I suppose, although I can't quite think in what circumstances. But when you're with a woman, it's complicated because you don't know who she's talking to when she tells you to fuck off and die. Her dad? The boyfriend she loved who dumped her ten years ago? Herself? Or even, just possibly, you?

If you don't have a strong sense of yourself, you may take yourself at her assessment, which can be a disaster. The law of the jungle is eat or be eaten. The law of love, and in fact of life, is to define or be defined.

As for my ex-wife-to-be, she has decided, after ten years of perfectly OK but not-really-good-enough-for-either-of-us marriage, that I am pure evil, that I am the bastard son of Rosemary West and Pol Pot. The fact that I have tried, during our separation, to be a good father to Poppy and that I have given Beth everything she has asked for in terms of money, house, car and record collection and, I think, *respect* seems to count for nothing.

It now occurs to me that I've just been clubbing my head with the cudgel of reason. As ever, reason is inadequate. Introspection reveals deeper, more atavistic reasons for my wife's hatred. She hurts, so she wants me to hurt too. She's punishing me for not loving her, but she's also punishing me because she doesn't love me. The world has gone wrong for her, not for the first time, and it's all broken, abandoned and piled up like rubbish in the corner of a wide, windy boulevard, and she needs someone to blame for all that mess. It's the most primitive of instincts. It's the most female of instincts.

I read in some museum exhibition on the Spanish Inquisition that the soul of the torturer is male. I suspect that's true.

But the soul of the revenger is female.

I suppose it's got something to do with those millennia of slavery and abuse. Right now it's payback time. Why? Because now, and for the first time, they *can*.

Pointless, I suppose, to point out that *I* didn't enslave them. I wasn't even *born*.

That's another nightmare thing about women. That pain they pour down on you: half the time it's what you had coming, but the other half it's the accumulated compound interest on someone else's crime, someone who's quite possibly *dead*, who's had their good time at women's expense and, being dead, yet surviving as part of some residual *culture*, is now permanently off the hook.

I don't know why men, on the whole, manage to resist that instinct, that pull of the past, more than women. But they do. That's one of the good things about them, an offshoot of their much-mocked literal-mindedness. Literal-mindedness can be a disaster, disconnectedness with the past can be a disaster, but there are circumstances in which it is priceless.

*

*What do you think of this, Poppy? 'Titmarsh Toilet Tissue –
The No-nonsense Wipe'. Catchy, don't you think? They're
going to love it, I know they are.*

If they like it, will you be able to buy a new house?

Aren't we cosy here? Don't you like it?

No. I hate it.

Do you, poppet? Why?

It's too small. It smells like wee.

*I know it smells, sweetheart. That's because the drains
are clogged up and I can't afford to pay for a plumber at the
moment.*

I want to go home.

*This is your home too now, darling. You've got two
homes, you lucky thing! The big nice one with Mummy.
And the small smelly one with Daddy.*

I want to go home to my real home.

Is that a new dolly? What's her name?

I know what you're doing, Daddy.

*Yes. That's right. I'm trying to tickle you! Yes, I am. Yes,
I am.*

You're trying to detract me, Daddy.

Yes, darling. I suppose I am trying to distract you.

Are you still married to Mummy?

Yes, poppet. But we are going to get unmarried very soon.

Why?

Why?

Why?

You'll understand when you're older.

When I'm seven?

Maybe.

Do you still love Mummy?

Of course I do, darling.

57

Then why are you getting unmarried?

*So what **is** the name of that new dolly?*

If you get unmarried will I still have a daddy?

Of – of course you will, darling.

Are you crying, Daddy?

Would you like to watch a video? Do you like the Tweenies?

I can't decide whether to call her Princess or Lucy.

Who?

My new dolly.

How about Princess Lucy?

Have you got a girlfriend, Daddy?

No.

Why not?

Because nobody wants to sleep with a forty-five-year-old failure with a six-year-old kid who lives in a bedsit that smells of piss and has too many sleepless nights and no money or prospects and cries in front of his daughter.

What I really said was, No. Has Mummy got a boyfriend?

Of course. I think Lucy's better, don't you, Dad? Dad? What's the matter? Why has your face gone all red?

It hasn't gone red. Better than what?

It has. Better than Princess.

I like Lucy.

Mummy likes Princess best.

*Will you shut **up** about that bloody doll?*

I want to go home. It's not a bloody doll! I want my mummy.

Sorry, darling. You mustn't say bad words. Oh, don't cry. Oh, God. Look, why don't you have . . . er . . . something to eat. I've got some . . . some . . . half a can of baked beans or something . . .

*You **hate** me.*

Of course I don't. I love you, Poppy, more than anything in the world.

*You **don't.***

I do.

You don't.

I do.

Then why did you leave home? Because if you still love Mummy, why did you leave home?

*I think Princess **is** the best name, actually. Princess Poppet.*

You're trying to detract me again.

What's his name?

Who?

Mummy's new boyfriend.

Oliver.

That's a nice name.

Yes.

Do you think he's nice?

Yes.

Not as nice as Daddy, though.

Sometimes he is.

Is he?

He brings me sweets and plays with me and never tells me off and he gives me hugs and he's nice to Mummy and he bought me this bloody doll.

*He bought you **that** doll? Don't use rude words.*

Yes.

Poppy.

Yes?

What do you think of the name Jezebel? Shall we call the doll Jezebel?

That's pretty.

It is, isn't it? Tell Mummy that Daddy thought of it, will you?

OK, Daddy. I need to go poo. Daddy?

Yes, poppet?

Can I use the fluffy toilet paper? I don't like 'Tickmarsh Toilet Tissue'.

Titmarsh. Darling, I get it free. I haven't got any fluffy paper.

Mummy has fluffy paper.

Mummy can afford fluffy paper. Mummy can afford to wipe your arse with a pashmina.

What's a pashmina?

It's a very silly, very expensive scarf.

Mummy doesn't wipe my arse with a scarf.

Let's go home, Poppy. It's time for you to go home.

It's time to take Poppy to Beth's house. To take Poppy home. That riff about Poppy having two homes – it's advertising. In other words, it's untrue. She lives with Beth. She leaves home to visit me. I return her home after forty-eight hours, once every two weeks. After the handover to Beth the ache of loss is like acid accumulating in my throat, pooling around my chest until twelve days later I get another chance to drain the reservoir temporarily.

I dread this journey. I really want to leave Poppy at the end of the path, let her ring the doorbell, then walk away before the door opens. I can't, because Poppy wouldn't understand. Yet I'm frightened of being there when the door opens because Beth always finds a new way to hurt me. In the space of the few seconds between the door opening, and me giving Poppy a farewell kiss, and turning to leave, she always finds a way of getting to me. A sentence is enough, and often it's so subtle that I don't even get it until ten minutes later, and then I'm seething, but it's too late to do anything about it. Not that I could have done anything about it anyway.

The weekend before last, just as I was handing over Poppy, she said, *That was good for Tom, wasn't it?*

And I said, *What?* I didn't have a clue what she was talking about.

She said, *Never mind*, and was gone.

A few minutes later it started playing on my mind. *That was good for Tom, wasn't it?* Out of all the things she could have said to me, all the unfinished, unsaid business that we have, she chooses that phrase.

The revenger's soul. It took me a full hour to decrypt. The cleverness was in calling him Tom when everyone knows him as Thomas. He hates the name Tom, so Beth always called him that. I always called him Thomas, even when he was my art director at Cazenove Allen & Silver. My talented, handsome, ambitious art director, the art director who stabbed me in the back and took all the credit for the Jimson's Jelly Beans ad, who is now earning £300,000 plus per annum and living with an It girl in a penthouse on Shad Thames.

What had she meant, *That was good for Tom, wasn't it?*

The genius of the thing was that she made sure the wound was self-inflicted. She knew that, when I had figured out that Tom was Thomas, I would rack my brains to work out what could possibly be 'good' for that worm-like, treacherous, maggot-like wormy maggot. She would also have known that I would quickly work out that this was the month of the D&AD awards. I don't get *Campaign*, the advertising trade journal, any more because I'm trying to put all that behind me. My past, as well as my hopes. Beth knew, all the same, that I was going to have to buy it. She made me pay several quid for my misery, with the offhand delivery of what might easily have been a generous remark.

The investment produced the result that Beth had expected. The page-two photograph of Thomas made him look like the happiest man alive: beaming, tanned from a no doubt recent expensive foreign holiday, It girl draped round his podgy little shoulders. Category winner for Sam's Satsuma Surprise, the soft-drink sensation of last summer. I know the product well – because I started developing the pitch. I know it because I came up with the slogan, the high concept and, indeed, the art direction, since Thomas is at best a technician who wouldn't know a good layout if it shot itself on a sidewinder missile up his sphincter. Then my marriage broke up and the drinking started, and the rest of the story is a hackneyed, discarded first draft, too crass and predictable to make it even as a half-arsed pitch for a clueless client, but perfect as a representation of real life, authentic in all its tawdry predictability.

Those simple words, *That was good for Tom, wasn't it?*, did exactly what they were intended to do. They reduced me to an apoplectic, pillow-biting, wall-punching psycho.

No recourse. No appeal. No restitution. For so much of my life I have imagined, wordlessly, almost thoughtlessly, that somewhere, somehow, there is a semi-celestial court of justice that makes sure things turn out OK in the long run, if you do the right thing. That someone, or some impersonal force somewhere, is in control, making sure that judicious outcomes ensue from the appropriate behaviour. The good are rewarded, the bad are punished. That there is nevertheless, in this transparently godless universe, a kind of God-bias built into the way things work.

It's not true – obviously. There's no one and nothing to appeal to. No one to judge. There's only what you can get away with. Thomas Spencer De'Ath of Cazenove Allen & Silver has got away with it. With my rewards and my salary and my kudos. He's got it all. Just like Beth's got my daughter and my house, and Oliver, whoever the fuck he is, has got Beth and is no doubt *working* on my daughter. Meanwhile what have I got?

I've got a drain that smells as if Dennis Nilsen was the last plumber to attend, and a ready-to-fill-out form for the Lonely Hearts column in *Time Out* on the kitchen table.

But I can't afford the luxury of bitterness because I'm too nervous. I'm heading home to the house in Hammersmith where we used to live, holding tight to Poppy's hand as she quietly mangles a Britney Spears song. She looks up at me: big hazel eyes, white-blonde hair like her grandmother, tall and slender like her mother, feet rather too big like mine. There it is. A lovely little cottage with a garden and a swing, three bedrooms, loads of natural light and a big kitchen. How happy we were there!

Really, it does seem that way, as I walk down the street towards the red front door.

In contrast to how I feel now, we really were happy.

Memory plays tricks, though. Memory's a leading prac-titioner in the Magic Circle, you could say. If we were happy, why did we split up? Didn't we know we were happy? Can you be happy, and not know it?

My mother always used to say this to me when something bad happened: *You can't change the past, Danny. It's no use crying over spilt milk. What's done is done.* She was wrong.

My sessions with Terence have achieved that much at least. Terence insists you *can* change the past. The past is changing all the time. The memories you select, the values you attach to them, are in constant flux. Inner life is like writing a product slogan, a constant series of revisions that are never finished, only refined or abandoned. What was true six months ago, that my marriage was a disaster, is no longer true today. *Divorce* is a disaster. Then again, maybe it won't be six months down the line. Nothing ever stays the same.

Daddy?

Yes, poppet?

Will you come inside the house today?

A terrible thought strikes me: *Beth put her up to this.* She's got something set up inside the house that's going to set my stomach churning. She's using Poppy as a weapon, as a lure.

Poppy looks up at me, clutches at my hand. *Will you, Daddy?*

I'm being ridiculous. Paranoid. I've been visiting a child psychologist, as well as an adult therapist. I'm gradually becoming a world-class expert on the various stages of development in the human mind. The child psychologist is there to advise on how I can minimize the effect of the separation on Poppy. One way is to try to be with her and her mother in the old house at the same time. It's good for her to see that we're OK together, that we don't actively hate each other.

The therapeutic orthodoxy is that it's good for her to witness lies.

All right, poppet. All right. If you want me to.

We walk down the path. The red door is the same as ever.

Everything is the same as ever – the scrubby plant pots beneath the bay windows, the wheelie-bin with the wheel missing, the hedge that always needs trimming. It's easy to imagine that I'm just going to walk back into my old life, that Beth will greet me with a friendly nod, even a kiss, and a hot cup of something dull but reassuring.

But it's a man who opens the door. A good ten years younger than me, good-looking in a dissolute way, with a flat stomach and a full head of medium-length, sun-flecked brown hair. It's six in the evening but he's wearing a dressing-gown – *my* dressing-gown – and smoking a ciga-rette, which he discards when he sees Poppy.

Oliver! Poppy throws her arms around his neck and gives him a kiss.

Oliver smiles, hugs her back. *Hello, poppet.*

He calls her *poppet.*

Still holding Poppy in one arm, he looks at me. Brazenly inspects me. I can read his eyes: there's judgement, com-plaint, a certain critical guardedness. I have a feeling he's been hearing a highly edited version of our marriage. The director's cut.

You must be Spike.

Daniel.

Oliver, can we play that game again?

What game, poppet?

The throwing-in-the-air game! Please please please please!

He calls her poppet. He has stolen my dressing-gown and my child's nickname.

A light footstep sounds from inside the door. A cautious but bright unmade-up face appears. It's the primary swag, the first of the looted spoils of my marriage – Beth. Once a little on the heavy side, she has lost weight. Her blonde hair

65

is piled up on her head and secured with clips decorated with silver butterflies. Her face is oval, still relatively unlined for her age. The mouth is wide and thin, but not without sensuality. There is a guardedness in her expression that she has only recently acquired, yet she looks healthy and pretty. She is wearing a thin silk dress that I last remember on a silver beach in Australia. There was an indigo twilight. We watched a pelican fly until it disappeared. Her head rested on my shoulder.

She looks happy today. She is not angry for once, but there is something in her face that suggests disdain, triumph. She puts her hand on Oliver's shoulder. The three of them make an attractive tableau.

Would you like to come in? she says, innocently.

Please, Daddy, please, Daddy, please, Daddy, please, Daddy . . .

OK, pop – cupcake. Just for a moment.

For the first time since I left the house, more than a year ago, I walk inside, following Oliver and Beth. Oliver is still carrying . . . poppet. I wish he would put her down. I wish he would put her down and never touch her or speak to her again.

I wish he would not steal her. I wish he would return my life to me.

It's a warm spring day, and there is a large circular wrought-iron table set out in the back garden. There are other children in the garden. Their mothers, benignly ignoring them, are sitting around the table, chatting happily, eating cake, home-made cake not cake bought in supermarkets like I have. It's the set-up, the sting I feared. It's a tableau arranged to show the sharp contrast between Beth's life and mine. Those present, all women, smile indulgently as I appear. Miranda Green is there, and Charlotte Hughes-Milton, and Lizzy Grist. There is milk in a jug, and bone china. It looks lovely. It looks like a home. It looks like a scene designed to make me feel lonely and sad. It works.

Hello, Danny.

Hello, Miranda.

Hello, stranger.

Hello, Charlotte.

Look who's here.

Oh, it's you, is it, Liz?

I've never got on too well with Lizzy Grist. She's dull and shrewish, and thinks all men are bastards anyway, evidenced by the prompt failure of every relationship she's ever had. The collapse of Beth's and my marriage is further satisfying evidence for her working theory of gender politics. Charlotte and Miranda are all right, but I haven't seen hide or hair of them since Beth and I split.

I've not seen them because I'm outside the network. It is a network. When a marriage splits up, it's hell for everybody – that's a given. But for women there's a whole structure, an entire culture of single parenthood. They get custody of the kids because that's what mothers get. They get the house, or the key to the council house, because they've got custody of the kids. They get maintenance for the same reason. Men are required merely to go out and work to pay the bills. In the eyes of the law, men are little more than an ATM, a hole in the wall.

In contrast, the women, the single mothers who are now in the majority at the school where Poppy goes, meet before school, after school, at weekends. Women have a talent for connection anyway, and are even more connected when in distress, because they can solidify as a group around it.

67

There is nothing more satisfying in times of stress than a common enemy, and the common enemy in this instance tends to be men. Also, if men are *a priori* bad, it saves a lot of painful self-scrutiny. Culprit identified, no confusion to add to the general misery.

On the other hand men, the crude mechanicals in the equation, the ATMs, are alone. They can't allow themselves a common enemy – at least, not if they're guilt-ridden, gender-politics-sensitive liberals like I used to be. Further-more, they don't have a talent for connection – quite the reverse. Their talent is for aloneness. Men mistake it for strength.

You're looking tired, Danny.

Am I, Liz? I wonder what the explanation for that might be.

Liz's eyes are small and black, and close together. She has pale skin and mousy hair that falls down her back in a dull cascade. When she says I'm looking tired, I take it to mean that I am looking old and ugly in comparison with Oliver. This is true, but it's not helping my digestion. The fresh cake tastes very good. Tastes of love.

How's the work going?

This time it's Charlotte speaking. A nice woman, rather lost for words most of the time, shy and nervous, with a paradoxical extremity in her choice of dress. She is wearing a 'Barbie Is A Slut' T-shirt and a pair of boots with huge heels. I'd thought we were friends until the split happened.

So-so. I've been . . .

I have to be careful what I say here. Actually, I've just been given a small job for Hopkinson's Perfect Plastic Buckets, but if I show the slightest sign of worldly success, Beth will be on to her lawyers looking to prise an even larger chunk of my depleted income out of my Lilliputian coffers. They insisted on taking my last year's total as indicative of my earning power. It didn't cut any ice that my work comes in dribs and drabs – and it was my bad luck that I had my best year for four years when we separated. Now the most profitable work has dried up again, and I'm stuffed. Already I work six days out of seven simply to pay my rent, spousal maintenance and child support.

Another slice of cake, Danny?

No, thank you, Oliver.

It's nice here, with the sun beating down, friends together in the back garden, the sound of Poppy's laughter from her room.

How's Caleb, Miranda?

Caleb is Miranda's seven-year-old, a charmless child with appalling manners and an enthusiasm for acts of extreme violence. Out of the corner of my eye I can see him gleefully dissecting a still wriggling worm with a lolly stick. Miranda is a brisk, no-nonsense middle-class professional, with a flourishing public-relations business. Even her small-talk snaps out as if she is hectoring one of her three secretaries.

He's fine. He's a boy, you know. Lots of rough-and-tumbling.

And when he gets older, lots of shooting and mugging, I imagine. The worm is in what looks like six pieces now. Caleb's smile has grown wider.

That's nice. Does he see much of his dad?

The atmosphere sours a little. Liz rattles her cup on its saucer.

He's gone abroad for six months. Never get so much as a phone call.

Bastard, I mutter.

To abandon your kid because you're having trouble with a marriage is unforgivable, unacceptable and shit in every way. Although I have to confess that, at one point after the separation, after what seemed like the two-hundredth screaming match that week, I could see the appeal, and savoured the fantasy: to disappear, to be away from it all, to distance myself from the wreckage and start again. It looks good, from a distance. It probably *is* good, especially if you find yourself a new woman, a new life. But it's wrong. Simple as that.

I think he's adjusting reasonably well.

The worm is in twelve pieces now, and Caleb is chuckling to himself. He's eyeing a trundling snail that is making ponderous progress across the masonry rabbit that decorates the rockery. The rockery I built, in the garden I dug and planted year after year.

Go on, have some more cake, Danny.

Fuck off, Oliver. You're trying to poison me. Poison me with the love in that cake, the love you know you possess, which I stopped wanting. But now you've got it, it's suddenly become mysteriously appealing.

Did you bake it specially? I say, curtly.

Oh, I can't cook! says Oliver, crinkling his eyes in a fashion he obviously thinks fetching.

Oh, poor little me, I say, parodically, half under my breath.

Well, I can't, says Oliver, simpering a little.

Men are hopeless, says Liz, fondly, and with a predictability that the circling sun might envy.

Are they? I say, draining my teacup.

Oh, she's only joking, says Charlotte, smiling her anxious smile. *We love men. Don't we?*

Of course, says Miranda. *You're too sensitive, Danny.*

You *don't love men, do you, Liz?* says Oliver, throwing me a conspiratorial look. I almost like him for half a split second.

I don't dislike them, says Liz, constructing herself a smug roll-up with a drug addict's ease. *They're just a bit messed up. They don't really have much of a clue.*

All right, it's nothing, and all right, I'm being a baby. But I'm sitting here outside what used to be my house, in a happy, sunny garden that used to be my garden, which is now full of friends and cake and laughter and Poppy screaming in delight at something Beth is doing with her in the kitchen, and my fuse is short. I've heard this sort of thing just one time too many. I turn to Liz, who is focusing on her roll-up.

Do you think men and women are equal, Liz?

She looks up, surprised but unperturbed.

Of course I do.

We all do, says Charlotte.

Yes, says Miranda.

I nod.

Tell me some of the things women are better at.

What?

We all know there are things that women are traditionally better at. It's not controversial. Name some of them.

Well, says Liz, sitting forward in her chair a little, beginning to relish the task, *I think they're probably better at multi-tasking.*

Definitely, says Oliver. *Men tend to focus on more specific goals in a linear way at the expense of everything else.*

Women are more in touch with their feelings. They have

an emotional intelligence that men lack, I suppose, says Charlotte.

Yes, says Liz.

They're better at nurturing.

And communicating. Men find it so hard to speak of their feelings, don't they? says Charlotte, mildly.

That's so true, says Oliver, shaking his head and tugging ruminatively at the cord on his – *my* – dressing-gown.

I think, says Liz, stroking her chin thoughtfully, *that women can read social situations far better than men. That we're sensitive to other people's feelings in a way that men simply aren't.*

Yes, says Oliver.

Yes, says Miranda, nodding calmly.

Women are more capable of love, aren't they? says Charlotte. *They've got a knack for it. For giving. For sharing.*

Men are so emotionally constipated, says Oliver.

Women are diplomats, says Liz. *They know how to sort things out, how to make the peace. Men just blunder on.*

I hate to say it, says Oliver, in a way that suggests he is in fact delighted to say it, *but I think, when all is said and done, women are simply more grown-up than men.*

More evolved, I suppose, says Liz.

But that's not to say we don't like them, says Charlotte.

Of course, men are responsible for most of the sexual abuse and the casual violence.

And war.

They can't find things when they lose them.

And they don't do their share of the housework.

And they can't iron.

And they never get what it is we're trying to say unless we spell it out in six-foot-high capital letters.

There's a brief hiatus. Tea is sipped. Mouthfuls of cake are primly consumed.

Is that it? I say, getting ready to leave.

I think so, says Liz, a faint, satisfied smile on her face. All the faces round the table wear similar expressions.

Good. And what kind of things are men better at?

A current of faint surprise seems to travel around the gathering, earthing itself on four suddenly furrowed foreheads.

What?

We've listed all the special virtues of women. We can all agree on them. Me included. But what are the special virtues specific to men?

Silence. More silence. An embarrassed giggle from Charlotte. I turn to go. *I think I've made my point about the female definition of equality.*

I'm a man, says Oliver.

Then you should try behaving like one, I reply.

Liz opens her mouth to say something, but I cut her off before she has a chance to speak. *I'll tell you one thing men are better at*, I say, flatly. *Putting up with things. Biting their lip, and putting up with things. Putting up with bucketloads and bucketloads of absolute shit being poured over their head. And not fighting back. They're better at not fighting back. They're better at taking it, taking it, taking it, and then just walking away.*

Without another word, I turn on my heel and walk through to the kitchen, where Poppy appears to be making rock cakes with Beth.

Poppy, Daddy has to go now. I put my hand on her shoulder.

Daddy! Look what you made me do, she says, angrily. A small drumlin she was forging out of the cake dough has lost its peak, and become flattened. *Not fair. I hate you Daddy! Go away!*

Children are gay and innocent and heartless. So says J. M. Barrie, and who am I, one of a million Peter Pans, to disagree?

'Bye, poppet.

She says nothing, but begins to cry. Not about me leaving, but about her cake dough being the wrong shape.

Beth looks at me sternly. *I think you'd better be off.*

See you, then, I say, in my best impersonation of nonchalance.

I walk away, out of the house alone and unregarded, the taste of sweet crumbs in my mouth.

I flee the trouble: a man's greatest talent and his greatest temptation.

4

I fell in love for the first time when I was eighteen. It had been five years since my experience with Sharon Smith, and I had built on that box-room epiphany and extended it through other clandestine experiences in cloakrooms, alleyways and empty parks. I was still a virgin – I had still not been, on my own definition, 'out' with a girl properly, although I had experimented with several, trying fitfully to get the measure of them in all their blithe unfathomability.

Such an odd relationship, the boy–girl one seemed then. It was as though you were in a room with one other person and you were trying to talk normally and pretend everything was absolutely unremarkable but there was a huge, terrifying, overwhelming and exciting presence just out of sight of both of you, yet you could hear its breath, you could register its footstep, you could sense it at all times. This shadowy golem was sex.

It's hard to remember what it was like to fall in love for the first time. The reality here, like everywhere else, has got twisted up with received information, the diet of first-love drama, fictionalization, cinema, TV. Over the decades, where I start and the collective, electronic and otherwise mediated world ends has become increasingly unclear to me. The memory, like the self and the memory of the self, is no longer pure.

If I were to point to one thing that feels first-hand and genuine, I'd say this: it was *easy*. One's antennae in middle age, so taut and sensitive to potential for damage, were then innocent and thus anaesthetized. Love seemed entirely good, without drawback or price tag.

The love of women seemed a right, an anticipated pleasure, and a certainty. That's not to say I wasn't terrified of women – though for a different reason than I'm terrified now. Then I was terrified of the golem, of their strangeness, their potential for evoking my most dreaded emotion – embarrassment.

But I also sensed that it was part of the way the world worked that girls wanted boyfriends, that it was culturally demanded that they should have one, and that, sooner or later, I would be one of the boyfriends they wanted. Young people fell in love with each other, that was what they *did*, sooner or later. Not like now, nearly thirty years on, when you're so stripped down to the bones by pain and failure, so wrinkled, slack and tired in body that it's hard to imagine anyone ever loving you again.

Then, it was a cinch: you simply had to wait, and the much-vaunted magic would self-conjure. You would be loved. And for a man, back then, there was an inbuilt conviction that you would not only be loved, you would *allow* yourself to be loved. Women sought out relationships. Men struggled for sex, but otherwise manoeuvred to stay free. Thus the exchange always involved a certain degree of sacrifice for the man: going out with a woman represented a dilution of masculinity, just as for a woman going out with a man represented an increase in femaleness. It was a hang-over from history, I suppose, which has disappeared now to a degree, though by no means entirely. It would be good to think that it had, because all forms of inequality in a rela-tionship tend towards dysfunction.

But then, in the mid-1970s, I was – despite being a virgin, despite being awkward with girls – cocky and sure of my-self. Sooner or later I would fall in love. Sooner or later I would be adored, promoted from geek to god in the twinkle of an eye.

At the time I was at college. In those days, there were two courses that outranked in fashionability all the others: sociology and social psychology. Helen Palmer and I were on the social-psychology course.

It was a polytechnic in the south of England, about as far from any dreaming spires as you could imagine. The nature of the students was pretty standard for that type of establish-ment – essentially Philistine, with a high degree of political affectation, mostly concerned with getting a good degree in order to land a decent job, and getting drunk. I've never liked students, even when I was one, but being at college had its compensations, Helen being the chief one.

I was not a fan of sleeping around – not that I'd had the chance. I recognized that perpetual promiscuity, even at eigh-teen years old, was an unrealistic fantasy, and that the act of penetrative sex was too intimate to be shrugged off as a leisure activity like table football. I just knew that it was something awesome. It was common to read in books and magazines, and to see in films (all the *Carry Ons*) back then that sex was fun, it was a *laugh*. That didn't ring

77

true then and doesn't now, although laughter came into it. Sex at its heart was the most deadly serious enterprise there was. How could something be thought trivial when its result could spread down through time and as yet unimagined generations?

It was after a seminar on Milgram's experiments with conformity that I finally got up the nerve to speak to Helen. I had been watching her out of the corner of my eye, glimpsing her through the sheet of blonde hair that drooped down from her crown when she was making notes. She didn't say much, but when she did it was honest and to the point. Also I liked her voice, which was coarser than her pale, delicate face suggested it might be. It had a sour tang of inner London, a knowingness that held a powerful attraction for suburban me, a reverse form of social climbing (during that epoch, the more working class you were, the cooler it made you). She wore Wrangler jeans and cheese-cloth tops, no makeup. Her at-rest expression was puzzlement. I found this endearing: everyone else on the course seemed to be trying too hard to display certainty.

Stanley Milgram was a psychologist who devised a series of ingenious tests to gauge the extent to which people were inclined to defer to authority. He invited the subjects of his experiments to a laboratory and placed them on the near side of a glass screen. There, they sat and observed another 'subject' – actually an actor – in a sealed-off room on the other side of the glass. This nervous-looking stooge was strapped into a chair, apparently to prevent his escape.

A man in a white coat instructed the *real* subject of the experiment, the one on the near side of the glass screen, that they were taking part in an exercise to test not obedience to authority but the ability to perform tasks under stress. They were then given control of an impressive-looking device and told that it was capable of delivering powerful electrical shocks to the person on the other side of the screen, should that person fail to answer certain questions correctly. The shocks, of course, were phoney, and the actor faked his screams of pain when they were delivered. But, in the overwhelming majority of cases, the subjects were prepared to administer the shocks to the point of apparent unconsciousness in the victim simply because a man in a white coat had told them to do so.

I had wanted to talk to Helen ever since the seminar had started, but had never found the courage or the right excuse. It takes quite a deep reservoir of courage to ask a woman for a date – and it remains stubbornly conventional for the man to do the asking, for the woman to do the accepting or rejecting.

The way in which this courting ritual is portrayed dramatically is rather like the way death was once shown in Westerns: a grisly and agonizing event that is passed off as essentially painless and even bland. However, those were the rules, and I was stuck with them.

I took a deep breath and sidled over. (I'm not sure what the precise definition of sidling *is*, but I've got a strong impression that this was what I was doing. It was a wafting, a muffled manoeuvring that meant I interrupted her clear passage to the door so that she would have to stop before she could get round me.) I smiled at her. She gave a little nod that might have meant anything, including 'Fuck off.' Therein lies the need for courage: you have to keep going, even if there's a sizeable chance that you're about to make a fool of yourself.

Hi.

Pardon?

She was on her way round me when this exchange took place. I could smell her now, an odd wet-hay scent that I imagined emanated from her body rather than any kind of cosmetic. She hesitated. She could have kept on walking, yet she hesitated. This also might have meant anything.

What do you think you would have done?

Sorry?

She frowned. I had not noticed her frown before. It made little furrows in her otherwise high, smooth forehead. I wanted to kiss away those furrows. But what was happening now was mere theatre. My voice suggested only measured indifference and academic curiosity.

If it had been you sitting there. If it had been you pressing the button. Would you have given the shock? Would you have kept going until the man behind the panel was unconscious?

Oh. She seemed surprised now that the question bore framing. *I'm sure I would. I'd like to think that I wouldn't. I'd like to pretend to myself that I was more independent of thought. But you can't be sure. It's easy to imagine yourself in a more virtuous light than you actually are. It's hard to know yourself. Do you?*

No, I said. *No, I don't. And you don't know me, either. My name's Danny Savage. Some people call me Spike.*

At this point, it must have been clear enough what I was after (not sex, not just sex, but that was involved). It must have been transparent that I fancied her. Otherwise, why would I have walked over and started talking to her like that? Why not to a man? Why not to one of the ugly girls? (She knew perfectly well, I could tell, that she was attractive.) The moment for me to be crushed was already there, looming. I had only asked her whether she would push the button, but the subtext was plain. So, would she push the button? Would she administer pain to the stooge?

I'm Helen Palmer.

Still no movement, no sign of a bolt, just a silence that needed to be filled, another possibility of rejection to be surmounted.

Do you fancy a cup of coffee?

I've got another seminar in an hour, and I really should prepare for it . . .

My gut churned slightly. A vision swam before my eyes of kicked teeth. The awareness of my own clumsiness, my own lack of physical charm pressed on unprotected nerves. Rejection. The hated heartburn of foolishness.

. . . but what the hell.

She smiled. The churning in my gut reversed itself; the premature self-hatred and doubt converted to premature triumph and joy.

She'd said yes.

But only to a cup of coffee. There was much work to be done before I could fall in love for the first time.

At the coffee shop, I spoke a little too fast, a little too eagerly, not only from nervousness but also because this was, if not a courtship ritual, then the possible preamble to a courtship ritual. I was seeking to establish a number of crucial facts. Did she have a boyfriend already? If so, did she love him? Did we have anything to talk about other than whether plain or chocolate digestives were the best accompaniment to instant coffee? I didn't find out all I needed to know – that would have required me to be more direct than such a pre-ritual allowed – but she made no direct *reference* to a boyfriend. Also she sat quite close to me – closer than she would have if she had found me wholly repulsive – and we kept reasonably steady eye-contact.

The first half-hour was on the relatively safe territory of Milgram. Then I found out that she was from Peckham, that she had a younger sister, and that she wanted to be a social worker. Not so interesting, but it didn't matter. It was personal, it transcended the purely functional. I had breached her armour. This was sufficient for my purposes. We made no plan to meet again, but a precedent had been established. The coffee ritual would be reprised.

In those days, everything I 'knew' about women was cobbled together out of prejudice, received information, propaganda, and stuff I'd picked up from TV, movies, gossip and magazines. These are the sort of assumptions I would have made:

Women were nicer than men.

They didn't want sex as much as you did, and only granted it to you as a gift if you managed to crack some code that only they knew.

On receipt of that gift, women required you to sign up to a certain set of obligations, which were never made explicit.

Women were as clever as men academically, but not necessarily in other, more important fields, like playing poker and getting quiz answers right.

They were less daring than men.

Women, with the sole exception of Carol Moon, liked awful music.

Women had a sense of humour, but they forgot the punchlines to jokes.

They remembered birthdays and knew how to wrap gifts.

They did things like tidy up and cook and take responsibility for things that you were too cool to think about.

That was that. Such was the gender-related knowledge of Danny 'Spike' Savage at that time.

Armed with this knowledge, I had coffee with Helen again a week later. Again, she had to go to another class shortly afterwards, but this time I took the plunge.

The Exorcist had just opened and Christians were demonstrating outside the Gaumonts and Essoldos of Britain, because the film 'would promote devil worship'. Fleets of St John ambulances were parked outside cinemas to minister to those who fainted. Highbrow film critics dismissed the movie as disgusting trash. Clips showed a young girl's head rotating on her shoulders.

Terence found it 'interesting' that I had picked for a first date a movie about a pubescent girl who is possessed by the devil. He found it less interesting when I told him it was my second choice after *Bambi*, which had been sold out. I take his point that it was not, perhaps, the obvious film for a first date, and it stands as further proof that my knowledge of women was rudimentary. All the same, Helen went for it. I asked and she said OK, just like that. Eight o'clock outside the cinema.

I say 'first date', but even then that concept was muddying as the lines of demarcation between the sexes blurred. The idea of women as friends had crept into the mainstream. When my father, or any man of his generation, asked a woman out, there was no doubt that a courtship ritual was being observed. It wasn't a potential friendship that was being sought but a potential mate.

But I wasn't sure that what I had was really a first date. Perhaps I was just making a new friend. Certainly, she was a girl and I was a boy, but it was possible that we were doing no more than seeing a movie. Then, I didn't understand the language of signs, gestures, silences and hints, only crude reason. I didn't see the beauty of the game of seduction, only a series of obstacles to what was a practical goal. In short, I was literal and Helen was symbolic.

Obvious to the point of cliché, but it took me a long time to get *that* Love Secret. Some men never get it. Women never admit it. Why? Because they are symbolic. If they want to tell you something important they may give you the means by which to divine it, but they will almost certainly fail to spell it out as a man would. This drives men to distraction, and it gets women pretty steamed up too, because men never really do get it the way they're supposed to. Feminism seems to have done little to erode this fundamental distinction. I don't know why. I was being taught that culture was everything, but perhaps it isn't. Maybe our ruination is biological. Who knows? Either way, we're ruined.

It hardly matters, anyway. What does matter is that at that time and on that date – or non-date – I didn't understand this difference at all.

No teenage girl, let alone Helen, would ever have been so crude. I do not know what she did on that evening before she met me to see *The Exorcist* because I never asked her, and if I had she wouldn't have told me. However, from where I stand now, I am almost certain that she would have called one of her friends about our assignation. She would have worked out whether it was a friend thing or a date thing. She would have had a conversation along these lines.

HELEN'S FRIEND: *What do you think? Are you excited?*
HELEN: *I don't know. Maybe.*
HF: *Do you like him?*

84

H: *He seems nice. I'm not sure what he wants.*

HF: *Do you think he fancies you?*

H: Laughs.

HF: *Of **course** he fancies you. How could he not fancy you? You're beautiful. What does he look like?*

H: *Ordinary. He's OK. I've seen worse.*

HF: *Tall, short, dark, blond, fat, thin, what?*

H: *He's about average height, brown hair, slim. Quite nice-looking.*

HF: *So how far have you got?*

H: *We've been for coffee a few times.*

HF: *Did he flirt with you?*

H: *I'm not sure. I think so.*

HF: *Did he sit close? Did he touch your clothes? Did he hold his look?*

H (laughing): *All of the above.*

HF: *There you are then. Do you fancy him?*

H: *I don't really know him. He's got nice eyes. Pale brown. Yellow flecks.*

HF: *You **fancy** him. What are you going to wear?*

Then she would have told her friend what she was going to wear, and they would have discussed whether it was appropriate, what messages it would send out – *No, that's too obvious . . . too subtle . . . too trashy . . . Yes, that's exactly right.* The grasp of the symbolic.

HF: *What are you going to see?*

H: *The Exorcist!*

HF: *You're joking! What was he thinking of?*

H: *God knows.*

HF: *I can't believe he's taking you to see* The Exorcist!

H: *There's nothing else on.*

HF: *Go for a walk in the park. Take a boat ride on the lake. Go on a date that doesn't involve vomit.*

H (laughs): *It's not really a date. We're just going to the pictures.*

HF: *Would you let him snog you?*

I suspect that this imaginary conversation would have gone on for a long time, might have encompassed several other friends chiming in. It would have involved advice, planning, strategy, according to whether she wanted to go further or not. The subject would have been examined from multiple standpoints. I know some women who would have done none of this, they would have just read their textbooks on Lacan and Melanie Klein and considered it too trivial to matter, just as some men would have approached the date/meeting-with-a-friend with no thought of sex, just the potential merits of the cinematic experience.

But I think they would have been in a minority.

Anyway, I also had a conversation with a friend, a male friend, about the forthcoming date/purely-social-non-sexual occasion.

I'm going out with Helen Palmer tonight.

That one with the big tits?

Yeh.

Reckon you can fuck her?

Yeh.

Give her one for me.

Right.

That was it.

Men were like that then. Many men still are. But there are important things to grasp about this conversation. Allow me to translate.

I'm going out with Helen Palmer tonight.

I don't know what to say.

Yeh.

*I have **no idea** what to say.*

Yeh.

Phew.

Right.

A more advanced translation, using the improbable assumption that the men involved were party to their unconscious thoughts, might be:

I'm going out with Helen Palmer tonight.

*My **God**. You're going out with a **girl**. How exciting and how strange. I am envious of you, and yet relieved it is not me. Envious because there is a possibility of sex, but relieved because you might enter into an emotional transaction with another human being that will take you to a strange and possibly frightening place in your head and your heart that I can still only fantasize about but undeniably fear as well as desire.*

Yeh.

I hope when you're finished, you will find some way to tell me something about women, because they bewilder me: the only one I've ever known is my mother and she can destroy me just by withdrawing her love. Are all women like that? Oh, God, I'm so paralysed with insecurity, can you say anything to help me?

Yeh.

I'm going to keep the conversation purely distilled into its sexual element because this will establish the one form of connection that we have, which is that we are both heterosexual men – or so we would at all costs have each other believe.

87

Right.

One could keep going like this for some time, delving deeper into the measureless strata of human unknowing, but it gets too depressing.

As a matter of fact, I had the rare privilege – for a man – of speaking intimately to a woman before my date with Helen. I had a confidante, a non-sexual, non-romantic, genuine friend who was female. I had known her since my early teenage years, and our friendship was born of mutual affection and our lack of attraction to each other. Not a rarity now, but quite something then. That conversation was very different from the one I had with my male friend.

FEMALE FRIEND: *So who is this woman?*

ME: *She's Helen Palmer.*

FF: *And?*

ME: *She's special.*

FF: *How is she special?*

ME: *I don't know. It's just a feeling. Stupid, really.*

FF: *Not stupid. Feelings count. Are you nervous?*

ME: *I'm looking forward to it.*

FF: *Really?*

ME: *Absolutely. It's a dead cert.*

FF: ***Really?***

ME: *I'm terrified.*

FF: *Don't be nervous, Spike. It'll be absolutely fine. Just relax. What are you going to see?*

ME: *The Exorcist.*

FF: *Interesting choice.*

ME: *They'd sold out of tickets for* Bambi.

FF: *Right.*

ME: *I've made a proper cake of myself, haven't I? She'll probably stand me up now.*

FF: *I doubt it.*

ME: *You don't think I messed up, do you?*

FF: *I'm sure it doesn't matter. She's going to be so excited about going out with you that she's not going to be thinking about the film.*

ME: *She's probably just too embarrassed to say no. I'm not even sure it's a date. All we've done is have coffee.*

FF: *How many times have you met for coffee?*

ME: *Twice.*

FF: *How did the first happen?*

ME: *I accosted her after a lecture.*

FF: *And then?*

ME: *A few days later.*

FF: *Was the next coffee meeting arranged in advance?*

ME: *Sort of. She knew I'd be at the lecture. She probably expected me to ask her again.*

FF: *Now, Spike, think carefully. Was there any difference in her the second time you met from the first?*

ME: *Difference? Um. I don't know.*

FF: *This is important. Reconstruct the scene in your head. What was she wearing? The same as the previous meeting?*

ME: *No. She was dressed a bit better, I should say. The first time she was a bit scruffy. Her clothes were nicer. She was wearing a skirt and blouse, I think.*

FF: *Did you notice any particular smell?*

ME: *Now that you mention it, on the first occasion it was a kind of wet-hay smell. The smell of her hair, I think. But the second time, it was muskier . . . like a . . . a . . .*

FF: *Perfume?*

ME: *Could have been.*

FF: *One more thing. Her lips. Were her lips any different?*

ME: *Her lips? I don't know.*

FF: *Shinier?*

ME: *A bit shinier, maybe. Yes, definitely shinier.*

FF: *Lipstick.*

ME: *So where do I stand?*

FF: *It's a date. She made an effort for the second meet. Nothing too obvious. Just enough.*

ME: *Really?*

FF: *Anyway, Spike, there's not a girl in that college who wouldn't want to be in her shoes.*

ME: *Really?*

FF: *Of course.*

And so on. Support, encouragement, perception, loving lies. It was exactly what I would expect from a woman.

It was exactly what I expected from Carol Moon.

I'd got to know her well since Sharon Smith's party. There was something about her that just made me want to be mates with her – her openness, her intelligence, her lack of artifice, perhaps. And the complete absence of certain female staples – charm, flirtatiousness, coyness, 'sweetness'. Carol was tough, thoughtful and down to earth. That was probably why she could never keep a boyfriend. Even though I wasn't attracted to her, I could see she was good-looking, with an athletic, slightly gauche body that looked terrific in a swimsuit, but men were afraid of her ability to see through them. Even then, she was frustrated with men and what she called their 'silly games'. Strange how different it looks from that side of the gender gap – how each side is suspicious of the other, how each caricatures and characterizes and demonizes.

Her love of music remained a powerful bond. We went shopping for records together, then rushed back to one or other of our houses to listen to the latest Leon Russell or Janis Joplin, Jackson Browne or J. J. Cale, or some obscure blues import. She was a genuine fan. Her passion for music was the same as mine – a strange love of sadness, a taste for the pain that was at the heart of all roots music. There was something peripherally melancholic in Carol, as if she sensed that her life was somehow the wrong shape to fit her carefully considered desires. She said the same sort of thing about me, although for a long time I didn't believe her.

Yes, her suspicions were well founded. And, yes, it was Carol Moon who gave me my nickname.

I remember that warm, dusty blue night – leaving the halls of residence where I lived, three miles from the cinema, and running all the way. Running and laughing. It was just like in a film. There have been few times when my life has taken on all the colour, definition and *reality* of an artificially mediated experience, but this was one of them. I was Young Man on First Date played by a character actor with, in fact, very little character at that age but plenty of curiosity and enthusiasm.

With Carol's help, I had convinced myself that I really was going on a date, that Helen quite possibly fancied me. I recognized that there was work to do, that I had to be charming, fascinating, witty, mildly suggestive and so on and so forth. But something was going to happen – I could feel it. I couldn't articulate it, though, because I thought that if I did I would bring down retribution from the gods, that the act of expecting or anticipating such a thing would prevent it happening. This superstition, of tempting fate, has stayed with me, despite my countervailing belief that the universe is empty, cold and indifferent. It has nothing to do with being a man: it has to do with being human and not being able to manage without God. Or so Terence would have it.

Anyway, I ran and I laughed until I reached the edge of the precinct, at exactly the time we had arranged.

Helen wasn't there.

I didn't understand that women were always late for dates. Carol Moon, my sole source of reliable information in these matters, hadn't mentioned it. By ten past eight I was frightened. I thought she'd stood me up. I thought there were going to be two horror movies in town that night.

There were Christians outside the cinema, carrying placards reading 'Satan's Work' and 'Stop This Evil Filth'. I had purchased two tickets and I clasped them in my increasingly sweaty palm. (One thing I did understand about women then, as now, is that on a first date I had to cough up for the tickets.)

Then a chant went up from the protesters – I heard it as 'Close this town', but I think it was probably 'Close it down' – and I looked at them and thought how pathetic they were, how completely they were prepared to deny reality, how absolutely they were determined to impose their version of the truth upon others. I found myself chanting back, *God is dead, God is dead, God is dead.*

The protesters seemed to hear what I was saying. They turned towards me and then it was as if they were chanting at *me*, not about the film: *Close it down!*

I was chanting back, a one-man ranter stood up on a date

and turning his rage on the Lord and his band of fuck-wit believers: *God is dead, God is dead.*

It dawned on me that these Christians didn't look as meek and mild as was customary. One or two were the standard-issue little old ladies, but there were several large, middle-aged men, one of them enormous, with a head like a genetically modified tomato. I had heard that in America fundamentalist Christians sometimes attacked abortionists, but I hadn't realized the Anglicans could get so worked up. However, Tomato Head was moving towards me in a very threatening fashion. I kept chanting, *God is dead, God is dead*, in a voice that was beginning to falter. I didn't like the look of Tomato Head one bit.

A few seconds later, he was three or four feet from me, bellowing, *Close it down*, almost into my face. It was clear that he was furious.

Then he stopped, sneered at me, and moved a step closer. When he spoke, it was in a voice far grimmer and rougher than I could have imagined issuing from a disciple of the Lord: *Do you have a problem with Jaysus, boy? Because if you hate the Lawd, then you hate me. Yea, you have offended me and my friends. Where I come from, we believe in an eye for an eye and a tooth for a tooth.*

The voice, sure enough, was American. By the sound of it he was one of those nutty Midwest fundamentalists. He took a step closer, so that I could smell his breath, which reminded me of luncheon meat and stewed tea. I looked into his eyes. Suddenly I could see that whoever this man was, and whatever his religious persuasion, he was insane, and poised to do me harm. I blinked once, twice. I considered the plausibility of a rapid Pauline conversion. Then I heard a voice behind me.

Are you a Christian?

It was soft, but rough at the edges, stippled already with the effects of cigarette smoke. I smelt the aroma of Marlboro, mixed with some perfume that I would soon come to know very well. Tomato Head looked puzzled as Helen came and stood between us.

Are you a Christian? she repeated, slightly louder this time.

The fat man looked at her. *Missy, I think you should keep out of this.*

Could you answer my question, sir? Are you a Christian?

Missy, that's a pretty dumb question.

Humour me by answering it.

Am I a Christian? You bet, missy. Jaysus be praised.

And Helen gave an innocent smile, shrugged her shoulders, and said, plainly, *Then forgive him.*

With this, she grabbed my elbow, and steered me away. I glanced behind me. Tomato Head was standing there, glaring. I felt Helen's hand on my elbow, pushing me towards the cinema entrance. Then we were inside, safe in Satan's lair.

It was a quarter past eight. I'll always remember that as the exact time I fell in love with Helen. I have always fallen in love quite easily. This, introspection is beginning to show me, is not very clever. This may be the first step in making sense of my high failure rate with women.

Yet it's also, in a way . . . right. Although I fall in love quite easily, I haven't fallen in love very *often*, and when I have, it has always been obvious to me, with the benefit of hindsight, that the love was real.

What is real love? Here language fails me. Here my thinking erodes into the vernacular of advertising: a young

94

couple consuming Häagen Dazs in front of a flickering hearth/TV, hooded looks concealed behind steaming Gold Blend. Love is the central association behind a vast array of products. Meat is love. Ice-cream is love. Perfume is love. Diamonds are love. My understanding of it, therefore, is ersatz. But, like failure, I know it when I see it. And at that moment I was in love with Helen.

When Helen next spoke, she seemed simultaneously motherly, piqued, slightly cross and sexy as hell.

What did you ***do****?*

I don't know. They were annoying me. It's only a film.

They just started threatening you?

No. I started shouting at them.

What were you saying?

'God is dead.' I thought it was safe. I thought they were Christians.

Christians invented the Crusades and the Inquisition. Don't underestimate the violence of belief.

Want some popcorn?

I changed the subject, because although I had fallen in love with Helen, I felt humiliated. Helen had saved *me*. In my mind men saved women, certainly in situations that involved the threat of physical violence. I knew this because I watched Hollywood films and English TV. From my earliest days, before I carved out a career in advertising, I confused media messages with life.

The template of men saving women was pretty much invariable, if you didn't count Emma Peel in *The Avengers*. I should have stuffed that God-botherer's tomato head up what his countrymen would have called his ass. Instead Helen, with her smoke-stained voice, had defused the situation.

No popcorn, thanks.
Ice-cream? Everton mints?
No, really.
Smarties?

By the time we sat down to watch the film, I was still desperate for my equilibrium to be restored.

Although at the time *The Exorcist* was widely derided as a ludicrous work of exploitative schlock, it was plain from the start of the film that it was going to be frightening, rather than simply horrific. It was all the quietness before anything happened: the long stretch of build-up before the devil finally revealed himself in the child's body. By the time the famous head-swivelling scene took place, half of the women in the audience had been having a fine old scream, and Helen was no exception. She might have been a match for a bulky Christian redneck, but when it came to a thirteen-year-old girl puking pea soup she turned to jelly. Half-way through, and thereafter every time the Exorcist approached Regan's bedroom, she clutched my arm, and on three occasions she let out a considerable shriek. Although I suspect I was at least as terrified as her, I sat stony, unmoved, nonchalant, occasionally letting out an ironic laugh. Some order had been restored in the gender universe. I was the brave one now, and she the delicate soul who needed protection. It felt good.

I wanted her to be brave, and yet I wanted her to be afraid.

Introspection – it's quite a product: it really does what it says on the tin. Suddenly, one of the most important secret places in my hinterland of doomed relationships heaves into view. The epicentre, perhaps.

At that epicentre is the double standard: the ability of the human creature to both desire and believe simultaneously things that are, in fact, mutually exclusive.

This *is* interesting. Sitting back, mulling it over like this – it illuminates things. I had previously believed that it was a particularly female failing to want two virtually opposite things at the same time: a man who is tough – but vulnerable; a man who is powerful – but helpless; a man who is handsome – but uninterested in appearances; a man who is wealthy – but indifferent to wealth; a man who allows his partner freedom – but who can dominate on cue; a man who is serious-minded – with a sense of humour; a man with a six-pack – who isn't vain; a man who is thoughtful – but never melancholy; a man who is dynamic – but who knows how to relax.

And I wanted a woman who was brave, but fearful.

What else do I want and not want at the same time? What other things does my right hand know that the left hand does not?

I have to find out, and soon: this weekend, I've my first date since Juliet Fry.

5

This time I'm going to take the middle position. I'm going to be myself – but I'm also not going to be myself. A little bit of spin, perhaps, but not enough to invalidate my inauthenticity.

I should have learned all this a long time ago. Only I haven't been that kind of person. Now I am. I have to get this right.

The woman's name is Talia Corke. I got her from the same place I got Juliet Fry, the personal columns. The date is tonight. And I have barely started my flip-chart, barely compiled my Love Secrets. I have not learned my lessons. I have not yet begun to introspect.

This is how the flip-chart reads so far.

THE LOVE SECRETS OF DON JUAN

Problem: Mother – withheld affection. Result: Fall in love too quickly. Constant disappointment. Anger. Solution: Be cooler – less needy. Abandon search for unconditional love.

Problem: Sex = power *(The Sharon Smith Principle).*
Result: Helpless, infantile rage. **Solution:** *Saltpetre, self-blinding, castration. Otherwise, none.*

Problem: Women full of impossible paradoxes. **Result:**
Bewilderment. Misunderstanding. Anger. **Solution:** *Not known. Complicated by fact that you are also full of contradictions.* **Solution:** *Also not known.*

Problem: More than two people in relationship. Shadow/ doppelgänger theory. Women symbolic, men literal.
Result: B, M, A. **Solution:** *Learn to speak chick. Watch behaviour as well as listening to words. Get to know shadows. Plus: words don't mean what they mean anyway. But listen for clues.*

Problem: Women flock to indifference (Martin's Law).
Result: Women don't flock to me very much. **Solution:**
Fake it.

It's not much to go on. My eye dallies on the first love secret. *Problem: Mother – withheld affection.* This starts a train of thought on which I catch a ride.

There's something odd about my parents. Odd, that is, if I'm working on the presumption that the reason I mess up all my relationships is not down to luck or women but down to some distortion of me, some blind spot, some fundamental lack of perception inherited from a family that in turn inherited it their family and so on down the centuries.

The odd thing is this: my parents had, and still have, a happy marriage.

Terence doesn't believe this. He hasn't actually *said* he

doesn't believe it, but he doesn't have to. In fact, Terence hardly ever says anything. Sometimes we have sat together for close on an hour and barely exchanged a word, other than my parting shot: 'For this I'm paying seventy-five pounds an hour?'

I can read his face, which I find smug and irritating. I expect this is 'displacement' or 'projection', but displaced and projected smugness and irritation still look pretty bad. Anyway, when I'm talking about my parents' happy marriage, a little part of his right eyebrow elevates by half a degree, his mouth curls very slightly and he shifts about a millimetre in his seat. I know what he's thinking – I may be an extrovert, but I'm not a fool.

He's thinking, *There's no such thing as a happy marriage.*

He's right, in a limited way: every marriage involves pain, anger, frustration, confusion and conflict. But neither my brother nor I can remember hearing a cross word between my parents, or them showing anything other than consideration and respect for each other. That's enough evidence for me that they had a happy marriage, regardless of the ideology of a therapist who often looks as if his own life is so dried up (he's pale, weedy and nervous) that he *wants* there to be no such thing as a happy marriage. Because then the unhappy marriage that undoubtedly produced him will seem less distressing.

Of course, I'm not the therapist. Nevertheless, this insight is occurring to me. If I am right, and my parents had a happy marriage, then happy marriages have their downside too – from the point of view of the progeny.

Many imagine that people like me (damaged people? emotionally unsuccessful people?) come from dysfunctional backgrounds. And, yes, Iris froze me out – although she never hit me, locked me in a wardrobe, chained me to a radiator or made me do a paper round. On the whole, I imagine my childhood was much like most – except for the happy marriage.

On casual inspection, it seems terrific never to have seen your parents argue, or scowl across the breakfast table or lob sarcastic barbs from their easy chairs. But there is something agonizing about it from a child's perspective.

The main disadvantage is that your parents come to seem, after a fashion, godlike. Not like two gods, but one god with two heads. One god, because those heads never disagree, never take a different point of view on anything. When you do something that is deemed wrong or unacceptable, there is no question that you *are* wrong or unacceptable. It is simply incontrovertible. There is never any division in the ranks to qualify the verdict. You are in the wrong. It is a fact of reality.

That's what it feels like to be me. It feels like being in the wrong even when my mind, conscience and instinct tell me that I'm in the right. If someone confronts me and challenges me, especially if they're angry (my parents never got angry – not in an overt way anyhow), my first instinct is, *I'm in the wrong.*

The second instinct that is umbilically attached to this is, *How **dare** you try to make me feel I'm in the wrong?* Like Mum and Dad always did. It is always associated with an emotion: anger. And the conversation always deteriorates from that point.

I remember when I was a child walking on a mountain somewhere, on holiday with my family, and there was a fence up protecting some sheep. (Bear with me: this *has* got something to do with me and women.) I don't know why I

101

remember it, but I can see the sign in my mind, etched in black into a silver grey plaque. It read, 'Electric Fence'.

This excited me. I had visions of touching it and being frazzled to a cinder there and then. However, I was old enough to realize that if an electric fence really did that, they wouldn't put it close to a public footpath where children like me went walking with their mother, father and brother.

Or maybe they did. Certainly, my older brother, Sam, was trying hard to convince me they did. I said it wasn't possible. So he dared me to touch the fence while my parents weren't looking. I battled between competing impulses: to show my brother I was brave, to demonstrate that the fence was safe, and to do something forbidden because it was forbidden. I was in a sweat about it – literally. My hands dripped. I was afraid, excited. I just *had* to touch that fence.

Go on, then, scaredy cat. Fry yourself if you want, said Sam.

It's probably not switched on. And if it is on, it's probably about as strong as a torch or something.

Scaredy cat, scaredy cat.

If you're so brave, you touch it.

I'm not going to touch it because then I'll blow up. You think it's safe. Not me.

Well, it is safe.

Isn't.

Is.

Touch it then.

All right, I will.

All right, then.

All right.

Go on then.

ALL RIGHT!

I clamped my hand around the wire.

The sensation that followed was rather hard to describe. It was certainly unpleasant enough to knock me backwards on to the ground. It was hard, like a thin baton being rammed along my tibia, but also soft-ish, like a hard slap from a fleshy hand. It was unquestionably an electric shock, but too mild to harm me. Nevertheless, it gave me a hell of a surprise. I yelled in alarm. Sam crumpled up with laughter. My parents turned simultaneously. Iris spoke first, in her normal quiet, firm voice, as recommended by the childcare manuals of the day.

What are you doing, Danny?

I got a 'lectric shock, I said, rubbing my arm, fighting back the tears that I had been told by my father not to shed if I was to grow up into a man.

Now my father spoke.

Don't be silly.

I did, Dad. I got a 'lectric shock. From the 'lectric fence.

They wouldn't switch an electric fence on so close to a walkway.

*It **hurt** me.*

My father grasped the electric fence, then released it. *Stop fibbing, Danny. Get up.*

I wasn't old enough to think of it then, but now I suppose a little boy with a wet hand would experience a mild electric shock differently from a grown man with a dry hand. As far as my father was concerned there had been no shock, I was just making a nuisance of myself.

At that moment I saw a flickering of recognition on my mother's face that it was unlikely I would be lying in the mud, rubbing my arm and making up stories about shocks from electric fences. It had certainly occurred to *her* that a child would experience an electric shock differently from a man. That I was probably telling the truth. But then marital loyalty meshed gears. My mother said, in a cold, distant voice, *Do what your father says, Danny. It's wrong to lie. Get up this minute.*

The pain in my arm diminished, nearly extinguished by the pain of the truth being denied. Although I was right, I was in the wrong. I'm still always in the wrong, in my heart.

What use is this perception going to be to me on this date with Talia, at eight thirty tonight, in the bar at the Lanesborough Hotel, Hyde Park Corner? The answer must be: almost certainly none. But if the date with Talia developed into a relationship, and if it went from a relationship to a serious relationship, and if it went from there to marriage . . .

Christ, I haven't even met the woman yet. That's how much I want to put it all right. That's how much I want to obliterate the mistakes of the past with the Snopake of the future. That's how eager I am to change.

The Lanesborough Hotel is on the fringes of Knightsbridge. I don't know why I suggested it, except that Talia lives on the other side of town from me, and it is central, intimate and luxurious, yet relaxed. Also, I'd just got another piece of work, this time quite a decent contract to develop a campaign for Stiffy, a soft drink that allegedly increases your sexual power. It was all a bit post-modern, a bit jokey, a bit 'we don't really know if this works or not but it'll be worth a pop anyway'. I tried the stuff and it certainly didn't work on me but, then, very little would nowadays, short of a ten-megawatt current shot into my pubis. Anyway, I'd got a nice fat cheque from the Stiffy Corporation burning a hole in my bank account.

Talia was there when I arrived and, like Juliet, she was attractive. You'd be amazed at the women who read the personals every week, just waiting for a vivacious, witty ad. This tilts the scales towards the writer who's literate and imaginative rather than stupid and drunk, but well dressed and a good dancer. When I saw Talia sitting there in a terrific pair of raw denim three-quarter-lengths, a figure-hugging black-leather jacket and two-inch fuck-me-then-propose-to-me heels, I was more than all in favour of this.

I'd come in my best clothes, determined not to be outclassed. I was in Nicole Farhi, a blue serge three-button suit, a white T-shirt and a pair of Prada shoes. Hair carefully washed, gelled and preened. We seemed like equals. I bought her a drink. Five pounds for a gin and tonic. Jesus.

We hit it off right away. Talia had the great saving grace, the ultimate virtue, of not taking herself too seriously. She laughed at herself at least as much as she laughed at anyone or anything else.

Are you Danny?

Are you Talia?

Of course I'm Talia. Otherwise I wouldn't be asking you if you were Danny.

It struck me that it *had* been a dumb thing to say, but also that it didn't matter. I was comfortable with Talia.

Sorry. I'm a bit nervous.

I'm pissing my Provocateurs. This is just so weird. Get me a drink, for God's sake. Get me two drinks.

We had a few gin and tonics, and talked. I successfully

avoided the nervous man's mistake (talking constantly
about oneself, getting a little too drunk a little too quickly)
and Talia successfully avoided the nervous woman's mistake
(putting up with it). There was a nice balance.

Within five minutes of talking I nailed her down with five
key personality traits. She was confident. She was a little bit
vain. She was ambitious, but did not see work as anything
other than a means to an end – so she had a sense of
proportion. She liked kids. She wasn't a fool.

So, you like ER do you? said Talia.

*Wow. Doctors. Brave. But tortured. Incredible dialogue.
Sharp characterization.*

What did you think of last week's episode?

I missed it.

*Do you think Carter will be able to get over the trauma
about the ice pick and the bag lady, though?*

I'm not sure.

You don't like ER, do you?

Pause.

No.

Why?

It's slick, sentimental crap.

*I'm with you. It's all too polished. The Yanks have got a
blind spot for rough edges. When they bring in some tramp,
it's like you can see he's a struggling actor who's spent not
long enough in Makeup getting his hair mussed. Real life is
all rough edges.*

That's right.

So you tell lies to get dates with women.

Yeh.

I can respect that.

I really connected with this woman. And I could sense

106

that she liked me too. There was a current running between us, although whether it was sexual or not I couldn't say. But we *liked* each other. That was a good start.

We had a couple more drinks, and then I suggested taking a cab into the West End for a meal. She insisted on buying the extortionately priced drinks, so I offered to stand us dinner. Within half an hour we were in Joe Allen, me ordering the hamburger off the menu, so that she would know I was cool, and she ordering steak and chips and a huge pudding. I *love* women who dig food, who aren't afraid of their bodies. We drank a litre of wine, and by this time we had shared our family histories, some of our traumas and triumphs, and had a bloody good laugh. She had grace, Talia, and I fancied her, I confess. Things couldn't have gone better.

Until it came time to say goodbye.

Even though I was quite drunk, I felt under no temptation whatsoever to try to kiss her or make any sexual overture. That could wait. One of the great things about being forty-five is that the driving, pounding insistence at the heart of you beats at a slower rhythm – I had been unchained from the gibbering lunatic of my libido some years previously. I felt optimistic about the future. I felt sure that Talia and I would meet again – why wouldn't we? It had been fun.

We left the restaurant and walked down the street. I felt as relaxed as could be, and was readying myself to hail her a cab and possibly shake hands when she turned to me and said, *Danny*.

Call me Spike.

Spike. I've had a really nice evening.

Talia. So have I.

You're a terrific guy. Funny, intelligent, warm. I like you a lot.

I felt myself puff up a little.

Well, I like you a lot, Talia.

Can I say something?

Of course you can.

Maybe I was going to get lucky, after all. And I'd come out without the condoms.

I'd like to meet up again.

Me too.

But that's not all I want to say.

Oh.

Spike, I don't fancy you.

Right.

I hope you'll forgive me for coming out and saying it like that. I wanted to spare you any embarrassment in case you were thinking of trying to kiss me.

Oh. Right. Thanks.

It's not that you're not perfectly attractive and everything, it's just that you're really not my type.

OK.

But it would be great if we could be friends.

Terrific.

Look, here's a cab.

Great.

Give me a call, eh? There's some new theatre thing I'd like to see next week.

Superb.

I look forward to it. Great evening.

Great evening!

See you, then. 'Bye.

'Bye, Talia.

You don't mind, do you? About the . . . you know?

Me? Mind? No, of course not. That's absolutely fine. No worries.

I stood and watched the cab pull away. What Talia had said was perfectly reasonable. She was only being honest and fair. Anyway, it wasn't personal – I just didn't fit her particular selection criteria.

So why did I feel like the worst piece of shit in the world?

I went home, took my copy of *Time Out* and threw it in the bin. There was something screwy about this way of meeting women, I decided. It all made sense on the surface, but underneath it poisoned things.

Of course, this was simply an initial, defensive impulse. It wasn't the personal columns that were at fault. It was me.

Or not exactly me. It was my circumstances. I'm going through a long, messy divorce. For the pheromones to function, for the responding pheromones to splutter, what any man needs is confidence, self-belief. My stocks of both are at an all-time low, and all the funny *aperçus* and intelligent insights in the world aren't going to change that. I need to get better before I can get a serious relationship.

Perhaps what I need is a bridging relationship, one of those women you hook up with to get you through to the next serious relationship. They don't have to be that great – just great enough to convince you in a deep emotional way, not a dry cerebral way, that you are OK, that you are a *man*. Because marriage, or at least the prospect of divorce, has somehow emasculated me. I need to re-equip myself, and I need a neutral ground on which to find my feet. Until that opportunity comes along, I'm going to sit at home and introspect, I'm going to do my homework. You can learn all the lessons in the world but they aren't going to do you any good if you never get a chance to sit the test.

Helen Palmer and I slept together about six weeks after our date with the devil. It was quite tough to get her into the bedroom. It turned out she *did* have a boyfriend, back in Peckham, some plumber she had been with since she was at school. And this struggle to lose my virginity to Helen taught me the first thing I learned about women. If you're completely determined – and you've got it *right* to a certain extent, even though they may not realize it – they usually cave in sooner or later. You can wear them down. With enough charm, and perseverance, you can bulldoze them.

Nowadays I don't bulldoze. The prize no longer seems big enough to chase, the chalice seems too poisoned. Also, it seems undignified, now that holding on to dignity has become a desperate project. To pursue and be rejected, to pursue again and be rejected again, I just don't have the energy any more, the belief in myself or the belief in the woman, or the belief in the whole courtly-love hall of mirrors. But in those days I chased them down, the hound and the fox. I knew Helen liked me, and I wasn't going to let a little thing like her boyfriend get in the way of that.

She said no, and she said no again. But she meant yes. Everybody sometimes says no when they mean yes. No one is fully cognizant of their own desires. Sometimes their own desires have to be dug out of them, excavated by a kind of soul-mining, by unreasoned persistence. People sometimes don't *know* what they want. *Nobody* knows *everything* they want. We're not that powerful. Sometimes it takes others to reveal it to them. Often it's the only way.

So, Helen and I went to bed, because I pestered her and

bugged her, and made a complete nuisance of myself. I pulled it off because I had enough insight to understand that it was what she wanted – to be freed of responsibility for the consequences and to cast herself, in the private drama of her inner life, as subject to forces more powerful than she was. This made it possible for her to hurt her boyfriend – because she had no choice. This made it possible for her to take me inside her – because she had no choice. It was a lie in both instances, but defused the guilt.

How did I find the strength to win her? Because her boyfriend was a plumber called Gordon, and I just couldn't see her ending up with a plumber called Gordon. For one thing, she was too clever, and however she felt about him, I knew she would be torn, like I was torn between the desire to belong and the desire to escape. She wanted her plumber, because he was her first love, and she wanted me because I was on my way out of cuppa-and-a-Garibaldi-biscuit land. I knew she wanted me more because I was the future. Dislocation was the future.

We got drunk, naturally. When I entered her bedroom for the first time I had a premonition of doom, even though our relationship hadn't properly started. It hit me the moment I saw the garish soft toys arranged on her bed.

There they were: a bunny, Carrots, a bear, Huggy, a hippo, Harry, a pig the size of a small cat, Pinky, and a giraffe, Gerry. My image of Helen as tough, edgy, sophisticated and strong took quite a knock. Though not enough of one to stop me sitting down on the bed with her, pushing her back on it and fumbling under her dress.

She didn't say no. Well, she did, but not with any conviction. She didn't say yes either. She didn't seem to know what she was doing. Which made two of us. I had assumed that because she had a boyfriend she was fairly experienced, but this was not so. She was nervous, and her fear communicated itself to me. We both had to master it. But by now I was beyond listening to the demands of anything other than the sound of my own heart, beyond smelling anything but the rich, earthy, unnameable smell that was her half-hidden desire.

Clumsy, frightened, excited, it took me a while to find the correct aperture, but then, in a single stroke, I was inside Helen. Not just a part of me, *I* was inside her. My self, then so overblown yet hollow, melted away, and I was Helen and she was me, and neither of us was there at all. I pulled back. I pushed forward. Helen gasped; I looked into her eyes.

Eyes: the strangest tissue, the mystic skin. That which watches, that place where we live, somehow, behind our eyes, our vantage-point for the entire universe, *of* the entire universe. To look directly into someone's eyes is an awesome thing. Were Helen's eyes beautiful? I suppose so, but I didn't really see them. I was reaching for something beyond them, something beyond speech or seeing, which was also reaching out for me. I held her eyes, one, two seconds. I pushed at her again, and then – an extraordinary thing.

She was absent behind her eyes; she was gone. There was an almost terrifying blankness there, a giving up, an interior disintegration. It was animal, as old as time, and it scared me, but I was still beyond fear, and she let out a long, low sound from the back of her throat. I moved inside her once more, sensing that absence was what we were seeking here, but that I was still *there*, I was still, despite it all, holding on to my self-consciousness, and I didn't know then what I know now: that I would never have the abandon women can muster, the ability to get lost, to enter nowhere. I would always be *here*, ecstatic, abandoned, excited – but *here*. The literalness of the male mind, the tragic, unshakeable focus.

I pushed once again, and then it was over. She touched my hair, and I felt it clearly, with all my senses: I truly loved her.

But it didn't last. I don't know how to make it last. So began the first great failure of Don Juan.

After that, we were indisputably girlfriend and boyfriend. The plumber was flushed away. I loved Helen. She loved me. It was as shallow and as fragile as only true love at that age can be.

Suddenly, this exquisite thing, Helen Palmer, was 'mine', as the language of romance *circa* 1975 would have it. I had conquered her, subdued her, won her round, out of her boyfriend's faltering orbit and into mine.

I suppose it was then that I also began to hate her.

How was this possible? She was kind and giving, clever and beautiful. Yet as the months went on and our relationship became more and more familiar, the seeds of disappointment grew into weeds.

If I can understand this, I can begin to unravel the knots in my history. If I can understand the impulse to lay waste the innocent, I can take another step forward. When I find the next putative, provisional Right Woman, I can start to get it right.

Is there something deep within men that wants to crush what they love? Is it the cause of war, of all discontent? Is it primal? Is it self-hatred, the completion of symbiosis for those women who love bastards?

All I knew was that part of me wanted to crush Helen

113

Palmer as soon as I began to love her. I would never have admitted it to myself, but the rage was there, at her gentleness, her finally submissive nature.

The woman I remembered from that night at the cinema, who had turned on the threatening Christian, was becoming harder and harder to square with the interior Helen. It was true that she was possessed of a certain public courage with people she did not care about: she would berate traffic wardens, fight her way through police lines on demonstrations. But in a relationship that courage deserted her. In loving me she became afraid – that I would hurt her, that I would discover some nothingness she imagined to be within her, that I would leave her. In being afraid, she somehow sealed her fate, and mine.

Because I was seeking strength. Men always ache for a show of power. I wanted her to be herself, to tell me to go fuck myself when I was tardy, or unkind, to throw a glass of wine in my face, to kick me out and tell me never to return. When I was insulting her, or putting her down – and I did these things, I am ashamed to say – I was angling for her *spirit*. I was pushing at her boundaries, seeing what she'd take before she turned on me.

What was Helen's defence against my cruelty? She did nothing. She looked at me, eyes filled with tears. Her perpetually puzzled expression, which I had initially found so seductive, deepened to unfathoming confusion. She never looked like leaving me, not for a second. She took it all.

And it worked – for her. In terms of power, not love. It was at that point I discovered about guilt and its many applications. I discovered the martyr's gambit, and its power over little boys who want to please their mothers. The martyr. It's so deep in the culture – the memory-trace slave culture

114

of women. A culture left over from the long dark wash of history that they were excluded from and written out of. How do the powerless get power? By violence. Psychological violence if no other kind is available.

But at that age, and with Helen Palmer, I had not learned anything. I had not learned about female masterblaster no. 1, the light sabre of Guilt, the Kalashnikov of the powerless.

Helen.

Yes, Spiky.

I'm going out with Martin tonight.

Oh, OK.

Is that OK?

Sure.

Fine, then.

Fine.

During this conversation, I experienced a wide range of emotions. First, apprehension: I knew I was going to end up feeling distressed. Then when she said, *Oh, OK*, the guilt kicked in. To understand why, you have to hear the tone of voice, observe the facial gymnastics. You have to know that the *Oh* is not just an *Oh* but an **Oh**. That the pause between the *Oh* and the *OK* was just half a beat longer than it needed to be. Together they say something quite different from *Oh, OK*. They say, *But don't you want **me** to come?*

I don't know how long it takes for one emotion to generate another but . . . actually I do. It takes the time between Helen saying, *Oh, OK*, and me saying, *Is that OK?* The emotion generated in this case was fury: fury that I was being manipulated, fury that Helen was being pathetic, and fury that I didn't have any defence against feeling bad. I was too young, my sense of self was too incomplete. It worked. I felt guilty.

Of course you can come if you want.

Oh, no. That's fine.

Pause.

Come on. I'm sure Martin would like to see you.

It's OK.

*Come on. **Please**.*

You don't really want me to come.

*I **do**.*

Well. If you're sure you don't mind . . .

Of course I mind. You're just too pathetic to sort your own life out this evening, and I'm too pathetic to force you to accept responsibility. The weak torture the weak: another fact of life, just like the strong torture the weak and the weak torture the strong. Only parity equals stability.

So she came out with us. And through the entire evening, since I was incapable of saying, *Helen, I don't want you to be here*, I just had to punish her out of the corner of my mouth, as it were. I was sarcastic, distant, aloof. She became more and more small in the corner, as I rapped and laughed with Martin, as we drank, told jokes and talked about football. The smaller she got, the more I hated her, and the more hateful I became.

Until Martin and I finally said goodnight, and Helen and I were alone together and then she burst into tears. At that point I stopped being horrible and angry and started feeling absolutely lousy for being so vicious. I said sorry, and she put her arms around me, and I began to cry, too, for being so horrible, and then . . .

Then I started to feel angry again because we had just been through an absurd pantomime that had forced me to be untrue to myself and reduced my respect both for her and me. And it was her fault.

Except that it wasn't. It was my fault, because I didn't make it plain to her that she had to get her own life. Because I wasn't brutal enough. So here's a thing . . .

Here's a note for The Love Secrets of Don Juan.

To have a successful relationship you have to be ruthless.

The alternative is cowardice. When Helen and I felt love slipping away from us, we did what cowards do when faced with calamity. We pretended it wasn't happening. That's how we moved in together – although our relationship was in trouble, although I knew it wasn't going to be happy-ever-after for me and my first love, although the last thing I wanted to do was live with Helen Palmer. But I was trying to be good. And I was afraid. Those two impulses have governed all my relationships with women and, finally, ruined them.

Helen was kicked out of the flat she shared with two former college pals. She had nowhere to live. I had a flat. She could come and live with me, or she would have to . . . I don't know, go back to her parents or something. She said it would only be for a month or two.

I believed her. She probably believed it herself, although I have learned that one of the Nightmare Things about Women is that they can be extremely calculating when desperate, weak or frightened. More calculating than men customarily find it useful to admit to imagining. Women can be sneaky and it can be dangerous to trust them. That's an important Love Lesson.

Perhaps she *didn't* plan it that way. I can't be sure. The powerless – and if women weren't powerless in the 1970s, to many it still felt that way – will do anything to assert who they are, will do anything to *survive*.

6

Only Martin Gilfeather thought I was a fool to let Helen move in with me. At least, he was the only one with the courage to tell me so. Carol Moon doubtless thought it too, but was too polite, or politic, or too much of a friend to Helen to say so. But Martin, who was then, as now, moving effortlessly from one woman to another, thought I was being weak and manipulated. Although he was a ditherer and gave the appearance of being hapless, he had a hidden toughness. Appeals to guilt never moved Martin. He had absolute confidence that what he did was OK, that it was right because he was doing it. There was no conflict in Martin between morality and self-interest. Somehow, despite this, he was popular and much admired, unlike me – and I worried and fretted all the time about doing the 'right thing'. Martin was one of those people utterly at home in his own skin; his easy charm and all-round tolerance of every-thing that happened to be taking place at the time, however difficult or stressful, more than compensated for his lack of interest in any moral fixed points. People felt comfortable with Martin because Martin felt comfortable with himself.

He never judged himself, so he never judged other people. He informed me about Helen's 'scheming' without malice – in fact, with amused affection.

I'd met Martin in my college holiday job. We were working in a DIY shop in a small provincial shopping centre. He was studying at some teaching college – nowadays he's an English teacher at a comprehensive in south London. He looked then much as he looks now – boyish, fresh-faced, innocent. We quickly achieved the intensity that teenage friendships somehow generate, and I fell under his spell like nearly everyone who met him.

They say that in every marriage one partner loves and the other permits themselves to be loved. Perhaps the same is true of friendships. I always needed Martin more than he needed me: his indifference attracted me much as it attracted women.

I've tried hard to learn through watching Martin with women, but I don't think *he* knows what he does. That's why whatever it is is so effective – it's natural, effortless. He meets a woman, likes her, asks her out – whether she says yes or no is of little import to him. He is unoffended when he's rejected – which he almost never is. He doesn't take love *personally* – that's his genius.

I say 'love', but I'm not sure that Martin is capable of love in the way I understand the word. He always seems delighted with the woman he's with, and if he's not, then – with sadness but never regret – he lets them drift away and finds himself another. Women rarely leave Martin because they can never get him in the first place – they're always angling for his heart, but they can never quite locate it, which keeps them hooked. They can never quite locate it, not because it's not there but because it operates differently from most people's. It seems capable of a generalized love – Martin's always giving money to charity, or helping out street drunks with a fiver and a chat – and of a strong connection with and affection for a woman. But the giving up of himself that to me is love – I just can't see Martin doing it. Being with a woman is too low a priority for him. He's happy on his own; he has no need to build up his self-esteem; even sex is something he can take or leave.

To be a success with women I'd have to learn to be like Martin – but it's never going to happen. I could never fake what Martin does naturally.

The thing with Alice, his girlfriend – uncharacteristically he made a decision about her, thanks, in part, to my brilliant advice – was that whatever he did, from a long enough perspective, was bound to be right. This banal sophistry apparently impressed Martin enough for him actually to take action, in the face of Alice's persistent prodding: he told her, with a combination of nods, tics, twitches and other forms of emotional semaphore that he wasn't ready for the 'next step'. So they called it a day.

Martin, as usual, took it with apparent equanimity. About a month after the event he mentioned it to me in passing. Now he's going out with some twenty-one-year-old Brazilian samba dancer, and his feathers are, as ever, unruffled. After two years you'd have expected a few tears in the beer, or at least a manly shrug, but Martin is like a cat: he picks himself up from a fall that might cripple a lesser creature and carries on as before.

Alice – well, I can't think about Alice at the moment. Actually I'm finding it hard to think about anything. Because I've got mediation again today. The churning in my guts tells me this. I don't even need to look in my diary. It's this morning, at eleven o'clock. As if that wasn't enough, this evening I've got another date.

Psyching myself up for the mediation session I ask myself: what's with the date? Why do I keep trying? I've read so many articles in the newspapers telling me that the New Singletons are on the march, that the way forward is for people to be independent, strong, self-contained, to pick up relationships and drop them again, like cars when the spark plugs wear out.

It amounts to spending life alone, giving up. I can't help but see it that way. To make that a positive lifestyle choice strikes me as simply sad.

I've been struggling hopelessly for nearly thirty years to find love, but I still believe in it. I'm Robin Williams, the perennial, hopeful half-wit. I still believe.

Maybe tonight will be the night. Because this isn't a cold call. It's with someone I already know. Although it's not *really* a date. The woman is off-limits, to tell you the truth. Why?

Because she used to go out with my best mate. Because she's Alice.

I've been trying to work out the etiquette of this. This is my reasoning.

1. He dumped *her*. Or that's what it amounts to, anyway. After two years with Alice, he's already with another woman. He doesn't love Alice – or isn't sure, which amounts to the same thing.

2. I didn't invite her out on a date – not that it is a date, of course – she invited *me*. So, am I going after my best friend's girl? No. If anything, she's going after me. Which is fine because . . .

3. I don't really fancy her that much.

4. I don't even like her that much. Not that I dislike her – I just don't know her well enough to have an opinion.
5. So I'm definitely not going to try and have sex with her.

Nevertheless, we're meeting up, two half-friends (I never had any kind of independent relationship with Alice). She said she would be around my way that evening, and did I fancy going out for a drink? I didn't see any reason not to. I mentioned it to Martin, and he was cool about it. It's not going to lead anywhere.

So what's the harm?

It's true, I am naïve. But, then, I'm a man. We can be. We're trained to dominate and manipulate the physical universe, and to take risks. Our instinct is usually towards the straightforward. It's a strength. It's a terrible weakness.

I'm in the waiting room at the mediator's office. Beth will be arriving in a moment. I wonder if I have time to retch before she gets here. It would be best to get it out of the way. It might suggest vulnerability, and that's something I can't afford. You can't in a war.

Mediation seemed such a good idea. Symbolically speaking, mediators are the ruminants to the lawyers' carnivores. The job of the mediator is not about securing given weights of flesh, but about helping you separate in a grown-up, mature, herbivorous fashion. This involves regular meetings in which, consensually, you work out all the financial and childcare differences between you. Then you give the paperwork to the carnivores, the flesh-tearing lawyers, and they, in a uniquely non-carnivore fashion, meekly implement what you have already agreed.

Nice idea. Only it's wrong and it's futile. Because separation requires the warring parties to face up to their irreconcilable differences, and the erecting of disinterested structures between them that will allow the law to do its job. What separation does not require, and must be resisted at all costs, is the maintenance of the illusion of reason between them.

But consensus does not happen in war. That's why it's called war. And divorce, when kids are involved, is war.

The retching will have to wait. Beth has just arrived.

Hi.

Hello.

Beth shoots a glance at me, but I'm not prepared to catch her eye. I glance at her when she's looking out of the window. She looks tired – perhaps the glowing self she presented last time at the house was just the theatre of cruelty I imagined it to be. Her long blonde hair has been cut a good bit shorter – it suits her. She's wearing a new outfit, something in taupe linen. Perhaps this is meant to suggest neutrality. Or maybe she just likes taupe. All this introspection is fucking me up. Everything seems like it means something else.

I can see that, like me, she's tense and angry – we always are at these sessions. Her wide, thin mouth is set tight, her oval face hardened by a clenched jaw.

It's an absurdly surrealistic exercise in some ways, this formal sorting through of all that was once emotional, spontaneous, hopeful, loving. It's a rite of maiming. It's so strange seeing your wife on such neutral territory, after you've been separated for nearly eighteen months, and now that your relationship has transformed out of all recognition.

For years I woke up each day in bed with this woman

and, whether I liked her that day or not, she was *there*. It was the most intimate relationship in my whole tapestry of relationships; I was naked beside her, both physically and metaphorically. She was the mother of my *child* – our child, an indissoluble lifelong link between us. I had watched that child being born, the most profound experience of my life. Every day I had woken up with this woman, loved her and fought her, and I'd eaten my eggs and she'd had her muesli, and she'd drunk her tea, and I'd had my coffee, and that had been my life for ten . . . whole . . . years.

Now we face each other, strangers – no, more than that, *enemies* – in an empty waiting room with magnolia walls, and watercolours of muddy fields and shire horses plodding through them. I can see the weight of the haycart that the horses pull, the effort on their faces. Is this a metaphor the mediators have chosen deliberately? Since I started going to Terence I see patterns everywhere, some, I suspect, based on little reality but on the fact that I want to see patterns. It puts me at the centre of the universe, gives me a sense of control. It's the same impulse that makes so many women read astrology columns, believe in angels and the efficacy of alternative medicine. Patterns that show us the way.

How are you?

Just terrific.

Enemies, but enemies who share a daughter, who still love each other in a way that cannot easily be dissolved. How can you not love the mother of your daughter? I don't know.

We are nearly at the end of the mediation sessions. Last time, I agreed to sign over the house to Beth so that Poppy would have a proper home. Beth, of course, will be the primary carer. Why? Because she's a better parent? Because she's got a stronger bond with Poppy? No. Because she's a woman.

If you're not married you might save money when you and your partner separate, but you've got no more right in law to *see* your child than the man sitting next to you on the bus. Why? Because you're a man. Your wife might be a crack whore and you might be a secular saint, and the woman would still get the kids and could stop you seeing them at whim. It happens all the time.

Beth's lips are still tight. Those lips I once kissed, whose softness made my heart race, are pursed and ready for war. We are in the final stages of the battle. Today, with any luck, we will put our signature on the mediation document that will represent the finalization of our financial and custody agreements. Whatever it costs me, I will sign it joyfully: nothing is worse for mental equilibrium than an unresolved situation, and I decided at the beginning of this that I would give up anything to maintain a functional relationship with Beth after the divorce.

So I've let her have the house and the car. I've agreed to pay fifteen per cent of my net earnings to Poppy until she is eighteen, and forty per cent of what's left to Beth for the next three years. I keep the bedsit that I used to have as an office. Although I paid for it in the first place, and had it long before I even met Beth the bedsit had to go into the pot too. Beth has agreed not to try to go after it so long as she gets to keep the house. Fair enough. Sharing is what marriage is about. Money isn't everything, blah-blah-blah.

Now she's living there with Poppy, and when Poppy grows up and leaves home, it will still be Beth's: I will have no claim on it. Meanwhile, I will have my little bedsit, with an extra put-up bed for Poppy, who doesn't like staying there. And I don't know how I'm going to save up for a larger place when a huge chunk of my net earnings goes to Beth and Poppy in the first place, and I can barely hold down a job.

God, I've got to stop *whining*. Terence would put it differently, but that's the track he's trying to get me on: put it behind me; accept; forgive; forget. There's got to be another side to this that I'm not taking into account. The woman's side. I dare say Beth's about to point it out to me. She usually does.

Shall we go in, then?

Sure.

OK.

Inside the mediation room there are two people, a woman, Carmen, and a man, Giles. It costs £120 per hour, but it still seems preferable to us both than slugging it out with lawyers. They are nice. We like them. They are reasonable and focused, calm and rational – everything that Beth and I are not at the moment. They do not give us legal advice, only advise us of what the legal situation might be. Carmen is a lawyer trained in mediation, Giles a mediator and counsellor. They invite us to consult lawyers separately, but we have both agreed informally not to since it is likely to inflame the situation, lawyers being lawyers and trained in the ways of battle rather than conciliation. With any luck, today we will sign our agreement, hand it to lawyers and they will neutrally put it into effect, thus saving us even more bitterness.

Hello, Danny. Hello, Beth.

We smile conventional smiles, and adopt the masks of normal social relations. We are each anxious to please these people, and hope that somehow, in liking us, they will be able to make our circumstances less painful. They have power, because we are in their domain, and we come into it as supplicants. They are also powerful, because they don't care. Their interest is professional. And indifference, as Martin knows so well, moves mountains.

Giles speaks first. An avuncular figure, in his mid-fifties, with a white open-neck Ralph Lauren shirt and rumpled grey chinos, slightly too tight round the waist, he beams down at us as if we have come to him for pleasure rather than the endgame in a long, grisly battle between and against ourselves.

Now, if I may recap from last week.

He points up to the flip-chart we have been using to delineate capital, income, pensions, profits, interest, upsides, downsides, parenting time, nominal values of this and that, future incomes from here and there. It all looks scientific, neutral and painless.

We're nearly at the end of the road, I think. I hope. Unless I'm mistaken, we've taken this thing as far as we can. It hasn't always been easy, but today I think we should be able to put our signatures to the mediation document for you to present to your lawyers. I want to thank you both for your commitment to the process, and your very obvious concern and love for your child.

OK.

OK.

There was a pause before Beth said OK, a pause I didn't care for. When one is in the midst of a situation so sensitive to implication, back-pedalling, second thoughts, hints and malice aforethought, one becomes as sensitized to the spaces as to the words that surround them.

To sum up, then. As you know, the mediation document

*isn't legally binding. It's a codified assertion of your con-
sensus and agreement. Signing this piece of paper isn't
committing you to anything, but symbolically, at least, it
has force. You can take it to a lawyer – in fact, I strongly
advise that you do take it to a lawyer. But any good lawyer
nowadays is sensitive to the mediation process, and will use
this document to prevent the process becoming unnecess-
arily adversarial.*

Right, I say.

Beth nods.

Giles is chattering merrily on, outlining exactly how I am
going to leave myself impoverished for the next God knows
how many years. But I don't mind. In fact, I'm glad,
relieved. It is an unburdening. Although I feel sure that, had
I fought it out in the courts, I could have done better, I can't
face going through the legal system. The signing of this document represents another vital stage in getting beyond my
marriage, removing myself from the wreckage. In that sense,
at least, I expect signing this piece of paper, which renders
me a satellite to real life, confined to a bedsit, enslaved to a
maintenance cheque, will, paradoxically, make me happier
than I have been for the last few years. The possibility of a
new start – not that there can ever be anything such as a
new start for anyone who loves their child – is worth every
penny.

Shall we get on with it then? I say, hardly able to keep the
eagerness out of my voice. I want to be out of this office, out
of this building, walking down the street in the sunshine by
myself, away from Beth, towards my drink, my non-date,
with Alice this evening. The document is in front of me.
Without bothering to read it – we did all that last week – I
am reaching for my pen.

I've already been to see a lawyer, says Beth. *A new lawyer.*

Slowly, with theatrical reluctance, I propel the pen back into my pocket. I had half anticipated something like this. But that doesn't stop the dark, terrible heat that is swelling in my stomach, then surging up my spine, colouring my face, tightening my cheeks. When I speak, my voice is strait-jacketed.

We agreed that we wouldn't introduce lawyers at this point, Beth.

This is my whole future we're talking about. My future and Poppy's. I don't want to sign this without taking legal advice.

Well, of course, you are technically within your rights, says Carmen, carefully.

My voice remains strangulated. *But you said . . . you said we could agree this between us like grown-ups. We* **have** *a lawyer here. Carmen is a lawyer. We went to see lawyers at the beginning of the process. We went to see lawyers half-way through the process. And then we agreed that once we had thrashed out this deal, which I think you should remember has taken ten months to put together, we would take it to our lawyers completed and they would simply institute it. The reason for that was –*

I know what the reason for that was, Danny. Don't condescend to me.

I take a deep breath, count to ten, unclench my fists.

I'm not trying to condescend to you. I'm sorry if you got the impression that I was. Can we just discuss this in a reasonable –

Don't put on your **reasonable** *voice with me. I wasn't the one who broke up the marriage.*

Weren't you?

You know I wasn't.

We'll have to agree to differ there. I think we need to talk this through if we're going to –

Don't patronize me, Danny.

I'm NOT PATRONIZING YOU.

And there's no need for shouting.

Oh, my God.

Long pause. Body language as follows. Me: arms crossed, legs crossed, lips white with anger. Beth: elbows on table. Studied nonchalance. Face on hands. Releases face, picks up pen, makes a few notes on a pad in front of her. I can see Carmen waiting for her moment to intervene. I let it happen.

OK. Now these discussions, as Giles and I know only too well, can get very heated. And that's fine. Or, at least, it's normal. But, having come this far, it's important to focus on the issues. Now, what I'm hearing is that you, Danny, are upset that Beth has gone to a lawyer again, which is outside the guidelines that you established with her at the start of this particular dialogue.

That we all established with her. She broke her word, that's what I'm saying.

I never gave my word.

You never promised. That's something Poppy would say.

Never mind what my daughter would say.

Our daughter. Our daughter. Our daughter.

Hold on a moment. Beth, what you are saying is that whatever has passed between you and Danny informally, you have a right to exercise your legal privileges.

Our daughter. We all agreed it. In this room.

That's right. I have that right. In the interests of myself and my child.

Our child.

130

That remains to be seen.

Fuck you.

Hold on. Danny. Beth. Let's just cool down a moment, shall we?

I blink, take another deep breath. I'm beginning to hyper-ventilate. *Sorry. I didn't mean to swear. But she's the one making threats. And Poppy's going to be the one to suffer if we end up dragging this through the courts.*

I'm not making threats. I'm just saying that the process isn't finished yet. Not according to my new lawyer.

How can you come to this meeting having seen a lawyer when I haven't had a chance to consult mine?

When Beth speaks this time her voice is dark with sarcasm. *Oh, yeh. Sure you haven't.*

*What does **that** mean?*

Come on, Danny. Of course you've seen a lawyer. You're just keeping your mouth shut about it.

Yes, I've seen a lawyer. But we agreed that the last consultation five months ago was the last time for both of us.

Of course you've seen a lawyer since then.

I haven't.

I haven't. I've tried to play it by the rules. But I'm only just learning that in this game there are no rules, beyond pure and simple survival. Women understand this instinctively. Whereas I want to be good. Mum, am I being good?

Can I suggest something? says Giles, matily, in his rich, consoling voice. Why don't we just listen to what the lawyer has to tell us? It might be nothing too problematic. We may be seeing problems where there are no problems. So why don't we all just calm down and see what's on the table. Danny? What do you think?

*I think . . . I think she's **cheating**.*

Nevertheless, the situation is the situation. We have to deal with it. Beth?

Beth speaks briefly, in a clipped, businesslike tone.

My lawyer advised me that in court I could achieve twenty per cent for Poppy and fifty per cent of what's left for me for five years.

What? I can feel a wave of coldness moving up my back.

Poppy is still a very dependent child. I have to look after her. My statement of my financial needs makes this quite clear. The stress of this whole break-up is causing me to suffer depression. I've got a doctor's certificate.

*You're depressed. **You're** depressed.*

It's going to make it hard for me to find a proper job. I need proper support so that Poppy's needs can be met.

What about my needs? You've already got the house and the car.

Typical. Completely selfish.

My needs are valid. My need for a home big enough to share with my daughter. My need to have enough money left to take her out to the cinema from time to time. My need to try to build, one day, some kind of new future.

My lawyer says –

***Fuck** your lawyer.*

I'm just thinking of Poppy. I can't manage without help. You have to bring your anger under control. If you can't control it with me, then you can't control it with Poppy. And if you can't control it with Poppy –

*Then **what**?*

I'm just saying.

Did you hear the threat? Did you hear it?

I think you'd both better –

If you're just thinking of Poppy, give me the house, give

132

me care of Poppy. I'll give you spousal maintenance. You
can still have your pound of flesh. I'll have the house, you
can have the flat. I'll be the primary carer.

A child needs her mother.

A child needs her father too.

That's not what the law says.

Then the law can suck my dick. Which is more than you
ever did.

I'm making up for it with Oliver.

Hold on now. Calm down. Carmen is holding her palms
out in a placatory gesture. *I think we need to talk this*
through.

We do talk it through. And, using a tactic that in house-
buying is known as gazumping, in the loan industry as
sharking, and in poker as shit-or-bust, Beth secures for
herself a compromise. I'll continue to pay fifteen per cent
of my net earnings to Poppy for the next twelve years
minimum and fifty per cent of what's left to Beth for at least
four years. If at that time she hasn't got a job, she can go
back and ask for an extension.

I choose to give in because I know that Beth *will* do it.
One of the things that separates men and women in most
domestic negotiations is that women are ready to push the
button marked 'nuclear'. Men, historically trained through
the culture of commerce to deal with compromises and
negotiation, have no defence against this other than bewilderment, inchoate anger and, finally, submission. They are
not good enough poker players because they won't go
nuclear. It's too irrational, too destructive. They are always
outbid by the fanatic. There is no defence against the suicide
bomber.

*

133

Did I fail my wife? Of course I failed my wife. I failed her because I fell out of love with her. Does she therefore have a right to be so relentless? It's a non-question. Rights have nothing to do with it. A marriage break-up is about cutting a deal. Forget good faith: good faith is a burden here. Good faith was what Neville Chamberlain showed Adolf Hitler.

Not that I'm comparing my wife with Hitler, God forbid. Although she has got a bit of a moustache.

I'm sitting in a coffee bar with Martin a few hundred yards from the mediation offices. He works nearby. Martin always offers to come round and meet me after a battle has been fought. This time he finds me sitting in my chair, shaking, blinking, my hand trembling as it fights to control the vanilla latte I ordered, thinking all that sweetness and fat might comfort me. He watches me through a curtain of floppy brown hair falling in front of one chestnut eye. His pale skin is still young, despite the onset of middle age, and his lips are softly curled in a way that suggests wry kindness or sympathetic inquisition. Tall, of course. The faint imprint of laugh lines now etching themselves attractively at the corner of his eyes. A man-boy, a boy-girl, a delicate strength.

I love Martin. He has always been a friend to me, always looked out for me. I wish I could marry someone like him. He and I actually like each other enough to get married, and I know that we wouldn't argue or bitch or secretly destroy one another.

God, sometimes I so wish I was gay.

*Look at you, Spike. What **happened**?*

Almost without pausing for breath, I spill it all out, a great hawking of pain and anger, distress and confusion.

*It's not the money. I'll do whatever it takes. It's just that
it's all so ruthless, so unending. Even now I know it's not
over. There'll be some new thing in a week or two, contract
or no contract. She always **cheats**. She won't let go. She'd
rather make all of us suffer, than let go. At least making me
hate her is getting a **reaction**. She can't face the prospect of
indifference. She'd rather blow up the world than face
reality. It's so stupid, so unfair.*

All this time, Martin just looks at me with his large
brown eyes. I take a sip of the latte. It's cold. Now, at last,
he speaks.

*The trouble with you is that you're turning into a
woman.*

What do you mean? I look up from my coffee, shocked.

He smiles gently. Martin has this amazing ability to
criticize people quite harshly without causing offence. He's a
human version of my vanilla latte.

*You're getting into all that victim shit. 'Poor little
me, nasty, cheating, oh, boo-hoo, why is the world so
wicked?'*

So?

So you're missing the first principle of grown-up life.

Which is?

He laughs, and puts his arm round my shoulders. *There is
no God.*

I nod, recognizing this commonly ignored yet incontrovertible truth and allowing myself a wry smile. Of course I
know there's no God, but, then, I both know and don't
know. There's still that God-shaped hole. The infant
craving for justice.

I forgot.

People do what they need to do to get what they need to

*get. When it comes down to it, when people's very survival
as people, as identities, is at stake, they will do anything.
Beth sees this as being about her survival, about winning
out over you, since you left her.*

I didn't leave her. It was mutual.

*He takes his arm from my shoulders and sips his coffee.
He checks his watch – he's in his lunch break.*

*Come on, Spike. There's no such thing as a mutual
separation.*

Honest, it's . . .

How did it end?

I don't know.

Make an effort. Try to remember.

I think I asked her if . . . I asked her what was more
important to her in the marriage. Me. Or Poppy.

And she said Poppy.

But that wasn't it. It was how she said Poppy, how she
actually spoke the word. Because the way she spoke the
word meant that it had never been any contest, that of
course Poppy was far more important to her than me, that I
was, in fact, of staggering insignificance compared with
Poppy. This was not news to me – I had seen what little we
had of a relationship shrivel and dry up after Poppy was
born, after, in a sense, I became unnecessary. But it was the
way she said it. With a kind of . . . soft contempt, I suppose.
Actually, not that soft.

And then?

And then I said, 'Well, maybe you don't want to be with
me, if I'm not all that important.'

And then?

And then she said, 'Oh, don't be such a baby.' She was
always calling me a baby. Whenever I dared to disagree with

136

any of her points of view, or challenge her essential world picture, she would just reduce me – call me a child.

And then?

And then . . . I didn't lose my temper.

*You **didn't** lose your temper?*

That's when I knew it was over. Because a hundred times out of a hundred, when she tries to neutralize me in that way, tries to make me into a non-person, I lose my temper. That's why she does it. To prove her point. That I'm a baby. But that time I just felt icy cold. Then I said, 'Do you still love me?' She didn't say anything. So I pushed it. I said, 'Do you? Do you still love me?'

What did she say?

She didn't say anything. She just shrugged. Then she went back to playing with Poppy. That's when I went upstairs and started getting packed. Something deep inside me just gave way. So I packed.

So you did leave her.

Only technically.

Why didn't you tell her you loved her?

Why? How could I love her? How can a baby love a wife?

That's what she wanted you to say. She was scared to tell you that she loved you. Women test men by putting them on the rack. It's the way they think they can find out if you really love them. She wanted you to say it first. After she'd given you every reason to hate her.

Why?

Don't ask me. It's just what women do. They think strange thoughts.

*That's what I wanted **her** to say. Then I could have said . . .*

What would you have said?

I don't know.

Well, it's too late now, I suppose.

I suppose so.

I stir my coffee, think about ordering another. Martin stares out of the window – he has a tendency to drift off. He's never quite all there. But he's sharp, too.

Martin. If a separation is never mutual, how about you and Alice?

He blinks, shifts in his seat, refocuses.

I suppose you've got a point.

You left her, then.

Uh. Well. It's never that simple. Is it?

Isn't it? Did you leave her or not?

Now Martin looks at me, with a certain affable curiosity.

I don't, uh, know why this is so important to you, Spike.

I'm not sure either. Terence would be disappointed in me. Given how obvious it is.

Did you? Did you leave her?

Um. Well.

If you'd offered to move in and have a kid with her, would she have stayed?

I, er . . . She'd have stayed with me if I'd given her the chance. Yeh. I suppose.

You left her, then.

I left her. Yes.

Now it's Martin's turn to stare ruminatively at his coffee. What he seems to be experiencing is mild nostalgia rather than loss. All his negative emotions seem to be innocent parodies of real sentiment: anger is vague irritation, pain is being slightly under the weather, outrage is feeling that it's really not on. He's toned down, modulated.

What Martin needs, what he's always wanted, is a

woman who'll accept his indifference as a long-term prospect, and who'll be smart enough not to try to convert him to the world of emotion. Also, a woman who doesn't want kids – one's enough in any relationship. I'm reluctant to add to the stereotype that all men are overgrown infants because they're not, but Martin is, and he'll never change. He wants the lightness of life to last for ever – so no kids, no clingers. No ballast.

When he looks up again, he gives me a warm, rueful smile. *What about Poppy? How's she doing?*

What *about* Poppy? Where does she stand in this long, terrible war between two selfish adults vying to have their own needs met?

She stands in the middle, a victim, also selfish but innocent. She stands on earth that is falling away from her, the foundations of her universe rocked, because I can't stand to be with her mother and her mother can't stand to be with me. She is suspended between us, learning the toughest lesson of them all, the one lesson we spend a lifetime failing to learn: there is no God. There is no Santa Claus, there is no Tooth Fairy.

Forces larger than all of us operate, and not all of them are benevolent, Poppy. *Most* of them are not benevolent. We are caught up in storms. We are all going to die. We don't go to heaven. We just rot. So we want to make our brief stay on this earth worthwhile, and we will hurt others in order to do so. We will even hurt our children.

This is the truth, Poppy, although, God help me, the day I walked out of that house where I lived with your mummy the heart was ripped out of me. This is the truth, Poppy, although I love you more than I can tell you, although you are the greatest joy I have ever known. This is the truth, although the break-up of my marriage was – is – crucifixion, the most painful punishment known to humankind.

There is no God, Poppy, and we are all trying to save ourselves.

She's OK. God, I miss her. It's not natural for a father not to see his child every day. I get a glimpse once a fort-night. Sometimes it's so bad I park outside her school just to watch her go in or come out. It's one of those things that you think will make you feel better but actually makes you feel worse, yet you keep doing it anyway. I ache. All the time.

But what about **her**?

Children are amazingly resilient, I suppose. So they say. So I need to believe. More resilient than adults, anyway. They're the strong ones, because they have no memory. Oh, she and I have an OK time. She gets on my nerves some-times. Sometimes I think that if she says 'not fair' one more time, I'll . . .

But what about her? You keep turning it round to your-self. Do you feel guilty about what this is doing to her?

I suppose so. What use is guilt? I'm trying my best to do the best I can, given the situation we're all in. I'll never desert her.

You already did.

I stare morosely at him. *Yeh. I already did.*

Martin puts his arm round me again. He's not afraid of showing affection. It's one of the reasons I love him. *It's OK. You're a good man. Good enough, anyway. This will be over one day. Perhaps sooner than you think. Just ride it out. Everything goes away if you sit still enough for long enough.*

Yeh. I know.

Where are you going with Alice tonight?

I don't know. Just down the pub.

I look up at him, scanning his face for signs of suspicion or concern. There are none. *You're cool with this, Martin, yeh? I mean, I don't want to . . .*

Sure. It's fine. It's nice that you two can be friends.

It's not a date, Martin. We're just . . .

Martin laughs. It is clear that he thinks the possibility of me and Alice having a date is rather outside his scope for worry. Martin is tall, cool, dark, handsome and irresistibly indifferent, and I am a desperate forty-five-year-old near-divorcé. He doesn't feel remotely threatened. Anyway, he trusts me, and he doesn't love Alice.

You two have a good time. She's a terrific woman. You send her my . . . and with this he puts his fingers up to make inverted commas in the air . . . *love.* He takes a final swig of his coffee, puts his thumb up and heads out of the door.

Be good to yourself, Spike.

I'll try.

*I know you will. I know **you**, Spike.*

No, you don't, Martin. You have no idea.

7

I never expected, planned or imagined that I would end up in bed with Alice. It took me by surprise.

No – Terence didn't buy that one either. After all, as he pointed out, she's a woman and I'm a man. We're both available. So I cannot say that the question of sex did not fleetingly cross my mind. But I had answered no. I wasn't going to bed with my best friend's ex-girlfriend. And I certainly wasn't going to start it even if it did come up. Not that it was going to.

However, we went to the pub, and we got drunk, and we ended up in bed together. It was nice, and it felt comfortable, and in the morning neither of us regretted it. By then I had already decided two things. One: it wasn't going to happen again, or if it did, I wasn't going to institute it. Not that it was going to. Two, and this was something we were both agreed on, neither of us was going to tell Martin, or if we did, it wasn't going to be me. What was the point? It was a one-off, we were both emotionally threadbare, the one from the impending divorce, the other from losing Martin. (Alice still loved Martin – she had made that clear from the outset.)

So I didn't think much more about it. Until I got an email from Alice a few days later asking if I wanted to go out for another drink. I hesitated, to make a gesture towards my better self, then said yes.

The guilt I felt was surprisingly manageable. I knew that, as far as Martin was concerned, it was over, that he had left her, and I knew, too, that Alice and I weren't going to get seriously involved, so it would all be over soon enough, no harm done, two lonely souls finding brief consolation in each other's arms.

Except that by the end of the second night we had fallen in love.

Who knew where it had come from? A truck, no head-lights on, straight out of the night. This woman, whom I barely know, who had been Martin's girlfriend, a nice enough woman, to whom I hadn't given much thought. Now I can't get her out of my mind.

It's suspicious, I grant you. I know that the emotions of a man going through a divorce and a woman just after the break-up with her boyfriend are quintessentially unre-liable, yet what's real is real. One thing women are right about, which I once, in my very male way, doubted, is that there *is* such a thing as intuitive knowledge. That, in fact, intuitive knowledge is the only kind that is really true, the kind of knowing that isn't worked out in the chilly air-conditioned spaces of your head, but in the furnace of your heart.

I am in love with Alice. And she, I know, is in love with me. I didn't have to ask. The fact is, we could look into each other's eyes for minutes on end. I don't think I did that with Beth for the last five years of our marriage. Too honest. You can see too much. You glimpse too many lies.

But there, in Alice's eyes, I could see there was nothing to fear. We had entire conversations with our eyes.

Oh, God, it was like balm.

Now I have a real chance to use everything I've learned from talking to Terence, introspecting, raking over the ashes of my old relationships. I've learned a lot – and this time I'm going to get it right. Alice is going to be the first woman who isn't going to be disappointed with me. Alice is going to be the first woman who is not going to disappoint me. The Love Secrets that I've mined from the frozen fields of my past are my protection. I'm going to stick with them. I've grown up. I've learned my lessons. This time, everything is going to be fine.

Love is such an extraordinary force. To take a heart like mine, so torn and dried out and battle-scarred and, almost overnight, flood it, rebirth it, remake it, unfold its fiercely closed petals! How tough the human heart is. How endlessly renewable. And how poignantly trusting.

What are you looking so cheerful about? says Beth, suspiciously.

I'm at the house to pick up Poppy. It's my weekend. Poppy doesn't want to come, she's clinging to her mother, which is usually enough to make me miserable. She hides behind her white-blonde hair, screws up her big hazel eyes. She's crying.

But I'm cool about it. I try to josh her out of it in an uncharacteristically nonchalant and unconcerned fashion. This is enough to put an arch, knowing look in Beth's eye.

Come on, Poppy. We'll have fun.

I hate fun.

No, you don't. Tell you what, I'll take you to Teddy's Big Adventure.

144

I don't care.

Come along, poppet.

*So, what **are** you looking so cheerful about?*

*Why shouldn't I look cheerful? Come on, Poppy. Look,
I've brought you a lollipop.*

I've told you they'll ruin her teeth. Get her an apple.

Not fair! Apples stink.

With that she throws her slight frame into my arms, and
takes the lollipop. Good old-fashioned bribery. You can't
beat it.

Make sure you bring her back on time.

Of course I will, darling.

What?

I blink, confused. Sometimes I forget I hate Beth. Here we
are, in the porch of the house we spent so many years in
with our daughter. Inside, the furniture is the same, the
decorations are the same (we've been putting off the ritual
of dividing up our worldly goods but now the mediators
have pushed us into scheduling it for next Wednesday).
Sometimes it seems like we're the same, as if nothing has
happened.

Sorry. I didn't mean to . . .

Beth's expression is unreadable. Then it resolves into a
wry smile. *It's OK, 'darling'. Have a nice time.*

I'll try.

She kisses Poppy, who is concentrating on her lollipop,
then closes the door.

I'm glad I still provide her with such a rich source of
amusement.

Poppy gets into the front seat of my car, a crumbling
Nissan Sunny that I bought for five hundred pounds through
Exchange & Mart. It is rusty and smells bad, but it's all I

can afford. I just hope it will keep going long enough to get us through the weekend. I start up and we begin heading towards Teddy's Big Adventure, an indoor playground in a converted warehouse along Western Avenue. Poppy stares out of the window sucking her lollipop.

Why does your car smell bad, Daddy?

Because I can't afford a nicer one, poppet.

Mummy's car smells nice.

I resist the impulse to say, *That's because Daddy gave it to Mummy and it's only a year old, and it's got real leather seats, so why would it smell bad?* This one looks like it has spent its long, unhappy life being impregnated with cigarette smoke and fast food, and smells like a week-old bucket of Colonel Sanders' Economy Chicken Wings mixed with the contents of an airport ashtray. I spent all morning trying to get it to smell nice with deodorants, polish and shampoo because I was picking up my little poppet.

Why don't you just get some more money?

I'm trying, poppet. But . . .

What?

Never mind.

Daddy.

Yes, darling.

I feel sick.

It'll pass, darling, as soon as we . . . CHRIST!

The vomit shoots out of Poppy in a thick rainbow cascade and on to the carpet. I am astonished by the quantity, and the foulness of its smell. One half expects children to stay like their baby selves, when even their shit smelt OK, but they get older. They get human.

Sorry, Daddy. Don't be angry, Daddy.

Why didn't you tell me sooner that you felt sick?

146

Sorry, Daddy.

Poppy begins to cry, there's a pile of sick on the carpet, the engine in the Nissan Sunny is making strange noises, and suddenly I don't feel quite so good any more.

It takes a good fifteen minutes to sort out the mess, but now the car smells of chicken wings, cigarettes *and* vomit. Poppy, however, has made a full recovery, and is working at the dissolution of her lollipop. It's pouring with rain. We pull into the car park of Teddy's Big Adventure. I almost fall backwards as the cacophony inside assaults my ears. The downpour has brought in every family from within a ten-mile radius. There's nowhere to sit, food and sweet wrappers all over the floor, and the play apparatus is so crowded that it looks as if it's about to collapse. But Poppy wants to come here, although as she stares at the heaving mass of screeching bodies she's looking a tad nervous. Why wouldn't she? A Paras lieutenant would look a tad nervous.

Nevertheless, she takes off her shoes and socks, I pay the entrance fee and she's into the arterial arrangement of pipes, the soft boulders to crash into, the nets and pulleys and ropes and chaotic collisions that to me conjure up the shape of a child's mind if you could represent it in three dimensions in lurid plastic.

Fearless – Poppy has always been a spirited, outward-going child – she heads into a pipe that is already stuffed with a knot of infant bodies. If Beth was here she'd be looking out for Poppy and kvetching and making a fuss, but I think you've got to let kids learn for themselves.

I look for a place to sit, but there's nowhere. The people around me bring out the snob in me; the women seem slatternly, the men loutish. Almost all of the little boys have cropped heads and wear football shirts, while the little girls have pale, unhealthy skin – junkatarians. But a wet day for single parents knows no class barriers. All there is at the bedsit is a television, a video and a load of books, which I bought to fulfil a fantasy that Poppy might prefer them to the finely crafted characters and plots of Digimon. But she's bored by books. She's bored by the theatre. She's bored by vegetables. She's bored by violin lessons. She's bored by the whole middle-class fantasy package. She likes to watch TV and eat crap. So, today I will take her to McDonald's, which is where she wants to go, and at least at Teddy's she'll run around and work off the processed fat that she's about to add to the chocolate, fish fingers and oven chips that she will only eat when she's with me. I find it hard to deny her, because if I did she'd make an even bigger fuss about leaving Beth and maybe I'd lose her altogether.

I have made the fatal mistake of not bringing a book to read. I lounge against the wall, trying to ignore the screaming. I am bored. More precisely, I am in hell. I try to identify Poppy in the array of brightly coloured equipment, but cannot see her among the demonic bodies. Hieronymus Bosch would have dropped his paintbrush and run. Horrible pop music is being piped at a terrific volume through inadequate speakers. A portly young gentleman with a buzz-cut is sitting at a table next to me and having a sparkling Sunday-morning conversation with his blushing paramour.

Don't you fucking start.
Piss off, you fat cunt.
Don't you tell me to piss off.
Oh, I'm scared.
You should be.

I'm fucking shaking in my shoes.

You fucking should be.

And so on. I scan round for something to distract me from the demands of this Socratic inquiry. There are a few abandoned newspapers and magazines in the rubbish bin. It seems that the *Economist* and the *New Yorker* are not much in demand, but the *Sunday Sport*, most of the red-top tabloids and variations on *Hello!*, *OK!* and *Chat* enjoy an enthusiastic following. I pick up a copy of *OK!* and flick through it dejectedly. Lots of pointless toffs and so-called celebs parading around their country homes and chatting at endless pointless parties with herds of Hugos, Annabels and grazing flocks of Cholmondeley-Warners and Featherstonehaughs. Why do the lower classes get off on looking at this stuff? It's sick. Why are so few people just *normal*?

Because there's no such thing. There's no normal any more. Everyone's moronic in their own special way. Me included.

I put down the magazine, and start checking my Filofax-wallet to see what work I've got scheduled next week. Given the quality of my leisure time, I sometimes ache to get back to work. Then I hear a squeal that stands out from the squeal-saturated environment in which I am stranded. The ability of a parent to pick out their own child's special squeal of distress in a packed, airport-hangar-sized room is almost supernatural. Poppy is in trouble.

I scan the Heath Robinson In Hell array of contraptions and devices to locate the source of the cry. I cannot make out Poppy, but I can hear her clearly now.

Daddy! Daddy!

There are few more traumatic experiences than knowing

your child is in distress and being unable to do anything about it. I try to find an attendant to help me – they are just about distinguishable from the rest of the crowd by the fact that they wear tiny plastic badges on their otherwise non-uniform attire. I can't see a soul.

But I can make out Poppy. An arrangement of pipes and nets snakes up one wall. This area is meant for the over-eights, but Poppy has found her way into it, and is stuck in a narrow passageway through which a load of apparently deranged children, most of them boys, are pushing both ways. Her precociously big feet, naked of shoes and socks, push at the netting that traps her. Her hair is dishevelled and she looks terrified. She reaches a hand through the netting towards me, but I am on the ground, twenty feet below, and can do nothing.

Poppy! Hold on! I'll be right there, poppet.

Daddy! Help me!

I'm coming.

I look at the arrangement of pipes again. It's built in a number of complex helixes, and I realize there is no way I can find my way up to the spot in the maze where Poppy is stuck. I need an attendant, and there is no attendant. The only staff member, apparently, is the dimwitted girl mutely taking the money at the entrance. My sense of helplessness grows, coagulates into anger.

It suddenly occurs to me what parenthood has most in common with: childhood. The defining experience of both parenthood and childhood is the same: helplessness. And human beings can bear any other emotion more easily than that. For a child, it's the source of almost every tantrum. Growing up is all about coming to terms with one's own limitations.

As an adult, moments of extreme helplessness call up a memory of all those times when as a kid you were in trouble and ignored, sidelined, or unprotected by your parents. In such moments, the adult becomes the child once more, roaring at an indifferent universe. This is such a moment.

CAN I GET A FUCKING ATTENDANT HERE? WHO THE FUCK IS IN CHARGE OF THIS FUCKING HELL-HOLE?

I shout this at what seems to me an incredible volume. In a film or a play, it might have resulted in the entire room being silenced. This being real life, everyone ignores me. The man and woman are still carrying on their debate about the nature of fear and abjection.

You're fucking dead, you are.

Oh, boo-hoo. Call yourself a man? You're nothing.

You're nothing, you cunt.

Still no attendant in sight. I have no choice. I am reminded, should I have let it slip my mind, that there is no God.

I pull off my shoes and socks, throw off my jacket and, at random, plunge into the mêlée of shrieking, dwarfish bodies.

I'm not as fit as I used to be – I never was very fit anyway. In fact, in my middle years I've begun to develop a paunch, accentuated by the last year of comfort-eating, TV dinners, Jack Daniel's and Mr Tom peanut bars. It's not easy to fight your way through hundreds of yards of plastic pipes built for children, especially when you don't know where you're going, especially when some of the spaces you have to get through would be a challenge for Calista Flockhart, especially when you can hear the pitiful crying of your six-year-old daughter growing louder and more desperate by the moment.

It suddenly dawns on me that Poppy's screams are fainter. I'm stuck in a system of pipes separate from the snakepit she is lodged in, and it's leading me away from her. I change tack, go down instead of up. I can see a small bridge, covered with rope netting, that I will have to crawl through to get to Poppy's part of the apparatus.

The bridge is filled with small boys. I take a deep breath and try to get through, increasingly panicky. The boys are outraged.

Fuck off, fatty.

What the fuck are you doing, you old cunt?

These children, I swear, are the same age as Poppy. At this moment I decide that all the bad things Lizzy Grist has ever said about the male sex are true; that testosterone is cultural hemlock. The last boy to speak eyes me intently with a focused malice. I decide he needs to be put in his place by the deployment of a grown-up's superior sense of irony.

You fuck off, you little prick.

The kid looks momentarily taken aback.

I'm telling my dad.

I'm scared.

Yeh, you will be.

I push him away roughly and jostle through to the other side of the bridge. Now I can make out Poppy in a distant section of the pipe, her little arm dangling through the netting. I can see her face wet with tears; I can see her eyes full of panic.

Darling, I'm coming.

She looks around, but cannot see me. She screams, more loudly than ever, *Daddy!*

I push forward through the tunnels. My breathing is

heavy, my eyes are watering. Suddenly, at a turn in the pipes, I see another adult, a young man with gelled hair, a blue polo-shirt, and one of those little badges. He registers my presence wanly.

Adults aren't allowed on the play frame unless they are employees of Teddy's Big Adventure, he says sternly.

Fuck Teddy, I say. *Fuck Teddy's Big Nightmare. And fuck you. My daughter is up there and she's stuck and you'd better help me get up there if you don't want one of those little plastic balls stuck up your arse.*

This seems to penetrate the indeterminate padding that passes for brains in this postcode, and he leads me up three last tunnels to Poppy, who throws her arms round my neck and holds on to me so tightly I swear it will leave marks.

Are you all right, poppet?

She says nothing, but clings tighter than ever. Slowly, Teddy's Little Helper leads us back to the ground. Outside the rain continues to pound down, but I don't care any more.

Come on, darling. We're going. I'll take you to McDonald's.

Immediately Poppy brightens up. The prospect of sugar, fat and a shit little plastic toy galvanizes her. I grab my belongings and her shoes and socks. Even the rain and an appointment with Mayor McCheese looks appetizing after twenty minutes with Teddy. Just as I'm heading for the door, I hear a voice behind me.

That's him, Dad.

Right. Oi!

I beg your pardon?

I turn to be confronted with the Schopenhauer of the

school run, the man with the buzz-cut who was chatting so elegantly with his wife at the table next to me.

You tell my Daryl to fuck off?

He said it to me first.

He squares up. He's even bigger than he looked when he was seated. I expect him to land a devastating blow to my ear or chin, humiliating me and traumatizing Poppy, but in fact he does something worse: he looks me up and down and he says, in low, measured tones, *You should grow up, mate.*

Then he turns, takes his son by the hand and walks back to his table where his wife, or partner, is looking daggers at me. Then I'm out in the rain with Poppy, and I'm soaked.

Only seven more hours to go. The fat man is right. I should grow up.

But I can't. I can't be a man in a world full of children. I can't be the only one.

The local McDonald's is not what you'd call a flagship branch. It has that lifeless, end-of-the-line, all-hope-is-gone atmosphere. The customers look like they eat there every day. However, they're giving out free plastic representations of some Disney character this week, so Poppy is happy.

I order one Happy Meal with Chicken McNuggets, and a McStrawberry McMilkshake, with McFries, and a glass of McWater. I need to evacuate my McBowels, but I can't leave Poppy by her McSelf, so I'll have to see it out for now. I order the least offensive thing I can discover on the menu – a small fries and a bottle of water. At least it's cheap. I reach in my jacket pocket for my Filofax-wallet.

Gone. Of *course* it's gone. I left it on the table for a few seconds while I went to look for my terrified daughter. Why shouldn't I be punished? Clearly I deserve it. Still, it was only ninety pounds, plus all my credit cards, my favourite photo of Poppy and me, lost the negative ages ago, plus my video card, all the notes for my new ad campaign and my address book, which I've never got round to copying. Of course it's gone.

Daddy. I'm hungry. Can I have extra chips? What toy is it? I want the monkey one. Can I have the monkey one?

Just a minute, poppet. Excuse me. Yes. You. Look, I'm sorry. I seem to have lost my wallet. Would you mind if I came back later with the money? I just need to – I'll have to go back home. I've got some change in the kitchen drawer.

The man behind the counter looks at me blankly.

Look, I just need – my daughter is starving – if we could just – you've got four stars, haven't you? On your little plastic Hamburger University badge. That gives you the authority. You're a premier, A1 beef-patty flipper. You're management, you're practically the CEO. Please help me here. Please.

Nothing. I want to leap over the counter and thrust his head into the deep-fat fryer – McHead, Moron McHead, going cheap! – but instead I just feel myself collapsing, utterly defeated.

Daddy. Why are we going, Daddy? I'm hungry! I'm HUNGRY! LET GO OF MY HAND!

I'm sorry, poppet. Daddy hasn't got any money. We have to go back to the flat and get something to eat there.

I DON'T WANT TO GO BACK TO YOUR HORRIBLE FLAT. I WANT A HAPPY MEAL. I HATE YOU I HATE YOU I HATE YOU. IT'S NOT FAIR!

She throws herself on to the floor and refuses to budge. *Now then, darling. Try to understand. It's not really*

155

Daddy's fault. We can have a happy meal back at the flat. I'll tell you jokes.

I HATE YOU. I'M NEVER COMING TO YOUR HOUSE AGAIN. I WANT MUMMY. I WANT MUMMY. I WANT MUMMY.

Now, you know that Daddy loves you very much, but Daddy's just lost all his money for the week, but all right, when we get back, I'm sure Daddy can find enough so we can go to another McDonald's and I'll buy you some sweeties and then –

I DON'T CARE! I HATE YOU!

Yeh, well, I hate you too.

There. I said it. Because, right at that moment, I'm sick of people hating me – my wife, my daughter, the kid in the tunnel, the kid in the tunnel's dad – I'm sick of having lost my wallet, I'm sick of *trying*, I'm sick of being reasonable.

Now I look down at my six-year-old daughter, and see her anger and rage collapse into grief and surprise at what her father has just said to her.

Now she's taken her first tiny step towards learning that towering lesson: that there's no God. And if there is one, it isn't Daddy.

I pick up her now unprotesting frame from the floor, and she bursts into tears, and I apologize, God, how I apologize, but what has been said cannot be unsaid, and how can I explain that you can hate someone and love them completely at the same time? How could she understand?

For one thing she's never been married.

We're back at the flat, and Poppy's calmed down somewhat. I've placated her with the promise of a visit to her grandparents, my mum and dad, out in Yiewsley. They have

156

space, and old Iris is quite keen on her grandchild, as grand-mothers often are. I ring my dad while Poppy is eating what was left of a chocolate Angel Delight that I'd had at the back of the fridge for three days.

Dad.

Hello.

It's Danny.

Hello, son.

How are you, Dad?

OK, son. Just pottering around in the garden.

Good. Listen. I was just wondering if you and Mum would mind me coming over with Poppy for a few hours. You know, it's pissing down with rain, and there's nothing to do and, frankly, I'm going insane.

Well. It's a bit tricky, actually, son. I've got to get my weeding done, and you know how it is.

I know how it is, Dad. Children to you are forces of disruption you can do without. Men of your generation didn't have relationships with their children, they had contracts. *I pay for everything/brought you into the world/ work night and day to put food on the table, so you just shut up and do as you're told.*

Dad.

Yes, son.

It's pissing down with rain. How can you be pottering around in the garden?

Pause.

Actually, it's quite clear here. I can see some rainclouds in the distance, but they haven't –

You're four miles away. Can you put Mum on the phone?

Dad knows he's scuppered if Iris comes on the phone. Dad took Thoroughfare Number One in the relationship

maze a long time ago, the route signposted Complete Obedience. It's the eventual strategy of choice for about ninety per
cent of males, as far as I can make out. It's got a lot going
for it, as long as you can swallow your pride, dignity and
independence of thought for the rest of your life.

Well, she's just making a cup of tea.

I can wait.

Oh. Right.

Dad. Put. Her. On.

I can almost hear the sigh of resignation. Thirty seconds
later, it's Iris's brackish tones I hear throbbing through the
telephone wires from downtown Yiewsley.

Hello, Danny.

*Hi, Mum. Listen, I've got Poppy today, and what with it
pouring down with rain and everything and me stuck in this
bedsit I thought you wouldn't mind if we came and paid a
visit.*

*Mind? Of course we wouldn't mind. We'd be delighted to
see our granddaughter.*

Of course you would. Any thoughts about the prospect
of seeing your son? Would that bring you any pleasure
at *all*?

Good. About half an hour, maybe?

Lovely. I'll sort some lunch out.

God, that sounds wonderful.

*I'll only be able to do something simple. A roast. All the
trimmings.*

Mum. I love you.

Long pause.

See you in a little while, then, Danny.

'Bye, Mum.

                    *

Children have interior weather so turbulent that to track Poppy's emotional states reminds me of those time-lapse films of clouds unfolding, gathering, precipitating, dissecting. Now all the squalls have passed and Poppy has forgotten that I hated her for a millisecond two hours ago, she's forgotten that the car smells, she's forgotten that she hates me and that the world is mutable and irremediably unfair. We're singing songs in the car and having a wonderful time. She's teaching me some Britney Spears and I'm doing 'Anarchy In The UK' for her, which makes her helpless with laughter every time I do another verse. Poor old Johnny Rotten: if he'd known that his hymn to disorder was going to end up as a nursery rhyme, he'd have given up even sooner than he did.

We're heading back down Western Avenue towards my parents. I stop off at Teddy's Big Crap Hole on the way and, to my amazement, my Filofax has been handed in, ninety pounds intact. Perhaps people aren't so bad after all. I'm just full of bitterness, prejudice and anger, and if I could clear those out of my system, the world would be full of rainbows and light, like Poppy sees it most of the time – except when she can't get a fucking Happy Meal, of course.

Poppy's trying to sing 'Anarchy In The UK', only it's coming out too angelic. I make up a story to tell her, and she listens, and she helps me to make it up. It's a good story, and we're both having fun and we love each other, Daddy and daughter. Maybe it's the only man–woman relationship that can ever work.

Then we arrive at my parents' house, and Iris and Derek are out front. Dad is nodding – not for any particular reason, he just likes to nod – and Mum's hands are fluttering. They do that. They flutter in the air, little wizened butterflies, under thick canvas gardening gloves. I remember them flapping around me when she tried to comfort me after I had grazed my knee, or been bullied, or felt sick, and how she never quite got the hang of it. How, in a way, she always wore gloves.

The gardening gloves come off for Poppy. She drops them on the path as Poppy runs towards her, and she catches her granddaughter in her arms. In a show of surprising strength for a woman in her early seventies, she throws her into the air. Dad stands at a distance, watching, grinning – but not, I would say, spontaneously. Grinning because he feels that is what is required of him.

Iris lets Poppy go, and Poppy turns to Granddad. *Hello, Granddad.*

How's my little girl?

You've got a bogey.

What?

There's a bogey on your nose.

Dad takes a handkerchief out of his pocket and wipes it. Men of his generation carry handkerchiefs. It's one of their cultural tics, like emotional constipation, the capacity for sudden anger, and a counterbalancing self-contained dignity and strength. As is true of everything else, the consequences of being born into a certain generation are a mixture of negative and positive. My father was forged for the world into which he was born – tough, proud, ready to push aside emotions as so much weakness and chaff. He fought in the war, he survived, and his marriage has survived. Good. His children can't sort out their lives because although they want to be like him, and liked by him, they don't want to be like him at all and don't care whether or not he likes them. Another messy set of contradictions in a universe full of them, the ubiquitous and unseen dark matter of life.

Oh, look, Poppy, there's a bumble-wumble-bee. Look at it buzzy-wuzzing round the garden. Oooh, I'm scared, are you scared? Big nasty bumble-bee, he's going to bite Granddad. Oooh, buzzy-wuzz, buzzy-wuzz.

Poppy looks at me and I look at her. My dad doesn't really understand that children are just people. To him they're children, a different species. A species that requires you to make funny faces and put on silly voices, and generally lark about. He has put on his Poppy-voice now, sing-song and an octave higher than his usual voice, and it will barely leave him for the next five hours. I look at him fondly and think, as if it were a fresh thought, *My dad is actually very uncomfortable around children.*

It's not his fault. I love my father, and he was a good father by his lights. But he was never there when we were being brought up: he was out working about fourteen hours a day. When he was there, he was incorporated into the family pattern as a source of justice and authority: a benevolent but distant and sometimes angry god. Now, as a grandfather and trapped in a different time, he can no longer play the role he's been taught, so he caricatures how he thinks modern adults are meant to behave around kids. It's quite sweet, quite helpless. And it's bloody irritating.

Oooh, looky, Poppy. Dere's a pusscat. Nasty old pusscat is chasing the birdies. Nasty old pusscat wants to eat the birdie. Does Poppy like pusscats? Look, now the birdie is –

Granddad. The bogey's still there.

Iris takes Poppy's hand and leads her towards the kitchen. She says, in a perfectly ordinary voice, *Do you want to help me make some dinner?*

Yes, please, Grandma.

Good. You can help me chop the carrots and peel the potatoes.

Thank you, Grandma.

Eventually we sit down for dinner. Poppy is quiet, well-behaved. She loves her grandparents like she loves everything. How can an adult be so full of love and passion as a child? Poppy cries if one of her toys gets a scratch. She's genuinely upset, not because it's a possession but because she *loves* it. She cries to see an ant crushed, she cries when a butterfly she has been chasing flies away. Her body is so tiny, but her feelings are so huge. Growing up is just about getting smaller feelings, I suppose, until you're old like my mum and dad and all there is is benign indifference. This is the conclusion of our lives – an unstoppable diminution of scale.

We start on the Sunday roast. It's delicious – inevitably. One thing my mother can cook is a Sunday roast. She's made about ten thousand in her lifetime, and now she could make roasts for England. It's nice, but somehow I feel a bit pathetic. Back with my mum and dad. There's failure in it. I should be having Sunday lunch with my wife and child, not Mum and Dad. There's failure in *everything* at the moment.

Poppy accidentally drops a piece of her potato on the floor, but ignores it and carries on eating. Before I have a chance to say anything, I see my father's eyes flash. When he speaks he is in his other mode, the mode I remember, the patriarch.

I think you dropped something, young lady.

Poppy keeps on eating, ignoring him. I think she's too intent on the food even to hear him.

You pick up that food RIGHT NOW.

Dad . . .

162

Daddy, Granddad's being nasty to me.

Never mind that, young lady. You pick up that potato, unless you want a smack.

Daddy, Granddad wants to smack me.

I know that Poppy's being openly manipulative, I know she should pick up the potato, I know she's being rude. But she isn't used to being talked to like this – as ruler to serf, the only way my father knows in a power-broking situation. Also, Poppy's not Dad's daughter: she's mine.

Dad –

Just a minute, young feller m'lad. Now, listen, young lady. I'm going to count to three. If you haven't picked up that potato, you're going to feel the flat of my hand.

Daddy, please . . .

Dad. Stop it! Don't you ever threaten to hit my daughter!

What?

I don't smack Poppy. You're not going to smack her, either.

What's wrong with smacking? It never did you any harm.

Didn't it?

What do you mean?

Has it ever occurred to you that both your sons are living lives of miserable emotional failure?

Oh, come on, now.

Has it ever occurred to you that both Sam and I are unable to sustain a relationship with a woman? Has it ever occurred to you that that might have something to do with you and Mum?

Now, hold on just a minute.

It's the voice he used with Poppy: stern, authoritative, pompous, expectant of obedience by right.

First, you leave your mother out of it. Second, if you're

*saying that the fact that you can't keep your marriage
together is to do with me giving you a smack every once in a
while, then you're talking balderdash!*

It's not just the smacking.

What is it, then?

*Oh, I don't know. You never . . . talked to us. You talked
at us. You never treated us as equals.*

You weren't equals. You were children.

You made us feel small all the time.

*So it's all down to me, is it? Me and your mother?
Nothing to do with you, of course.*

I glance at Poppy. She is clearly enjoying this, and is
picking happily at her roast lamb. I decide it is time to show
my dad how to handle children in this day and age, how it
doesn't require threats of violence. I turn to Poppy and say,
very politely, *Poppy. Could you please pick up the potato?*

In a minute.

Not in a minute. Now please.

In a MINUTE. I'm just finishing my dinner.

My father looks on, a faintly mocking smile on his face.
All at once, those feelings from my childhood rush up, the
wash of helplessness, the tide of impotence, anger,
disappointment, sadness.

I'm not telling you again, poppet. Pick up the potato.

Poppy carries on eating.

PICK UP THE POTATO!

This comes out even louder than I'd intended. It is my
voice, but I recognize it as somebody else's. My father's. I
am my father. Poppy bursts into tears.

Not fair! I hate you, Daddy.

Just pick up the potato.

She throws it on to a plate so it splatters on to the tablecloth.

Go to your room.

*I haven't **got** a room.*

Go to Grandma and Granddad's room.

I'd rather she didn't. There are some rather valuable pieces of porcelain, says Iris.

She needs a damn good smack, says my father.

At this moment I'm inclined to agree with him, but my liberal conscience forbids any such thing.

Right, that's it, Poppy. You've got a black mark.

I have learned from the various childcare manuals I've read that reward is far better than punishment when dealing with children. So I've bought a sticker book in which I give Poppy gold stars when she's good. If she gets twenty gold stars, she gets a Beanie Baby. But if she gets a black mark, it means she has to cover up the black mark with a gold star before she gets the toy – so it might take it up to twenty-one, twenty-two gold stars to get the toy.

Unfortunately, since Beth and I separated, her anger and pain have been converted into rebellious misbehaviour and she's had so many black marks that she never gets the toy. So the carrot has somehow been replaced by the stick. And, as the books advise, it doesn't work.

Don't care, says Poppy. And she doesn't. I feel helpless.

There is a tense silence. Finally Iris speaks. *Would you like to come and help me do the washing-up, Poppy?*

Poppy gets up obediently from her chair and goes into the kitchen. I sit facing my father, thinking of the cycle of shit, and how mistakes just get passed down the generations and how I have no idea any more how to get it right with my parents, my children, my partners, myself. At least I have my friends, I suppose.

8

Not that I have many friends left. I think the ending of the marriage and the subsequent warping of my personality sent a good few running. But I don't mind too much because the two best have stayed – Carol and Martin. They're my real soulmates, nowadays – Carol especially. Martin is trustworthy, kind and well-meaning, but communicating with him can be a bit of an obstacle course, a Teddy's Big Adventure experience. You take a conversational tunnel to somewhere and end up somewhere else, or you get stuck in the netting. Carol, like most women, has the communicative gift that is rarely granted men.

Women are good at friendship – if you discount the bitching. Outside those two pole positions in the friendship premier league – Martin and Carol – I have probably five or six peripheral friends, and the majority of those are women. They're just so much more engaged than men. They're all those things that you hope women are going to be when you get into a relationship with them, but as soon as it becomes a relationship, everything degrades. Don't ask me why. Something to do with sex, something to do with children, something to do with power. But what was once a pleasure becomes a series of insoluble and usually painful conundrums.

Carol is the perfect woman. I don't fancy her, she doesn't fancy me, there's no sexual electricity between us whatsoever. She's just a mate – and she's brilliant at it.

I don't want to disparage the brothers. Men have come a long way, even in my lifetime, in terms of what they'll allow into a friendship. When I was in my teens, friendship was based on football, banter, the fantasy of sex, and music. Nothing intimate or personal found its way into conversation. Friendship was fun, but it was also about domination, about beating your friends, getting a peg above them. And the last thing you would ever do was talk over a problem with a mate. Too gay.

All that's changed. Men have taken twenty years of battering – seen their jobs go, their relationships go, their status go, their purpose go. They kill themselves a lot. They are unhappy. This unhappiness has a big upside. It has made them think about what it is to be a man, and it has made them reach out to other men.

But, nevertheless, they've got a long way to go before they're as good at friendship as women are. Point one: women friends know how to listen. Point two: women understand the symbolic, and life is almost all symbolic. Point three: women aren't afraid of intimacy or vulnerability, and men will still go only so far on that. (I once made the mistake of ringing up a good friend and telling him I was lonely. He was off the line in about fifteen seconds flat – it was like telling him I'd got cancer.) Point four: women understand other women, and most men don't. They either rely on their prejudices (out of date) or they believe what they read in the papers (ideology). Women will tell truths about other women that you will never read in a million years in a newspaper.

I'm meeting up with Carol tonight. We're going to have a real old heart-to-heart – about my pending divorce, about me and Martin and Alice. About her too – she's had a hard time with men. The broken heart I pinned on her all those years ago turned out to be remarkably prescient. The same age as me, she's been divorced twice, no kids, and now she's uneasily single. Her job as a successful management consultant keeps her busy, keeps her distracted. But she's not happy.

What went wrong? I don't know. I only know outside-of-relationship Carol, just as she only knows outside-of-relationship Spike. Perhaps we both buckle and distort, present different faces to those with whom we are partnered.

Carol feels about men like I feel about women – that they're a nightmare. But perhaps you conjure your own nightmares.

I don't know what men could object to in Carol, but I do know this: men are scared of her because she's so clever. I understand that. Clever people are scary. People who can see inside you, who can tell what you're doing before you know it yourself. It's a bit like having a burglar in your house, only the burglar isn't there to steal anything, they're there to rearrange the furniture, polish the mirrors, help you to move around more effectively and see yourself more clearly. A benevolent burglar. But it's still an invasion of your privacy. It's still an affront, having someone poke around inside your head.

Carol is fascinated by my own venture into introspection,

all the faltering steps I'm taking towards finding stuff out for myself that usually she needs to spell out for me. It's almost like she's set me a project, and I have to report to her. The only difficulty is, I don't know that I've got much progress to report. It's time to recap: this is what I've learned so far – this is what I've added to the flip-chart.

THE LOVE SECRETS OF DON JUAN

Problem: Mother – withheld affection. *Result*: Fall in love too quickly. Constant disappointment. Anger. *Solution*: Be cooler – less needy. Abandon search for unconditional love.

Problem: Sex = power (The Sharon Smith Principle). *Result*: Helpless, infantile rage. *Solution*: Saltpetre, self-blinding, castration. Otherwise, none.

Problem: Women full of impossible paradoxes. *Result*: Bewilderment. Misunderstanding. Anger. *Solution*: Not known. Complicated by fact that you are also full of contradictions. *Solution*: Also not known.

Problem: More than two people in relationship. Shadow/doppelgänger theory. Women symbolic, men literal. *Result*: B, M, A. *Solution*: Learn to speak chick. Watch behaviour as well as listening to words. Get to know shadows. Plus: words don't mean what they mean anyway. But listen for clues.

Problem: Women flock to indifference (Martin's Law). *Result*: Women don't flock to me very much. *Solution*: Fake it.

Problem: *Men try to crush what they see as weak.* ***Result***: *Lots of crushing.* ***Solution***: *Stop doing it. Avoid weak women.*

Problem: *Relationships continuing when already dead.* ***Result***: *Weak torture weak.* ***Solution***: *Be ruthless.*

PROBLEM X: *Can't remember what this problem is. Something to do with Helen Palmer. V. important, though.*

Problem: *Women test men's love by means of torture (The Gilfeather Paradox).* ***Result***: *Male suffering.* ***Solution***: *Put up with it – but only if w. is worth it.*

Now, what was Problem X? There *was* another. I just can't call it up. It feels important. I need to find it. Perhaps if I go back, I can dig it out again. Back to Helen, back to the 1970s in search of the missing Love Secret.

Helen and I started living together just as we were falling out of love. Or, rather, just as I was falling out of love with Helen, and she, becoming aware of this, replaced her love for me with a desperation not to be abandoned, with need, love's poor crippled cousin. Meanwhile, my love was replaced with a poor crippled cousin from the other side of the family: pity. The awful instinct to torment, but not quite destroy, the helpless.

Helen and I were in the suburb of hell that is a failing, dependent relationship. We still had sex, we still had the memory-trace of love. But we were gulled by the perpetual human capability for self-delusion. Our delusion was that this etiolated, frightened place was what all carnal relationships sooner or later degraded to. Thus, moving on was futile. Rationalization of our situation kept us nailed in place. That, and my inability to speak those heavy, heavy words, which would, like a warlock's charm, change everything.

I don't love you any more.

Years of averted eyes, of conversations constructed of lies. Being in a relationship you don't want to be in is as bad as sleeping with the next-door neighbour every night. It is bad faith, treachery. This leads you to inhabit a partial world in which truths become shaky, perpetually out of focus, because to confront the real truth means confronting your own failure and your own aloneness.

Not quite perpetually out of focus, though. Every now and then the world goes crisp on you, focused and sharp, and you see as plain as day what you need to do to unfreeze your life. You see the illusions illuminated, and the mendacity and the self-serving myths. You see straight. It doesn't last long, but it is as if a gate has opened through which beckons – you don't know what, only that it is the way out of your prison. Then you have to run like mad, or the gate will close again and you will fall back helplessly into your dream world.

I had seen this gate open many times during those years with Helen, and time after time I had turned my back and let it close again, stayed rooted to my place of dire safety. But then, one day, I ran through it. I remember the scene exactly.

We had both got out of bed in the flat. I was working as a trainee copywriter now, having started as a proof-reader, at a small advertising agency in Holborn. Helen was still training to be a social worker, a profession that in those days was thought worthwhile and rewarding. We both had trains to catch. It was eight a.m. Helen had had her bath and was sitting at the table with a cup of tea. She looked up at me and smiled. The gate in my imagination gaped. I turned the words round in my head, got them to the back of my throat.

Would you like a cup of tea, Danny?

No, thanks.

She knew something was up. Something about her blink rate told me she was nervous. She was wearing an old shirt, her blonde hair was messy. Her puzzled expression seemed to have deepened since college, her high forehead more deeply grooved than it should have been for someone of her age. She lit a Marlboro – her consumption had increased of late, so the smell of smoke wiped out almost entirely the wet-hay body fragrance I had always loved. She smelt stale, nowadays. This was fitting.

Is something the matter?

No. I'm fine.

Then I began to cry because I knew suddenly that the words in my throat were no longer impossibly heavy, that I was going to speak them, and I had already spooled forward to the moment after they had been spoken, to the moment when all we had, which was nothing except the past, was lost. I was thinking of me running to the cinema that warm night, I was thinking of the fire in my chest when I had first shared a bed with this woman, I was thinking of how shrivelled and shrunken we had both become in each other's dishonest company over the past few years. I was grieving already for something that was long gone. I was learning, for the first time, about loss.

It made me feel so old.

Danny? What on earth is the matter?

I looked up and, for the first time in God knows how long, I met her eyes, those lie-detectors, those mirrors. I saw that she knew. She didn't want to know, but she knew. Her puzzled expression had disappeared for the first time that I could remember.

You want me to move out.

I nodded. I was unable to speak through the tears.

She seemed calm and collected. She didn't cry. She even smiled. At that moment I loved her again, saw the flash of courage spark into life again.

Of course. I'll move my stuff out tonight.

I nodded again.

It was all over. And I hadn't even said anything. That night, Helen was gone.

There are few emotional states more strange or contradictory than those generated by the end of a relationship. The immense relief, the sense of extraordinary possibility and freedom that dawns. The falling away of scales from your eyes, the ability to look at the world with a fresh sense of honesty reclaimed, a raft of illusions out of the way, with all the blocks and blinds they put on your life. The euphoria, the strange weightlessness.

Both Carol and Martin had been amazed when they'd seen me a few days later. The spring in my tread, the new sparkle in my eyes. Martin was robustly delighted; Carol was sad for us both and tried to console Helen. Both warned me that I was a long way from being out of the woods yet, that the bubble of my euphoria would pop.

As Martin and Carol had known it would happen, sadness, fear, regret, panic, the dangerous weaving of new myths followed. The desperate wanting to believe that the situation was not irretrievable, that all we needed was a 'break' from each other to make things right. That we could split up yet not split up. The siren song, the lullaby of the past.

These illusions persisted, and there was no final ending to the relationship as long as they endured. Although I had stopped loving Helen, I missed her because we had woven ourselves into each other just by being proximate for such a long time. We did that thing you do when you're young, when you're stupid, when you're weak. We got back together briefly a couple of times, pretending that living together had been too early for us both and that all we had needed was 'space'. Lies, lies. There was only the reluctance to destroy, to be unshackled from the past. It led to collisions more pathetic than tragic. It never properly ended for either of us – until Helen met someone else.

That was not how I had imagined things playing themselves out. Since I was the one doing the leaving, it was axiomatic in my imagination that I was the one who would meet someone else soon. *She* was the discarded, abandoned one. I could have her back at the click of my fingers. When she phoned me one day and announced perkily that she and Conrad Carbon, an American I knew vaguely from college days, were together, it was all I could do not to retch.

I had left her . . . and now she didn't want *me*. It was unconscionable. The plan was that she should spend the short- and medium-term future pining for me, hoping I would come back to her, a temptation I would nobly resist, understanding that it was in the interest of us both to be mature, to accept that we were now separate people with separate futures. Now the rules had been disgracefully transgressed. Certainly, I had left her and I didn't want her back. But if I *did*, I knew she would be there, waiting with her cup of tea and her martyr's wounds. Now she was gone, beyond my reach.

I tried to get her back. I went round to her place (she lived in a tiny flat in Kilburn), banged on the door and yelled. This was a full six months after we'd split up. Eventually she came to the window. And I saw the look on her face. It was only there for a second – it disappeared as soon as she registered me registering it – but it was there.

Triumph. The same triumph I had seen on Beth's face when she introduced me to Oliver. The sweetest feeling: the victory of the formerly vanquished.

She invited me up for a cup of coffee, and we talked, and I told her how I had made a terrible mistake and how I still loved her and how we still had a future if we only worked at it, and that what I had done was crazy. She sat and listened, then said, *I have go to. I'm meeting Conrad.*

I begged and pleaded with her, but she went, and she promised she'd call me. She never did. In about forty-eight hours, the whole thing had died down again, and that week's particular shipment of illusions capsized, and I realized again, and fully now, that it was over between me and Helen. I was glad, and I wished her and Conrad well.

I never spoke to Helen again. Within six months they were married.

All this introspection and memory has failed to dredge up Problem X. But it wasn't entirely useless. It revealed to me that one of the secrets of any relationship is knowing, in the end, how to leave it. Even if you don't want to leave it, you have to know deep within yourself that you have the emotional equipment to do so, should it be required. You have to go forward from a position of strength.

Yet everything in relationships conspires to make you weak. Love makes you weak, desire makes you weak, the past makes you weak, fear of regret makes you weak, inertia makes you weak, tenderness makes you weak.

From where, then, does strength come? It comes from knowing that, whatever happens, you don't disappear. You will still be you. This is true of all change. You cannot imagine your parents dying, but when they do, you don't disappear. You cannot imagine having a child, but when you do, you don't disappear. You cannot imagine losing the woman you're with. But when you do, you don't disappear. You are continuous.

We are perpetually renewed. We are forever changed.

No luck. Problem X seems to be lost to memory for good, which means it probably doesn't matter that much. I check my watch. Late. I run outside, grab a cab. Five minutes later, I arrive at the bar. Carol is waiting.

Hey there, Spiky.

She stands up to kiss my cheek, then sits down again, regards me affectionately. She has aged well. Better than me. Women do age better than men nowadays – when did that happen? Her clothes are expensive. The badly cut, Marmite-coloured hair is long gone: now the cut is chic and modern, and her hair is carefully tinted. Her figure has retained its slight gawkiness, but is also still trim and athletic. She wears a cashmere sweater in much the same shade of pink she wore at Sharon Smith's party. Much of that version of Carol Moon has survived. But there is a tightness, a wariness that she didn't have at thirteen, before life had been battered out to the shape she now finds it to be, in luxurious solitude in a palatial flat in St John's Wood, where the litter bins are never full and the air smells of antiseptic and furniture polish.

Her stare has remained the most constant thing about her. Her eyes search my face blatantly, looking for news before I've had a chance to speak. It's a habit I still find disconcerting. She nods, as if she is confirming to herself what she already knew, then lets her eyes lower.

What's been going on, then, you reprobate? For once you look vaguely cheerful as well as sad and pissed off. Here, I brought you a present.

She hands me a small rectangular package, carefully gift-wrapped. It's obviously a CD. Carol's musical tastes have remained pretty stuck in the 1970s and 1980s while mine have moved on – or, to be precise, pretty much disappeared. The only time I listen to music now is when Poppy brings over a CD – *Now That's What I Call Music, Volume Infinity*. I prepare myself for a tactical smile in acknowledge-ment of some country-rock masterpiece or neglected white-soul classic that, in my hands, will continue to be neglected.

What is it?

Something that will chime with your emotional state. Or, at least, the emotional state I saw you in last time.

Jacques Brel? Nick Drake? Early New Order? Nico?

More bitter.

Bitter is good.

The CD is *Blood on the Tracks*.

I know you don't like Dylan.

Of course I do. This is great.

You hate him. But this will reach you. It's the story of his divorce. You need to listen to track four, 'Idiot Wind'.

Thanks, Carol.

177

Carol straightens her hair, adjusts her expensively framed spectacles. She regards me solicitously, her tiny eyes shrewdly assessing the hunched nature of my body language; her bull-shit detector is on full alert. We are in a bar in Primrose Hill. She nurses a drink – a vodka. I can remember her sipping vodka from that Donald Duck tumbler all those years ago. I order a large Jim Beam.

I sit next to her, picking at a bowl of pistachios, pretending I'm out of the woods. She knows better. I can also see that she senses the arrival of Alice – or, at any rate, that something has changed in me since the last time we met.

How are you, Belly-flopper?

In the middle of an unfolding disaster. Blood on the tracks doesn't come close.

That married man?

No other kind left. It's . . . What's the word? Shit.

How come you're so brilliant at decoding everybody else's life and make such a mess of your own?

Emotions. They distort everything. I've been trying to get rid of them.

Any luck?

They're quite persistent, it turns out. Particularly the negative ones. How about you?

The divorce is going ahead. It's with lawyers now. The mediation business didn't really work out.

That's too bad. When the bloodletting's over, things will calm down. There are demons to be exorcized for Beth as well as you. How are you getting on with her?

Fine. Except that I hope she dies soon.

She will die. Symbolically, at least. She has to kill you too. Also symbolically.

I get enough of this from Terence, really I do, Carol.
Anyway, you misunderstand me. I want her to die literally.

That's sweet. How's Poppy?

Hard to tell, really. Sometimes she seems very angry. I'm
scared of losing her.

You're doing your best. Don't punish yourself too much.
She's a nice kid.

Sometimes. She can be pretty difficult.

She's just a child, Danny. She's angry and sad.

Everyone's angry and sad.

Are you seeing anyone else?

I pause. I'm not sure I'm ready to tell Carol about Alice
yet. I don't like the shrewdness of her eyes, don't like the
truths she's so keen to tell me.

Not really.

Good. You're not ready, you know.

Aren't I? Then why do I want a woman so much?

That's why you're not ready. You're too angry and you're
too hurt. You need to get beyond all this. You're too down
on women.

I'm not 'down' on 'women'. I'm just angry with Beth
because of everything she's putting me and Poppy through.

It's all her fault, then.

The separation isn't her fault. The way she's conducting
it is. You know, I was thinking today. One of the real
secrets of relationships is knowing how to leave them. With
dignity. With courage.

Um-hum.

It's true, isn't it? Having the strength to do it cleanly, with
grace, without blame and bitterness. To cut the cord. The
weak torture the weak, don't they?

Um-hum.

179

To tell you the truth, I was expecting something better than 'um-hum'. Something along the lines of 'You know, Danny, that's very true. It's clear you've been giving this thing some thought and I respect you for that, and obviously next time you go into a relationship you're going to have a far better chance of making it work.' But all I'm getting is 'um-hum'.

You have to be poised to go, to cut your losses. Fear of separation is what keeps people together longer than they should be.

Um-hum.

Will you stop saying that?

Sorry, Danny.

And stop looking at me with those little eyes, like you know exactly what's going on.

I don't know what's going on. I was just thinking . . .

What? What were you just thinking?

Never mind.

No! You can't do this. I hate it when you do this.

OK, then. I'll shut up.

Too late now. Tell me what you were thinking.

The reason I'm not saying it is because I'm not sure I've got too much confidence in the thought.

Tell me anyway.

Perhaps . . . This thing about always having the courage to go. You've had that ever since you and Helen. Maybe it's become a sort of fetish. Maybe you smash things up before they're ready to be smashed up. Maybe you deliberately take the difficult option just because it's a difficult option, and therefore it seems to be braver to you. Maybe you're just someone who likes to make life difficult, because to you difficult is tough, difficult is brave and, above all, difficult is dramatic. We all learn lessons. Sometimes we learn them too late. But sometimes we learn them too soon.

There's a long pause as I absorb the irritating degree of truth that there probably is in this.

It must be wonderful being so clever.

It's awful, actually.

No wonder men run a mile.

I've been thinking of having an operation. Like breast reduction. For your brains.

Make sure they remove enough.

I will. In the meantime, as a short-term solution, how about another drink?

The Jim Beam has gone to my head. My resolution not to tell Carol about Alice is melting. I'm desperate not to hear what she has to say. I'm sure I'm not going to like it.

OK.

Carol orders, then smiles at me, scouring my face with her eyes again. I love Carol. I love her in the way you can only love someone whom you're not having sex with, who can walk away from you when they like, and vice versa. Friends are easy to leave. That's why we try so much harder to be nice to them.

Why can't I have a woman like Carol? Because if I went out with her, she wouldn't be Carol any more. She'd be my partner.

You know, Carol, I've been doing a lot of thinking.

Don't do yourself a mischief.

Don't laugh. I am capable of introspection, you know. I know you think I'm just a blundering, self-pitying, emotional dimwit, but I have been trying.

Don't be spiky, Spiky. How's the therapy coming along?

*How's **your** therapy coming along?*

Carol is thorough in her therapy, as she is in everything else. She's been going for ten years now, twice a week. I think she likes the intellectual challenge as much as anything.

It's hard. And rewarding. I'm slowly coming to the conclusion that I always go for the wrong sort of man.

How much is this guy charging you?

It's a woman. I know what she says seems obvious, but sometimes it takes a professional to point out the obvious to you. I don't feel good about myself, Danny. I don't know why. I could make up reasons, but that's all they are – made-up reasons. So I play it safe by making sure I choose people who feel the same about me. If I met someone who loved me I'd run a mile, because I'd want to know what they were doing loving someone with as little value as me.

God, Carol, you're the most wonderful –

I know. Thanks, Spike. I know you think that. And hey – I agree! But somewhere, in the heart of me, I can't feel that. It doesn't penetrate to the centre. Ten years of therapy has helped me to understand it. But in the end it hasn't changed anything. If a man loves me, I don't love him. So I always end up going for men who won't love me.

That's sad. But not inevitable.

I'm working on it. Perhaps I'll get there one day, says Carol, sadly. *Wherever 'there' is. How about you?*

OK, I suppose. Terence gets on my nerves somewhat, but maybe that's . . . you know . . . projection. Putting my anger on to him.

Um-hum. I mean –

It's OK. No, the real upshot of it all is that I'm learning to look inside myself. It doesn't come naturally to me like it does to you.

And what have you discovered?

Emboldened by the Jim Beams, I slurringly reel off the Love Secrets of Don Juan, point by point – except the one I've forgotten, Problem X, what the hell was it? – and sit back and wait for Carol to be impressed, but all she says is *Um-hum*.

This disappoints me. Why does she always seem to be expecting everything I tell her? I'd like to take her by surprise, just once.

God. You know, Carol, you really ought to meet Terence. You'd get on like a house on fire.

Sorry, Danny. Can I just get it straight what you're saying – what your 'Love Secrets' add up to?

Sure.

You seek women's approval too much, you fall in love too quickly, nothing's what it seems, your mother and father messed you up, life is full of contradictions, and you need to learn not to be so nice.

That's about the size of it, I suppose.

I realize how pitiful my lessons must sound. When Carol speaks again it is clear that she's through with the profound insights.

You'll find someone sooner or later who can make you happy.

Is that right? That's not what you said when you read my palm.

She laughs, that same sweet hee-haw, perhaps an octave lower than it was when she was a schoolgirl.

Maybe your palm has changed. Let's have a look.

I hold out my left hand to her, and she takes it in her olive-skinned hand, and inspects it for a good minute. Then she looks up at me, a worried expression on her face.

My God, Spike. Do you know what?

What? What is it?

I haven't got a fucking clue how to read anyone's palm.

We both burst out laughing and I nearly spit out a mouthful of bourbon.

Honestly, Spike, I do think you'll find someone. It's just a matter of time. Time and luck.

She intends this as a ritual closing-off of the subject, not a serious observation. I take another swig of the Jim. I knew I wouldn't be able to keep my mouth shut.

Actually, I already have.

Now, for the first time in our conversation – perhaps for the first time ever – Carol looks surprised at something I have said.

What?

I tell her about Alice, whom she's met once or twice, and Martin, whom she knows of old, and my nights with Alice, and my wild love, and for once it looks like Carol, the oracle, has nothing to say. The silence seems to last for ever. Then, at last, she speaks.

Be careful, Danny.

I know. I don't want to lose Martin as a friend. I will tell him, but I'm just not quite sure how to handle it.

That's not quite what I –

*But I **know** our friendship is bigger than that. He'll come to understand that Alice and I love each other. And you know something, Carol? This time I'm going to get it right. I'm going to keep right on with the therapy, I'm going to keep right on with the introspection, I'm going to keep pulling apart my life until I find the solutions. I'm learning my lessons – and I'm going to bear them in mind every day I'm with Alice. I'm not going to let this one go, I'm not going to fuck this one up. I'm forty-five. I can't afford to* *fuck up my life again. I know I've only been with her for a month, but I just feel it. I'm going to make this one last.*

Carol nods, looks like she's going to say something, then hesitates, takes a final swig of her vodka and says, *Good luck, Danny.*

Luck's got nothing to do with it, I say, firmly. *It's a matter of commitment. And learning the lessons I need to learn. Or, rather, applying the lessons that I've learned.*

Here's to that, says Carol, a strange twinkle in her eye.

Yeh. Here's to that.

Alice and I are in bed. While she breathes gently beside me, I'm running through the lessons in my mind. Have I fallen in love too fast again? Maybe. Don't care. Is Alice full of impossible contradictions? None that I can see, but I'm watching carefully. What are her shadows, her *doppelgängers*? I'll find out eventually. At least I know now that they exist. At least I know she's symbolic and that my literal self is capable of deciphering her. Now that she loves me, do I want to crush her? So far, no. Am I irrationally angry? Not with her: I could never be angry with her. Do I need to be ruthless? That only comes into play if we break up. And we're not going to. Never, never, never. Then there's the missing lesson, which I still can't remember.

We're at Alice's small flat in Putney. We spend a lot of time in bed. We're still in our horizontal phase.

She looks so different from how she used to when I saw her with Martin. Sex, the feeling made flesh, can transform the inner eye utterly. Her short, thick pale hair, her long legs, her creamy, marble-smooth torso tapering down to a wiry auburn forest. The mouth is wide and generous, the eyes hazel. I never saw her eyes when she was with Martin.

She's started talking about Martin now, in a neutral, careful tone, talking about how she still worries about him, how he's much more messed-up and confused than I understand.

We both love Martin, this we have repeatedly asserted. We are still trying to decide whether it is right to keep him in the dark about our relationship. Alice says she doesn't think he'll care. I think she's right – I know Martin doesn't love her. We've talked about it enough times, Martin and I. And I understand why Alice loves Martin so much. It's not just because he's a lovely man – and he is a lovely man – it's because he has no idea how to love women, or no wish to love them. He is content to *be* loved. It's his magical indifference at work again.

I don't get why this happens in a world where we are told that women are more emotionally sophisticated, more romantically knowing than men. Yet Martin is proof that the oldest cliché of all is true: women love a bastard. And all 'bastard' translates as is someone who doesn't care.

Nice guys finish last – and it's outrageous. If women want to start making their relationships work, they have to start *liking* nice guys. They have to understand that being nice is a strength not a weakness, that it takes resources and character and power and self-possession. In this respect, women need to grow up.

You're so beautiful, Alice.

Martin never used to tell me that. He never used to compliment me.

I'm sure he thought you were, though. How could he not?

He never told me he loved me either.

I love you.

Pause.

I love you too.

We hold each other close, and I hear birdsong through the window and I think, Finally my life is coming together. Finally, after years and years of shit, the sunshine is coming. Alice looks at me and smiles. *Shall we go out somewhere tonight?* she asks.

I can't.

OK.

I'm going out with Martin.

There's a slight change in the atmosphere. It's as if Alice has been knocked a degree off-balance. I can see her looking for a way to restore her equilibrium.

Shall I sort out some breakfast?

Have you got anything?

I don't think so, Spike. I'll nip down to the shops if you like.

I hesitate. *OK.*

Alice throws on a few old clothes, and takes some change out of her purse. I'm being unchivalrous, I know, but I have an ulterior motive. Nearly all my motives, in fact, are ulterior.

Part of her is still stuck in the past. I need to explore that past, I need to incorporate it. It's like a cannibal eating the brains of his victim. Martin is my victim here, and all the Martins before him.

Back in ten minutes.

OK.

The door bangs, and I'm out of bed.

I spotted them the other day, and although I know I shouldn't, I have to. Her photo albums. All piled up together inside a little cupboard off the hall. Ten minutes is enough.

History hangs like gravity around everyone by the time they reach mid-life. Relationships when you are in your twenties are so different from relationships in your forties. So vast a hinterland of time. So many other lovers.

I'm not ready to talk to Alice about her other lovers yet. The boy she met at school, the one she was serious with when she first left home, the one she almost married, the one who got away – whoever. I'm making this up, but all women seem to follow more or less the same pattern. It's time to meet the exes. It helps me feel more in control, because falling in love is to tumble hopelessly, randomly.

The photo albums, conveniently, are labelled in chronological order. Alice is in her thirties, so there's only about fifteen years or so to cover. I go to one of the earliest, from when Alice was about eighteen. Straight away I hit pay-dirt.

This one doesn't look much competition. Not bad-looking but a bit effeminate, dark curly hair, a bit of the brooding poet. Probably did a bit of busking and thought smoking dope was the apotheosis of rebellion. There are photos of them on beaches, larking about at respective parents' houses. I can imagine that Alice left him in the end when he got a job in a bank and sold his Tom Waits records to help with the down-payment on an Austin Metro. Probably had two or three years with Alice, and thinks of her still while living in a dormitory town in the home counties. As the photos move through the years, there are fewer and fewer that depict them with their arms around each other. Alice is increasingly straight-faced, and keeps her distance. No, this one's no threat. When she remembers me, I'll rank above this milksop. He's a starter-pack, an L-plate boy.

Sure enough, photos of Metro man disappear a few albums on. Now a long period of female-only friends in long-haul destinations – Vietnam, Thailand, Beijing? The lone traveller, girl-buddy years, boys flitting past like dragonflies, active life too short to show up on the film.

The next one appears about four albums on and looks like he'll be around for a while. He's tough, with rings and tattoos. He'd take me in a fight, all right. That South London look, stretched-tight skin, a bit wide, big biceps, high cheekbones, cropped hair. The macho trip, the half-tamed man. He'll be sensitive too – he'll make sure she thinks that. Maybe a taste for French films, I don't know, or Nick Cave and the Bad Seeds. Teeth bad, but she doesn't mind. He lounges on sofas, leans against walls, smokes cigarettes. Treats her mean and cruel, but she loves him all the same. Is this the one she still dreams of? Is this my competition? Is this the one she'll lie in bed thinking of when things are going wrong between us? *I love Spike, but he'll never be the same as Kirk.* That's got to be his name. Kirk. Or Mick. Or Rod. Something monosyllabic anyway. He fucks well. She'll think of it sometimes.

No photos of them draped together, he keeps his distance. She likes that, but it torments her. They go camping, they go on adventure holidays. He can put up a tent, strip a motorcycle engine in half an hour. But he can't express his emotions. That's why, three albums later, they split up. Everything reduced to anger. The inarticulate speech of the fist. Who dumped whom? In the end Alice saw through him. The late photographs show her distanced, bored, a little bit frightened. She won't haunt him. He's sunk beyond sight, his shadow lost in the petrified forest beneath conscious memory.

Another interregnum, two albums with nothing but friends and family. It can't be far off the present day now.

Alice is taking on her present look – the length of her hair is similar, the style of her makeup, the lines on her face. Here's another, a short stay. An older man, by the look of him, at least as old as I am now. Yes, here's the seer, the great man imposing his wisdom on his muse. Looks like a fucking artist. Yeh, here we go. Standing in front of his canvases, bleached-out landscapes, white hair pulled back in a pony-tail, lithe body, nut brown, handsome, at least fifty. Looks American.

Here they are in California. He's a fucking *surfer*. Christ, he should be going to bed early with a hot milky drink. He'll have that old-man smell. The aroma of distant death. Alice likes this one. *Really* likes him. But her practicality got the better of her, didn't it? She always wanted children. Teen-agers with a seventy-year-old father? It won't wash. He took it well, with a shrug, like Marlon Brando. He's still got his art. Waited with her at the airport when she got the plane, blew her a kiss and bought her airport flowers. He always knew the score.

Who else? Alice will be back from the shops in a minute. More blanks – office parties, casual kisses, lazing in the garden, barbecue smoke obscuring the lens. Two more albums to go. I hesitate before opening them. I feel slightly afraid.

The first photo in the next album is of her and Martin. They're in bed. You can't see anything exactly, the sheets are pulled up. Camera must be on automatic. They're having breakfast. In *this* bed. They'll have just had sex, won't they? Martin's got that look on his face. She's just finished laughing. Sunlight through the window. Looks like heaven.

A twist in my heart. A double-twist. I want to stop, but

can't. Turn the page. No automatic this time, I can see the shadow of the photographer, sun behind him, Martin and Alice squinting. Alice is looking at the camera, Martin's looking at Alice. I took this photograph. I remember it. But I don't remember that expression. What *is* that expression? I've never noticed it on Martin's face before. I've known him for more than twenty years. What does it mean? Turn the page. There it is again.

Fuck. Fuck.

I don't want to know this. I don't want this to be true.

I hear the key in the lock, and stuff the albums back into the cupboard where they came from. There'll be more time later, but I won't be taking advantage of it. Curiosity can be like jealousy or nostalgia, a sick fix, a debased emotion. Self-destruction, self-cruelty.

What do you want, Spiky? I've got sausages, eggs, bacon . . .

I don't feel so good all of a sudden.

Martin is on his third pint, and he's turning unusually gregarious. He keeps glancing at a woman with long brown hair in a tight skirt who is three tables away and returning his looks through hooded eyes. He's not been quite himself for the past few months – less emollient and relaxed. If I didn't know better I'd say something was troubling him. Yet I know that ripples on Martin's surface smooth out as swift as mercury.

We've got on to the subject of women. Martin is talking in his usual quiet, unconcerned way, but the length and rambling nature of the speech almost qualify it as a rant. Which is odd for him. He's usually rather diffident. Must be something in the beer.

Do you know the thing about women, Spike? The thing about women is that they want to be dominated. They think they want freedom, they think they want to be independent. It's not the case. Freedom is not what they want. Freedom is a nightmare. Some part of them gets that, understands it. All that potential for regret, for making mistakes. Understand this about women and you understand everything, Spike. They want to live by a myth, a double-standard. They want to have the illusion of responsibility, but not the actuality of it. That's why they like to be seduced – so they never did it. **You** *did it.*

Right.

Get us another drink, would you?

Don't you think you've had enough?

I'll tell you something else. They lay traps for you. When they feel bad about themselves. They don't . . . they want . . . they **punish** *you. Because* **they** *feel bad. What's that about? I don't know. But it's not like they want to hurt you, not really. They want you to see it as a cry for help.*

I've had that with Beth. You told me about that.

They want you to guess their pain. They can't **tell** *you. To tell you isn't* **it**. *You have to sniff it out, see? You have to put your arm around them as they're sticking the knife into your heart and tell them it's* **OK**. *It's OK. And then they'll* **twist** *the knife, but you have to keep holding on, keep your arm round them, tell them it's all right. You have to pull the knife to you. Because they're testing you, they're testing your love. It doesn't feel fair. It's not fair. But that's the way it is. You've got to know how it is, then you've got to find the strength to pass the test, again and again and again. Because it never stops, Spike, it never stops. You never pass the test, not completely, not for ever.*

I've not often seen Martin like this – maudlin, rambling. Instead of keeping it all packed inside, instead of being mysterious, knowledgeable and wise, he's letting it out. As if he's unpacking pain with words. I don't get it. Maybe he's going through a hard time with the Brazilian dancer.

I'll tell you something else. You can never . . . they'll never let you take the moral high ground. You can never seize it. However right you are. I mean, maybe for half an hour. That's the max. Make the most of it. Because they'll take it back. You'll be in the wrong again in no time at all. History rewritten. Women are all Stalinists. They control the past. You know that film. Did you see that film, Spike?

He drinks deeply from his glass.

Which film?

With Jack Nicholson. As Good As It Gets. There's a great moment in that, a perfect moment.

Can't remember much about it.

I've had three pints as well, and I'm feeling warm towards Martin, indulgent. The truth is, I am grateful to him for donating Alice to me, although obviously he doesn't know he's done it yet. Good old Martin.

Well, there's this moment when he's . . . I mean, Jack Nicholson is a writer, can't remember the name, they make him mentally ill so that he can say things about women and get away with it. Anyhow . . . do you want another pint?

I'm fine.

What was I saying?

He's mentally ill so he can say bad things about women.

But that's just a device for smuggling through certain truths, like, he can only say this stuff because he's mad, right?

Right.

So the thing is, Jack Nicholson is an author and he writes

193

*books about women. And, apparently, he's brilliant at it,
and has loads of women fans, and he goes to his publisher's
office one day, and there's this secretary there, you know,
this – this bim, and she goes up to him and she asks him, I
can't remember exactly, something like 'How do you create
such convincing women?' You know, as characters. How
does he do it?*

What does he say?

He says . . . he says . . . you know . . .

Here, Martin attempts a Jack Nicholson impersonation,
and it's not bad at all. I'm already laughing before he gets to
the end of the first sentence.

*'You want to know how I create such convincing women?
You really want to know?' And the woman smiles, and
looks all ditsy and adoring, plainly like expecting something
really flattering, and he turns and does that Jack Nicholson
what-the-fuck look, and says, 'I take a* **man***, and I subtract*
reason *and* **accountability***.'*

I remember that.

Of course you remember that! The whole **audience**
creases up. There's **uproar***. And I'll tell you, Spike . . . I
looked around the audience, and it was, like, half of them
were women. And they were the ones doing all the laughing,
they were the ones holding their sides. Because it was as if
someone had found them out and had the guts to tell it like
it was, and the truth was too much and when the truth is
that big it just makes you laugh.*

You think that women lack **reason***?* I take a long pull on
my pint, squint through the pub smoke. *But there are some
fucking clever ones out there, Martin. Millions of the
fuckers. Running rings round us.*

Martin's got a new pint, is sinking it fast. He puts his arm round me, pulls me close. I smell his body odour, beery, salty.

*Of **course** women don't lack reason. That's not why it's funny. It's not even worth suggesting – no one but a moron could suggest that women are dumb. What Jack's really saying is that women use reason or not as they see fit. They aren't hypnotized by it like men. That's why women laughed, because Jack was holding up a mirror to their own secret weaponry. They respect the dark forces. The dark forces, Danny, the dark forces.*

Of course, we don't say anything about the 'account-ability' bit. Because that's a given. Because we both know exactly what Jack Nicholson means. And so did the whole audience.

*For instance, what is it with PMT? You're not allowed to **mention** it any more. Testosterone, yes. Men are all killers because of testosterone. But pre-menstruals? Everyone knows it happens. Everyone knows half of all women go psycho for seven days out of thirty. But when they empty your breakfast cereal over your head because you put a heaped instead of a level teaspoon of sugar in their tea, you have to **pretend** that nothing out of the ordinary is happen-ing, that this is a justifiable act, generated by your self-evident thoughtlessness. Like there's no such **thing** as getting moody before you get the painters in. It's a crime to bring up the obvious. It's a crime to speak the fucking **truth**.*

Dangerous stuff.

What?

Truth.

*Yeh. You said it. You **said** it, Spiky boy.*

We drink on. I want to see Alice tonight, but I don't feel I can just turn up at her flat. It seems more of a betrayal of

Martin somehow now I've spent the evening with him. Not that it is a betrayal, of course.

Martin's good at listening, and I tell him about Poppy and my hopeless dates, and Beth, and the divorce, and I listen to myself and think how bitter and self-obsessed I remain, despite my good luck with Alice. So bitter that I've learned all the words to Dylan's 'Idiot Wind' and sing it to myself in the bath every night. Carol really hit the mark with that one. Fury made into sound.

Poor Martin. He's heard all this so many times before. I need to move on. Alice is going to help me do it.

How did that drink with Alice go, by the way?

I'm not sure whether I blush or not, but I say, rather too quickly, *Oh, it was fine. I like her.*

You know, sometimes I think we could really have made it together.

Why didn't you then?

Why didn't we?

Yes.

Martin screws up his face. His muscles work and stretch under the skin, as if questing for the solution to this conundrum. Finally, they relax back into something approaching equanimity.

Oh, you know. I'm not very good at that kind of thing, really. It's the way it's always been. Women come and go somehow.

For you they do.

Well. You know. I don't know. They come for you sometimes too, don't they?

Sometimes. Not often.

You should stop looking. Then they'll appear.

I have stopped looking.

And has anyone appeared?

There aren't that many great women out there.

*Don't be so **negative**. You're always – there's some fantastic women out there. I've known a few. Alice, for instance. Alice was a great woman. Is a great woman. Is. Is.*

Martin stares into his beer. He's definitely not himself. I feel the silence ballooning, search for ways to pop it.

I saw another film once when the guy says you only get to meet three great women in your life . . .

I know the one. By Chazz Palminteri. What was it called . . . A . . . A Bronx Tale?

That's it. It's weird, but he's sort of right.

You reckon? Have you reached your allocation yet?

I pull at the last of my pint. The room seems very fuzzy and Martin keeps going out of focus.

I suppose so. Yeh, I suppose so.

Who were they, then? Who were the Holy Trinity?

Well. There was Kelly Cornelius. There was Natasha Bliss, of course. I used to think Beth was number three, but I don't any more. Obviously.

So who holds that position now, then?

I look at Martin – and suddenly I can't keep it in any more, I want to share my happiness with him, and I want him to be happy for me, and we can all be pals together, and we'll embrace and we'll go out on foursomes with the Brazilian dancer, and we'll laugh at all the old times and how funny it was that we all ended up like this, and I look up from my glass and say, slurring a bit, because I'm somewhat the worse for drink, *Well, actually, Martin, it's Alice.*

What?

It is clear that Martin has heard what I said, but that it

197

hasn't yet reached the part of his brain that will produce the happy consequence of him clapping me on the back, congratulating me and buying me another drink.

It's Alice. We've been seeing each other. To tell you the truth, we've fallen in love.

There is a long, agonizing pause. Martin's face is suddenly the colour of a paving-stone. I hear myself beginning to burble: *It's like . . . I wouldn't have done it . . . you being my best friend and everything . . . but you **did** leave her. And you've told me enough times that you didn't love her. Or, at least, you never said you were in love with her. Which is the same thing in my book. So I didn't think in the end you would mind. Because, you know . . . anyway, it's not what I planned. I didn't do it . . . she kind of came after me, and I just went along with it, and then, you know, we fell in love. It was all out of the blue. I thought you'd be happy for me. You're happy for me, aren't you, Martin?*

Still Martin doesn't say anything. He hasn't moved since I said, 'We've been seeing each other.' He really does look ill. Eventually, he speaks in a very low, very soft voice: *That's great.*

Pause.

I'm glad you –

*No, that's great. That's really **outstanding**.*

A glass shatters behind the bar. Martin pulls on his beer. Shakes his head as if answering some long-pondered question. When he speaks again, his voice is brisk, bright, tarnished. *So anyway, Spike, how's work coming along?*

This wrench away from the subject is unnatural and awkward, but maybe we'll be able to get past it this way.

It's OK. I've got a chance of doing some new chocolate

thing. The krusha Bar™. Lot of money in it. I've got to make a pitch soon.

Right. Chocolate. Chocolate's good. OK. You sure you don't want another drink? Did you see the last Big Brother? Christ, I . . . How's your mum and dad, anyway?

Martin finishes three-quarters of his pint in one go. His eyes dart around the room furiously.

You're not upset, are you, Martin?

Martin looks up at me, smiles that little-boy smile. Pats me on the back. *Of course I'm not upset. Why would I be upset?*

*Well, I suppose . . . after all, even if you didn't love her, she **was** your girlfriend, and . . .*

Even if I was upset it wouldn't matter, would it?

I'm getting confused now. Martin seems to be in his own mind space, hardly hearing me now, speaking partly to me, partly to himself and partly to his beer mat.

*After all, it's not going to **last**.*

Well, this time, actually, I've got a feeling . . .

Anyway, what about your mum and dad? Haven't seen them for ages. Old Iris still sending you to Siberia? Bit of a Tartar, isn't she? Poor old Derek.

I saw them a few weeks ago, they seem quite –

Then Martin cuts me off, looks up abruptly from his beer mat.

*It's not going to **last**, Spiky, because you haven't got a fucking clue about women. Because you'll fuck it up like every other relationship you've ever had.*

It's as if someone has punched me. Martin is not saying this kindly or solicitously. He's looking at me through half-closed, suddenly violent eyes. His words come in spits.

I mean. What chance have you got? You're – you're like

one of **them**. *Always needy, always whining. 'Poor little me.'*

There's no need to –

Now he points a finger at me, jabs at the space between us as if to perforate it somehow.

You know when I met you for coffee after your last . . . whiny little mediation session, you said something about . . . Poppy. That she was always saying, 'Not fair, not fair.'

I don't think it's fair to bring Poppy into –

There you go again. 'Not fair, not fair.' Poor little Spiky. Poor lickle Danny. That's why you'll fuck it up, because you'll just spend all your time feeling sorry for yourself when things go wrong. You don't understand, you don't get it. Women don't give a fuck if it's fair or not. No one gives a fuck if it's fair or not. It's a fight to the death. It's the pro-creation of the species. You should know that. You've just **proved** *that. And you still expect it to be* **fair**, *like some whingeing, spiky little schoolboy.*

You've had too much to drink.

Something else. You'll never have a proper relationship with women because you don't like them. You think you do, but you don't. I like them. I really **like** *women. I take 'em as they are. With all their nightmares. With all their fucking shit. Because they're life. Because they're what makes things happen, they're the dynamo, they're the – whatever – source. But you think things can be made right, and they* **can't**. *Whatever that means, whatever 'right' means. No. It's not that. It's not so much that you're some kind of . . . naïve perfectionist. A disappointed idealist. That's too flattering. It's too untrue. It's simpler than that. It's that you're* **afraid** *of them. Of their difference. You want them to be like men, and that would be the worst nightmare of all. It's the* *scorpion and the frog. It's the . . . it's the . . . I don't know what it is, you cunt.*

I try to take in what Martin is saying. Of course I'm afraid of women. I'm afraid of everyone. I'm afraid of the man who sells me my newspaper in the morning. Because, like everyone else, I'm tender, all raw, all wound. Anyone can hurt you.

Martin –

He's on his feet now, wobbling about crazily. He looks like he's about to fall over. Terrifyingly, I see a tear overflow his eye, tumble down his cheek. His voice has changed now. It's softer, I can barely hear it.

I don't feel good. I don't feel good about this, Spike. I love you, Spike. You're my best friend. My best –

He stops mid-sentence, looks around as if for help.

I have to go.

What? This is about me and Alice? I thought . . . You said . . .

I rise, put my hand on his shoulder, but he shrugs me off angrily. *You think I care? I don't fucking care. What is she? She's only gash. There's another one, there's always another one, and another one, and another one. Down all the days. Tomorrow and tomorrow. Petty fucking pace of time. Fuck it. Fuck it.*

He steps away from me, a cornered, feral look in his eyes, steps towards the door. *I have to go. I have to go, Danny. I . . .* He's pulling on his coat, and before I can say another thing he's out of the pub.

I sit there for a few minutes, fighting with the effects of the drink, not knowing quite what to do. What is he doing? What's the *matter*?

But of course I know. I knew it the moment I saw those

photographs of him and Alice together. The unfamiliar look on his face, the look that made me snap the book shut in shock and despair.

The look of yearning.

The look of love.

9

I met the first of the three great women I have
known when I was twenty-five. It was the 1980s. I was doing
well. The advertising business was flying, and I was joy-
riding in the slipstream. I had moved to one of the bigger
agencies, was working on some major accounts. I was
wearing Armani suits, driving a 1967 VW Karmann Ghia,
and shoving an outlandish percentage of my six-figure salary
up my nose. I bed-hopped with a wide variety of shallow,
skinny, money-obsessed shoulder-padded Sharons. Aids had
not yet clouded the sexual horizon, although it wasn't far
away, and everything was a hedonistic disco-hustle of
expense-account lunches, ludicrously inflated Christmas
bonuses, nightclubs and champagne for breakfast. I was
having the time of my life.

Only I wasn't. I believed I was, I was *convinced* I was.
How could I not be having a great time when I was young,
had loads of money, was having sex as often as advertising
told me was mandatory, had a bulging Filofax, was
constantly going to meetings where I was being told I was
talented, the future, a prodigy. I had put the sales of G-Wiz

Energizing Cola up by twenty per cent with my clever 'Get Some Fizz With Mr Wiz' campaign, Mr Wiz appearing on TV as a kind of surrealist Jeremy Beadle, stopping people in the streets and asking them if they'd had any Wiz today. When they admitted they hadn't, he'd have a crane lower a twenty-foot can of G-Wiz in front of them, climb up the side, tug off the giant ring-pull and . . .

I won't go on. You had to be there to understand. Then there was my Puff the Magic Dragon campaign for Rozza cigarette papers, a Busby Berkeley pastiche with rhinos and hallucinogenic mythical beasts and my 'What You Mean You Like My Jeans?' campaign for Billy Bull Denims, which converted a generation to the delights of stretch denim. I was hot.

Yet somewhere inside I was unhappy. I was unhappy because I knew that what I did was nothing more than a trick, a childish knack, like juggling or cracking your knuckles. I got lucky once, then an insider mythology built around what I was doing, and I could do no wrong. But what I did was crap, and it was meaningless. And sleeping with loads of . . . *strangers*, although it had its compensations, wore thin. It just felt lonely. It had been a few years since I'd extricated myself from Helen; the lesson I appeared to have learned from it was, don't let yourself get hemmed in. So I'd started running, and kept on running. The moment anything threatened to become serious I was out of there before you could say 'What You Mean You Like My Jeans?'

It was then that I met Kelly Cornelius. I was at some fashionable restaurant that charged you an enormous amount of money for a tiny quantity of food with seven people I hardly knew, and with half a gram of cocaine burning a hole in my pocket and the other half scouring an extra partition in my septum. The chatter was tumultuous, vacuous, torturous. Despite the coke, I felt glummer and glummer. Everyone was prattling away as if their dreary clichés and trite observations would eclipse Dorothy Parker. Suddenly I had one of those moments of clarity; I saw the whole dinner table, the whole restaurant, as a freak show, a Tower of Babel, a whole Radio One of pathetic banter. And there I was at the heart of it. I wanted to run out of the restaurant, buy myself a battered Smith-Corona, move to Mexico and bash out the great novel. Only my certain knowledge that my writing ability extended to about eight buzzy syllables and a couple of paragraphs of infotainment stopped me.

I looked wearily around the table, grinding my teeth and toying with my miniature impressionist treacle tart and custard (£9.50, the size and flavour of a digestive biscuit), and it was then that I saw Kelly.

She'd been sitting there all evening, in fact, but for some reason she hadn't registered with me. She was resolutely unglamorous, and that was probably why I had ignored her. No makeup – this at a time when every woman in the business world wore makeup – no power suit, and her hair was a big bird's nest of curls, careless and untamed. Now, I saw a stillness about her, an innocent, bemused withdrawal from the circus, which lent her a strange dignity.

The man sitting next to her, an account executive from my agency with candy-coloured braces and slicked-back hair called Hugo Bunce, was telling her a joke in a loud, plummy voice. This gave me the opportunity to watch her face carefully without being noticed. Her skin was good, pale, almost ivory. A roundish face, a little tuck of a chin almost like a fold of fat, yet somehow appealing. She nodded slightly as Hugo reached the punchline. I could see she was uncertain as to when she was meant to laugh but that she didn't want to hurt his feelings. Not knowing, apparently, that Hugo's feelings had been cauterized by his years of training at a minor English public school. When her laugh came it was a moment too early and clearly forced, but it was an attempt to be polite rather than insincere. Then her eyes switched direction and caught mine.

I was shocked by how blue they were, and also that they were slightly crossed. I didn't mind – it was sexy. She held my eyes for one, maybe two seconds, enough, I imagined, for a crisp, and probably accurate, character assessment. I suspected that I hadn't fared that well – my red nose, the tooth-grinding, the uneaten food told their own story. Then she turned back to Hugo, who had started another anecdote. She raised a small hand – a tiny hand, delicate – to her mouth to conceal a yawn. I noticed her blouse now, that there was a small tear in it around the shoulder, and sensed that it was second-hand. She was wearing Oxfam clothes at a table where the other women had spent £150 on a scarf.

It intrigued me. When the bill came and had been settled, we all got up to leave. I did my sidling thing again. As luck would have it, she separated from the bulk of the crowd leaving the restaurant and I followed her. It was odd – I had never seen her before, and she seemed to have come with no one. We turned a corner, me ten paces behind. We found ourselves, just the two of us, in a small lane leading between two main thoroughfares. I felt seedy, but obscurely excited. I wanted to call out to her, but how would I explain myself? So I just kept following, through this alleyway, then another. Her pace was quickening, and I began to feel out of breath, but she showed no sign of having noticed me. Then a voice rang out, musical somehow, home counties, I would guess.

Why are you following me?

She turned and waited for me to catch her up. Her eyebrows, dark, were high and quizzical. The cold air in the street had cleared my head, but my nose hurt. She met my eyes, seemed unconcerned.

Are you a stalker? Is that it?

I sniffed a couple of times before I answered.

I'm not following you. I was just heading in the same direction.

Which is?

Holborn.

Holborn's in the opposite direction.

Chancery Lane, then.

That's in the opposite direction too.

All right, I was following you. But not in the way you think.

How many ways of following someone are there?

Several.

You sound like an expert.

Not really. I'm obviously not very good at it.

It depends what you're hoping to get out of it.

She pulled her coat round her. It was cheap, but it looked good, even though it was a little ragged around the sleeves. I was starting to feel slightly ridiculous, but I could tell that she was not offended. A little smile was working the corners of her mouth, either amused or contemptuous, I couldn't quite work out which.

I suppose so.

What were you hoping to get out of it?

I'm not sure.

Why me, then?

Because you laugh at the wrong moment in jokes.

Is that something you find attractive in people?

It sometimes betrays a kind of innocence, I suppose. A kind of sincerity.

I'm really not that innocent.

I'm really not that sincere. I'm following you because you've got a tear in your blouse and because you haven't been to a hairdresser for about five years. It made you stand out in that context.

What context?

The context of sitting next to someone like Hugo Bunce.

Now she smiled. *Hugo seemed quite nice. He wanted a date.*

Did you say yes?

I'm considering it.

Why?

Lack of better alternatives. Anyway, why would my dating habits interest a big-shot like you?

I'm no big-shot.

You're Mr Wiz.

So that's me accounted for. And you're . . . ?

She smiled, now, a full smile, showing rather crooked teeth with a little pink tongue poking through the gap in the yellowy white rows. *My name's Kelly.*

Kelly. Well, Kelly, can I buy you a drink?

The pubs are shut.

I'm a member of a little club around the corner.

Of course you are.

She hesitated for a few seconds, then thrust her hands

into her pockets, took out a packet of cheap cigarettes, and lit one. *OK, Mr Wiz. Show me the way.*

Kelly followed me up the stairs in the little club off St Martin's Lane. She got some odd looks – all the other women there seemed to be dressed at Joseph Bis, Ally Capellino and Margaret Howell. She looked a little unkempt in the bright light – shabby, even. But I didn't care. There was something intriguing about her, although I wasn't sure yet what it was.

She was an artist, as it turned out – a painter. I might have guessed. The relative poverty, the curiosity in the eyes, the strange animation and distance. Although I worked at the centre of a supposedly creative business, I had met few real artists – not, of course, that I was sure at that point that Kelly really was an artist, only that she had a studio, and that she had had a couple of exhibitions.

But whatever her abilities, she had a quality that set her apart from all the women I met in the advertising industry. It was the absence of the need to sell herself. There was also a kind of pause that she imposed when you said something to her, as if she was letting it percolate through to her very centre before she replied. She examined everything, scrupulously tested and weighed all input. Half of the time I felt pitiful when I was talking to her – the half of the time when I was trying to impress her. But when I stopped play-acting, when I relaxed into who I actually was, when I found the wherewithal to express my own feelings and opinions rather than the ones that were fashionable that week or the ones I thought would make me look good, she responded. Her eyes widened, her head came forward, she became engaged. She didn't say much, or feel the need to speak if she didn't have anything to say.

The other thing I liked about her was that, despite her self-possession and intelligence, she was also nervous and a bit clumsy. She knocked over the first drink I bought her, and almost did the same with the second. She shifted around on her chair, and blinked a lot. It was as if – I don't know if I thought this then – there was a thin layer between her and the rest of the world, that her protective coverings were only of the most gauzy fabric. This made her vulnerable, and for me vulnerability, even more than strength, makes love possible. People without weakness are easy to respect but difficult to feel much affection for.

After a few hours, she said she was tired and I called a cab to take her home. We exchanged phone numbers, and I promised to give her a call. She pecked my cheek before she disappeared out into the night.

Helping the hopeless and lonely, eh? It was Tom the barman, an old queen with a vicious tongue who had been watching us, frowning at her frumpy old clothes in the midst of all this opulence.

Yes, I said, quietly. *Yes, she was.*

A week later we went out on a date, and on the date after that we slept together. She wasn't terribly adept in bed, clumsy and unsure of herself, but I didn't mind. I felt I was with someone – I don't know . . . not better put together than me, exactly, but her raw materials seemed to be of higher quality. Although I was the one with the money, the power, the contacts, the success, I felt oddly crude next to Kelly. She would look at me sometimes, and I would realize that I had just said something pathetic, misogynistic, ugly or uncharitable, and I would feel ashamed. But she never accused me: she just knew how to hold up a mirror to me.

In this, she was gentle. She had no anger, or pride, just a vague diffuseness that observed the world uncritically, without judgement but with instinctive accuracy.

Interestingly, she was a terrible artist. This was in the days before most of the art world had turned towards installations and the creation of masterpieces with laundry and elephant shit. Kelly was simply a painter. Her tiny room in Wandsworth was full of canvases covered with what looked to me like the worst kind of sub-Jackson Pollock trash imaginable. The exhibitions she had had turned out not to have been her own but some 'New British Painting' season at a gallery near Marylebone. On neither occasion had any buyer shown any interest in her pictures but this had discouraged her not a whit. Kelly was unusual in that she possessed the spirit of the artist without the talent. She was determined to do what she did, irrespective of whether anyone thought it was good or not, irrespective of whether anyone bought a single painting. This wasn't pretension: it was a compulsion she was powerless to resist. I loved her for this purity of purpose, this singularity of vision.

She loved me back. I'm not quite sure why – as far as I can remember at the time my appeal was purely superficial, the suits, the car, the money. But I think she recognized that a piece of me – the tiny, truly creative piece that had been debased by money and worldly success – reached out to an identical piece of her. She was grateful that I was uncritical of her art and her artistic impulse, that it was enough for me that she had a true purpose. She saw also that, in a way, I was in awe of her, that the lack of a mediating force between her and the world was something towards which I aspired – I, who was all mediation, appearance and the placement of product.

We went out for three years, and found a kind of unosten-tatious, low-level bliss that I have never known before or since. True, the sex never got much better, and true, neither did her painting, and true, I never wrote the great novel I sometimes flattered myself was lurking beneath my brittle, flash exterior. But there was a synergy about us, a happy feeding by one upon the other. I found her extraordinary sense of calm a potent antidote to the edgy world of shifting surfaces I inhabited. Also, I had a kind of vital energy, I suppose, a determined wit and ambition that she found exotic, in a sometimes bemused, even horrified, way.

But, then, perhaps this is wrong. I sometimes think relationships are not about each other's merits so much as each other's faults, and one's ability to tolerate and dovetail with them. Kelly was always going to be a failure, I could see that, and was awkward, and socially inept, and not all that beautiful, and untidy and chaotic, but somehow I didn't care. I was a fake, a chancer, an advertisement for myself – but she didn't care either. We meshed, we melded. We were happy.

Three years, and we didn't argue, didn't fight, didn't hate one another. I paid most of the bills, but she couldn't have cared less if I hadn't – another reason I loved her. Money meant nothing to her, so long as she could get on with her terrible paintings.

I could see, actually, as the 1980s wore on, that the paint-ings took on a different quality of terribleness. Originally they had been jagged, separated and distinct lines and splat-ters, quite geometrical. If they spoke to me at all, it was in Cantonese or some other incomprehensible language in which one could only infer meaning through intonation and volume. The crude level of vocabulary that I was able to translate spoke of disintegration, chaos, loneliness. But as our relationship wore on, the pictures became more rounded, more connected-up. They started to change their language. What they were saying now was that she was finished with disconnection.

I read the change as meaning she felt happy, fulfilled, and settled in her life. What escaped me was that the paintings were saying she wanted to move in with me and start a family.

We were both twenty-nine, and my last experience of living with someone had been what I now characterized as self-inflicted imprisonment. I loved Kelly – loved her in a way I had never experienced with Helen, but I was also arrogant and felt more or less invulnerable. My experience of women still remained lodged in a child's world, a 1950s world, in which I believed that all women were grateful to men for having them. No one ever deserted me. Having got them into bed, which was the hard part, I either allowed them to love me or I didn't. I was typical of many men who thought women were out to trap them: women saw things in terms of a fantasy of absolute union, men in terms of a fantasy of absolute freedom.

Kelly applied to her life the singularity of purpose that she devoted to her art. Despite her apparent vagueness, she said what she meant and she meant what she said. So when she turned to me one spring day and said, *I think it's time for us to take the next step*, I should have listened. I should have watched. I should have looked at her paintings more carefully. She said she wanted us to live together and that, in a year or two, she wanted to have children. I nodded and listened, and said, as I'm sure a million men before me have said, *We're happy enough as it is. Why spoil it?*

213

Why indeed? I truly didn't understand in those days that life is fluid, in need of perpetual change and adaptation. I thought you could sort of freeze it at a point at which you are happy. Women don't have this illusion. Their bodies don't allow it.

Kelly being Kelly didn't argue the point, or try to convince me. She had told me what she wanted. I had refused her. Had I been watching, I might have seen her blue eyes searching me for clues – to the depth of my objection, to the obtuseness of my confusion. Perhaps the quizzicality of one of her dark eyebrows intensified for a moment or two. Conclusions were being drawn, not just about my fantasies of freedom but about the timbre of love that would let such a profound request be so casually deflected. She had spoken to me in her paintings; she had even said it directly. My only response had been the equivalent of a shrug. Was that the response of someone who valued her?

Her mind would have raced, checking and reviewing all the allowances she had been making for me. All the benefits of all the doubts were being reassessed and the process of withdrawal was set in train. An entire star nebula of change compressed into those few moments I spent saying, *We're happy enough as it is. Why spoil it?*

Already, I imagine, her mind would have started to move on, to make plans to get what she had determined she needed.

The ironic thing was that I was trying to do then what I am trying to do now. I was trying to learn from the past, and I had learned that living with a woman was a cage, the murderer of passion, the death of freedom, the beginning of the end. The trouble is that by the time you come to apply

214

what you have learned, life has moved on, and warped out of recognition, left you way, way behind.

After that we carried on in the same way for six months. As far as I could tell, nothing had changed. We still lay in bed doing the crosswords, still went for long walks on Hampstead Heath, still talked until all hours of the morning. Kelly never mentioned living together or children again, so I stopped thinking about it, believing I had won an easy victory.

Then, one day, Kelly stopped talking.

It was as simple as that. She went quiet. The groove we'd always had, that we'd shared so happily, had been lost – out of the blue as far as I was concerned. We'd go out for dinner and she'd hardly say anything, just pick at her food and stare out of the window. We'd do the crossword and she wouldn't solve any clues. She was folding in on herself. Her paintings had changed again: forms had begun to appear in them, almost like organisms, twisted and turned in on themselves, anguished, almost frightening in their intensity. I thought her work was getting better: it was less derivative, more passionate. I was just inspecting her latest, a kind of orgy of yellows and greens on an enormous canvas that almost covered an entire wall of the flat when she said – it was a few weeks after the silences had begun – *Spike. I don't know how to say this, but I'm just going to say it. I'm leaving you.* Her voice was gentle and not at all apologetic. I laughed at first. I didn't – I couldn't – take it remotely seriously.

What?

I turned away from the painting. She was standing there, hand on her hip, smoking a cigarette. As ever she was composed, sad but apparently at peace. She took a step towards me and embraced me, once, then took a step back. Then she regarded me neutrally. Her slightly crossed blue eyes were dry. She looked beautiful. And suddenly, unbearably unattainable.

I saw, then and there, that I had lost her, that she had moved beyond me and into another place in her heart, that I had dropped the catch, that I had queered my pitch, that I had made the worst mistake of my life. But all I said was *What do you mean?*

I'm leaving you, Danny. I've met someone else. We're going to live together.

She gave a small, violently kind smile. I don't suppose I've ever felt so incredulous as I did at that moment, because I had been happy, and if I had been happy it had to follow that Kelly was too. In those days I saw everything through the prism of my own ego – the attempt to throw myself into the mind of another, which comes so naturally to women (or if you prefer, so culturally), just wasn't in me. I was literal-minded – if Kelly had been unhappy she would have *told* me so that I could have done something about it. I was too blind to see all the clues that had been laid out in front of me – the change in the paintings, the emotional retreat accompanied by an incongruous increase in her taking care of herself (she had started to wear makeup and to work out in a gym). Even the silence I interpreted as some kind of passing artistic *ennui*. I had seen only what I had wanted to see – and now I had to pay the price.

Anyway, if a relationship was going to end, *I* was the one who was going to do the leaving. Nobody left *me*. I suppose, statistically, relationship break-ups must split about fifty–fifty, but I don't think the distribution is even. There are clusters. There are people who predominantly get left, and people who predominantly leave. I was a leaver. My arrogance was such – and it was partly informed by the underlying male arrogance that has only recently, historically speaking, been replaced by insecurity and doubt – that I thought it axiomatic that no woman would leave me. From the standpoint of where I am now, I find this illusion extraordinary. But in my twenties I was a man in a male-dominated world. I was about to find those things out that someone, sooner or later, was bound to teach me.

You've met someone else.

I've known him for some time actually. Hugo.

Hugo.

Hugo Bunce. As rich as Croesus and a legendary goon. If she was leaving me, she should go to a penniless artist, a doomed genius or someone crippled whom she had taken pity on. Preferably all three. But Hugo . . . If she wanted Hugo more than me, after all our time together, our history, our shared memories, our private jokes and passionate letters, our bedtime tricks and secret codes, and Hugo was a pathetic public-school pinhead, then what did that make *me*?

That's how I saw it in the narcissistic virtual world in which I lived. I didn't know then that love, in a strange way, isn't really *personal*. People fall in love with other people for the strangest reasons, often unrelated to virtue, personality, intelligence or looks. Something in us seeks out what we need. After years of being a penniless artist, something in Kelly had decided she needed a home, children, security, and someone who would be grateful for her in a way that I wasn't.

Or maybe Kelly was just another of those otherwise

217

brilliant women with a blind spot for bastards. Who knows?

How did I take it? Not too badly, I think. If you view not getting out of bed for a week as not too badly – not even to wash or shave. Not even, on one occasion, to piss.

This was the first time my heart was truly broken. It had been sad when I'd finished with Helen, and there had been one or two others whom I'd missed when they'd gone. But this was the real thing. The meaning of the phrase 'broken heart' came home to me then in a way that it never had before. The little packet of energy in the chest, which for the last few years had been sweet, cohered, knitted together, pulsing nicely, turned to jagged glass. Everything hurt. Every day hurt, every minute.

I lay in bed thinking of Kelly with Hugo, thinking of me slowly being written out of Kelly's history – or, at least, relocated in her emotional maps to the Antarctic, when only a short time previously I had been the equator, Greenwich Mean Time, the centre of it all. This redrawing of maps, this negating of our past together, was what hurt most. I thought of her lying in bed with Hugo, talking about me *in the past tense*. Danny was . . . Danny used to . . . Danny never . . .

I was being dismantled. I knew this. I was being taken apart within the soul and mind of someone I had come to believe was part of me. So strongly had I believed in that person that, as Kelly slowly let me seep away, I felt myself becoming invisible, lightweight, flyaway. And, at the same time, dried out, desiccated, frozen. There was a perpetual tension within me that sought to hold inside me everything I was losing. I needed to 'let go', as they say nowadays. I needed 'closure', as my therapist now puts it. But all I could think of was Kelly.

What lesson can I learn from this? The most fundamental for any man. Be watchful. Never, never, never take a woman for granted. The price of love is perpetual vigilance.

After a week I got out of bed and was back at work, though barely functional, a week later. I had a lot of healing to do before I was ready even to look at another woman. Which is why it was a crying shame that I had to get involved with Natasha Bliss.

Beth and I are sitting in the front room of the house in Hammersmith, each holding a piece of paper and a pen. I am twenty feet away from her – as far as possible. We each stare at the list in front of us. The time has come for the division of our worldly goods. This is one of the final acts in the long-running farce of divorce. I half expect a vicar to walk in stage-door left with his trousers round his knees.

The room even feels like a stage, the situation like the dying moments of a final act. There is a feeling of suspended reality, of a script being played out that was written by someone else. I feel my choices are prescribed by the script-writer, only I'm not sure who that is or what has been written. As so often before, I don't know my lines.

Yet there is a well-tested procedure for this, which is what we are about to follow. A list has been compiled by a professional agency that specializes in these matters of every-thing in the house. Now we choose item by item what we get to keep. Toss a coin to see who goes first. Like a party game, really. Except that what is being divided up is our history, our life together, our marriage.

Terence has tried to prepare me. He has given me a number of simple rules to follow: Don't shout. Don't cry. Stay focused. Get through it.

I gulp soundlessly, make pointless little marks in the margin of the meticulous inventory.

1 Bang & Olufsen stereo console
1 pair Bang & Olufsen speakers
2 'ethnic' style cushions
1 wood-framed mirror
1 large child's painting, framed, marked 'To mumy and
    daddy lov Poppy'
1 colander

I feel sick. I risk a glance at Beth. She is wearing reading glasses, with Dolce & Gabbana frames. The spectacles add to her brisk, businesslike persona. Her distance, her formal body language, her pursed and purposeful lips – it all depresses me. Yet it is necessary. She takes a swig of the coffee she has made.

5 coffee mugs, Habitat
6 wine glasses, make unknown
1 fake Persian rug
1 carriage clock with inscription, 'To Danny and Beth on
    their wedding day, from the bride's proud parents,
    Dorothy and Mike'
1 pair of worn child's ballet slippers
3 milk teeth in plastic envelope
Nest of coffee tables

Even at the eleventh hour, I'm not quite sure how to approach this exercise. There is an element of tactics in it, and the potential for malice. It's not as straightforward as choosing what you want in the order that you want it. I can achieve the best result if I guess in advance what Beth *doesn't* want. This will enable me to leave these items further down the list to make way for the things I do want that she'll want too. But, then, Beth knows this so she'll be making her guesses about what she thinks I don't want, and moving those items down *her* list.

It's further complicated because we're not just dealing in financial values: there's sentimental value and spite value. Spite value is Beth or me deliberately choosing something because we know it will piss the other off. I don't want to go there, but if Beth starts it I'll respond in kind. It's the only way to deter her. It's the iciest of Cold Wars.

Pair of ivory bookends in the shape of elephant heads
217 compact discs, various artists
Custom-made ivory lace and silk wedding dress from
    Harrods, London
Ofrex office stapler with staples

It doesn't matter who owned what before we were married. Once we signed the certificate they all became joint possessions. It only matters in a moral, not a legal, sense. And morals have run their course in this house, are run ragged, after a year of betrayed promises and bad faith.

Are you ready, then?

I look up. Beth's chewing the end of her pencil nonchalantly. It's part of the softening-up process. Like she doesn't care, like she's bigger than this. But we're not bigger than this, either of us. Life towers over us both, mocking.

I suppose.

Shall I toss?

Can I trust her to toss? Will she have a double-header, or some special flick of the wrist that will turn it the way she wants? Should we cut cards instead, or get an arbitrator in?

Sure.

She takes a ten-pence piece out of her purse, hurls it into the air, catches it on the back of her hand. I watch her movements, fluid, even graceful. She is dressed mainly in white today, as if this is the beginning of some new virginity, or a counter-wedding. As it happens, I am in black.

Heads or tails?

Heads.

It's tails.

Can I see?

Beth looks at me sardonically. First blood to her.

If it matters to you so much, you go first.

I just want to see the coin.

OK.

She shows me the back of her hand. Tails.

OK. Go ahead, then.

We haven't even started and already she's seized the moral high ground. I'm outclassed here. But I'm not going down without a fight.

I'll have that picture.

She points to Poppy's – 'To mumy and daddy lov Poppy'. God, she's good: this immediately raises the moral tone another degree – she's not gone for the most expensive item, but for the one that means most to her. But, of course, it's not that simple, because it also means most to me. It's the first thing I'd marked on my list. She knew it. That's why she went for it. So what looks like a moral act is actually an act of ruthlessness and spite.

Come on, Beth. Don't do this.

Don't do what?

Choose something else. You've got Poppy, after all. I just want something to remind me of her when she's not with me.

222

The picture is the first proper one that either of us can remember Poppy painting. It's remarkably good – of the house, with me and Beth standing at the window with big smiles on our faces and Poppy in the garden playing. There are sweets growing from the trees, and the sun has a surprised face. Bluebirds fly over clouds. Poppy did it on her fourth birthday. She's even dated it.

There's no point in getting into this, Danny. There's no point in discussions any more. It'll be best if we do this as quickly and clinically as possible. Let's make our choices and get out of here.

Fine. I'll take that clock.

I point to the carriage clock with the inscription from her parents on it. Beth blanches. She knows I hate it, and that I'm not very keen on her parents either. She also knows that I know it means a huge amount to her.

That was unnecessary. That was cruel.

You give me the painting, and I'll give you the clock.

I'll have Poppy's milk teeth.

I want to choke. I was always the Tooth Fairy, the one who made sure that there was a pound under the pillow. I always saved the teeth. Beth wants all of Poppy. She wants the precious superfluities of her body. She wants my memories for herself. She won't stop. She'll take the stakes higher and higher. She'll press the nuclear button. I feel myself sag. I shouldn't have started this game.

OK, I say wearily. I take up my pencil theatrically and stab at the list randomly. *I'll have the . . . stapler.*

Beth smiles incredulously, and my attempt to show I'm above it all backfires.

I'll have the Bang & Olufsen console.

Right. I'll have the speakers.

Obviously the console is no good without the speakers. But Beth doesn't flinch.

Poppy's ballet slippers.

Your wedding dress.

And so forth. Half an hour later we're finished, and it's a gruesome mess, as usual. We each now own separate essential parts of larger items, we've got things we never wanted, we're both full of resentment and anger against each other. No winners, only losers. We should start again. But that would be to ignore the bleakest law of our lives. You can't start again. Not now, not ever.

Alice and I are in the park with Poppy. Alice is pushing Poppy on a swing. I am watching Alice from a vantage-point to the side, perched on a plastic turtle with a winning smile. She is not looking at me, so I can inspect her at my leisure. The strength and sensitivity of her face, the narrow slope of her shoulders, the beacon of her smile. I love this woman, and this time it's going to work. For ever and ever.

It's going to work, because I've learned my lessons. I've talked to Terence, I've consulted the flip-chart, I've got it all mapped out in my head. No more prat-falls, no more dumb-shows. I can't afford them.

To run through the list on the flip-chart: obviously it's too late not to fall in love too quickly. I've done that, and if it's a mistake, I don't regret it. As for the Sharon Smith Principle, the problem of sex = power, it's not as true as it was when I was thirteen. It's been replaced by the Beth Principle: children = power. And as Alice and I haven't got any, it doesn't apply.

Alice's impossible paradoxes aren't clear to me yet, but

I'm prepared. When they come, I fully intend to transcend them, tolerate them, suffer them and even defuse them. As for the shadows and *doppelgängers* – well, clearly Martin is the chief shadow that I have to deal with here. And I am dealing with it. She still talks about him, still talks *to* him sometimes – or, rather, talks to me in the apparent belief that I am liable to behave like he does. That I am about to bolt (so she needs to be wary), that I am vulnerable (therefore I need looking after), that I am confused and indecisive (therefore she needs to take the lead). Slowly, gently, patiently, I am setting her right. I am me, it is me she loves. It's over between her and Martin. I think she's getting there. I will go with her the full mile here, I will wrestle with all her shadows, I will shadow-box her *doppelgängers* until they beg for mercy.

I've worked out the secret language of women. I've read *Men Are from Mars and Women Are from Venus* by John Gray, I've read *You Just Don't Understand* by Deborah Tannen. I'm interpreting symbols, sidelining the literal. I've got the whole territory covered. I'm proactive – I understand that women get angry with men for the things they *don't* do. I know you have to do what they need *without being asked*. I understand that one cannot overestimate the importance of the last three words of that sentence. I see clues and signs everywhere.

Women flock to indifference. OK, I'm finding it very hard to be indifferent to Alice. I love her, but I'm doing my best not to show it too much. This feels phoney, but I'm determined not to gush because it makes women nervous. I need to take things slowly. I can't apply Martin's Law exactly, because I don't *really* feel indifferent like he does. All the same, I'm rationing the loving looks, and curtailing the overwhelming desire to hold her, kiss her, be with her twenty-four hours a day.

Am I trying to crush her because she's weak? No. Because she's not weak. And if she was, I would try to look after her, not crush her.

What about the Gilfeather Paradox? That women torture you so you can prove you love them. It's true she has been a bit difficult, but I put this down to the switch between me and Martin. Sometimes, in fact, she's so cruel to me I think she wants me to leave her. But I know she wants me to prove my love. I'm going to do just that.

As for being ruthless at the end of a relationship – well, it doesn't apply. Because this relationship isn't going to end.

The only thing outstanding is Problem X. I've given up trying to remember what it is. I don't care, anyway: I've got enough of the ground covered now. We're going to be fine, fine, fine.

God, life is good.

I've still got my eyes on Alice. She even pushes a swing with a certain grace. She and Poppy don't know each other very well yet, but I feel pleased with the way they're getting on. Alice likes kids, and kids like her.

Then I think, This isn't just about me and Alice any more.

I've already hurt Poppy so much by taking away from her her most fixed point of reality: her mother and father living together in the same house, protecting and supporting her as a unit, a solid immovable force for good. Now the force is splintered, and Poppy, who is sometimes full of anger and outrage, is really just full of sadness. We put that there, Beth and I.

So here's the thing. I don't want to see it happen again. It *mustn't* happen again. I don't want to tell Poppy that I love someone else, that that person is going to be around for ever and then perhaps she'll fall in love with them, even though they're not her mother, or at least get used to having them around, and see them disappear.

I'm sure of my love for Alice, I'm sure of her love for me. But God forbid that anything goes wrong.

Alice has stopped pushing Poppy on the swing now and Poppy is on a climbing-frame. Alice comes over to me.

How are you?

Oh, so-so.

You seem a bit down.

Oh, God. You know. That splitting of the worldly possessions, it was like, Christ, you know? What a superbitch, what a bitch squared. Anyway, I told you how it was, didn't I? Yeh, well, I don't want to go on about it.

Right, well . . .

Of course, it wasn't the end. I had another argument with Beth today, and we've got the court case next week. It's all doing my head in. She's so inflexible. I'm tired of it all. All this fighting, all this anger. She never gives it a rest. You know, I really feel she's out to hurt me. The cunt. Sorry. Sorry. But – you know. Anyway, now she's instructed her barrister to go for a full court hearing. What's she playing at? As if this is going to do Poppy any good. What Poppy needs is to see an end to this as soon as possible. Don't you think? But does she care about Poppy? No. She says she does but, when push comes to shove, all she cares about is how big her bank balance is going to look. I'm just a – just a cash cow, really, not a father. You know, there's no reason for all this. Sometimes I think she just wants a fight – she doesn't even care if she loses. And it's just racking up more and more costs for both of us and that money could be going on, say, Poppy's education. Sometimes I can't see the light at the end of the tunnel, it seems so long that ... Christ, I'm eaten up inside. Poppy's tough, though. Do you know what she said to me today? It made me laugh, I tell you.

Danny. Have you any idea how much you talk about Beth? About Beth and Poppy?

What?

You're obsessed with it. The divorce, everything.

I'm obsessed with my daughter. Of course I bloody am.

There's no need to keep swearing.

'Bloody' isn't swearing. You're not listening. Christ, thanks for being so **supportive**. I'm just ...

I'm getting sick of it, Danny.

What?

Alice sighs. You know. I do love you and everything but I'm ... I'm not in your situation. Poppy's a nice kid. But she's not my kid.

What does that mean?

I just mean ... it's difficult. And it's not just Poppy I'm taking on when I take on you, Danny. It's Beth. She's always on your mind – she's on your mind more than I am.

That's not true.

It is true. I don't think you realize how much you go on about her. I try to be supportive, but sometimes I think, I just think ...

What do you think?

That I sometimes wish I wasn't in this situation.

Pause.

Well, you are.

Alice sighs, looks over to where Poppy has now come off

the climbing-frame and is running towards us. *I guess so.*

Alice! Alice! Lift me up!

And Alice lifts her up and swings her in the air, and there is an expression of pure bliss on Poppy's face, and Alice is smiling too, but the smile is tinged with sadness, and something else I cannot name, which frightens me. I brush away the feeling. It's a difficult situation. But we'll get over it. Love finds a way.

A couple of hours later we've dropped Poppy back at her mother's. Beth and I aren't talking at the moment, after she said something about me to Poppy that I consider unforgivable – that if I loved Poppy more, Daddy would not make Mummy go through the courts. Except that it's *Beth* who's making us go through the courts and, anyway, whoever it is, you don't bring Poppy into it, you don't slag off the other parent to the kid. So now I'm not talking to Beth because to see her makes me feel sick. I'm dropping Poppy off at the end of the path, watching while she walks up it until the door opens a crack. Then I blow a kiss and walk off.

Of course it occurs to me that this must be painful for Poppy, but the alternative, that we might end up trading insults on the doorstep, seems even worse. I return to the car, where Alice is sitting. I'm shaking now, and feel like bursting into tears, but I hold myself tight inside: after what Alice said to me earlier, I don't want to unburden myself on her. Yet the pain and the tension make my body rigid. I find it hard to speak. Alice sits next to me in the car as we drive back to my bedsit. We don't talk.

Inside, I make a cup of tea while Alice fidgets with her makeup. I bring the tea to her at the table. I'm about to join her when she says, *What's that thing you're writing on your flip-chart?*

What?

You know. The Love Secrets of Don Juan. Is it some kind of weird brainstorming for an advertising campaign? And why are there only nine?

There's actually ten, now. There's one I haven't yet put up, the fruit of my last bout of introspection.

> **Problem**: *Women don't always let you know when they want out. Cf. Kelly Cornelius.* **Result**: *Heartbreak, agony, regret.* **Solution**: *Be watchful. Don't take your eye off the ball.*

Yes. A campaign.

What kind of campaign?

I don't really want to talk about it.

Oh.

I see immediately that I'm not going to be able to sustain this line. Especially as Alice is right: I do talk most of the time about Beth and Poppy. It's hardly fair to cut her off from something she's curious about.

It's not an advertising thing. It's . . . I suppose you'd call it self-help. Terence, my therapist, suggested I do it. It's me trying to work out how to understand women and myself. It's me trying to learn a few lessons.

Alice seems lost for words at the futility of the exercise.

Well. At least I'm trying to learn.

Good luck.

She sips her tea. I sip mine.

Alice. You never asked about my night out with Martin.

Didn't I?

Aren't you interested?

Of course I am.

It's just that you haven't asked.

It must have slipped my mind.

I told him about us, you know. About me and you.

Long pause.

I know you did.

I look up sharply. *You know?*

Yes. He told me.

I didn't know you two were still in touch.

Martin will always be my friend and I will always be his.

Is that so?

I'm not sure I like the way this is going. There is something in Alice's eyes, some weird mixture of apology and defiance, that makes me nervous.

Yes.

So . . . what did he say?

He said he wanted to marry me.

I burst out laughing at the improbability of it. Alice's face doesn't change but I carry on in much the same vein. *Oh, my God. That's rich. I can't **believe** it. Last week he didn't love you, didn't care a hoot. All the time he's been with you, he's never told you he loved you. Now **I'm** with you, he wants to marry you. That's not just pathetic, that's the **definition** of pathetic.*

Alice doesn't move. Then she says, *I feel very confused all of a sudden.*

I bark an incredulous laugh. *Confused? What about?*

Danny, Martin and I were together a long time. Two years. You knew when we started going out that I still loved him . . .

Yes, but . . .

231

Well, then. And I know that Martin has a lot of trouble with his feelings. That he's out of touch with them.

I'll say he's out of touch with them. He's out of touch with them, because when it comes to women, he doesn't have them. I know, I'm his best friend.

I'm not sure about that. When I saw him –

You saw him?

Yes. He came round yesterday night.

Yesterday night?

That's right. And he was just so . . . I don't know. So sad, so confused, so heartbroken.

The deadly combination – vulnerability and inaccessibility. Only now he *was* accessible. The man that no woman could get was on the canvas. And Alice was going to be the one who . . . no. She wouldn't *do* that.

I presume you explained to him that he's blown it.

It's not that simple, Danny.

Isn't it?

No.

My panic is making me angry. *Why isn't it? What's so fucking complicated?*

You don't just wipe out two years of being together just like that. You don't just throw your feelings into the bin the day you split up. I think he's changed. I think . . . I think he needs me.

*I think I'm going to be sick. **Needs** you? Martin doesn't need anyone. It's just too big a blow to his fucking ego that his mate of all people is going out with his ex-girlfriend. It's all about **possession**, not love.*

I don't think that's true. I just think he didn't realize he loved me.

I cover my face with my hands, and sit down opposite

her. I peer through the gaps in my fingers, hardly daring to look directly at her. When I speak, my voice is quiet and tinged with desperation. *Let me tell you something, Alice. You're a clever and perceptive woman. But if you believe that, you don't understand men. You don't understand what power means to them. Even I underestimated it – I mean, I never thought Martin would . . .*

My words run out. Alice has started crying now. Bad sign.

And, you know, Danny, I don't think you're ready for a proper relationship at the moment. You're still too tied up with your wife. You're still climbing from the wreckage. I don't like all that wreckage. I don't want to be caught up in it, all the sharp metal, all the broken glass. And then there's Poppy.

What about Poppy?

She's fifty per cent Beth. She even looks like Beth. She's living history. And you want me to love her. It's a terrific responsibility.

Everyone has baggage.

But it isn't always so tangible.

You don't like Poppy, do you?

As a matter of fact, I do. Very much. That really isn't the point.

I know it's the truth. Everything she says is reasonable. Why should an attractive, desirable woman like her take on all these problems? There are plenty of single men out there who are unencumbered. And successful. Wealthy, even. Life's difficult enough. God knows, I see her point.

All the same, it hurts more than I know how to say.

We fall into silence. We have run out of words. Or things that we're prepared to say. Or prepared to hear. But the silence becomes too much. In the end I speak the words heavily, not wanting to know the answer. Already knowing the answer.

Are you going back to him?

Alice's eyes fill with tears, and she presses her lips together to hold back the sobs. It's enough.

You're a fucking idiot, Alice.

I expect you're right.

Now I fall to my knees, prostrate myself in front of her. I feel my world dissolving.

I'll marry you. You're all I want, Alice. Please. I . . .

She shakes her head. I'm crying too now. The third great woman. The last one. And I've lost her. *Whatever* happens I've lost her. Even though I don't think it's going to work out between them, whether Martin loves her or not. After this moment – too much damage between us. Her blowing it all to pieces, and for *nothing*. And I've done nothing wrong. I've learned all my lessons. I've been *good*.

But that's the problem, isn't it? Martin has never bothered with being good. That's how he gets results.

Then, another thought strikes me. Amazingly, it has not occurred to me before. I feel a terrible hot ball of rage form inside me. I get up, stand accusingly over Alice who is still at the table, cradling her cup of tea. When I speak, my mouth is curled with contempt.

You set me up.

She looks up sharply.

*You knew Martin would come back to you if you slept with me. You **knew**. You knew I'd tell him. You had it all worked out.*

Alice's expression becomes blank.

And you didn't care. You were prepared to do it.

Prepared to hurt me, prepared to hurt Poppy, prepared to do anything to get what you wanted. Weren't you?

I love you, Danny.

*I **know** you love me. I'm not wrong about that. That's where your plan went wrong, isn't it? That's one of several reasons why it's not going to work out with Martin, the other being that, metaphorically speaking, Martin is much more interested in fucking me than he is you. But it was a dirty little plan none the less. God, women are ruthless.*

Alice is silent for maybe fifteen seconds. When she speaks again her voice is a whisper.

We're all ruthless when we're trying to get what we need, Danny. You know that. You'd have done the same.

You know something, Alice, I say, dead calmly. I wouldn't. I really wouldn't.

I'm sorry, Danny. I'm truly sorry.

Get the fuck out of my flat.

What?

Get. The Fuck. Out of. My flat.

Oh.

She is trembling as she picks up her gear, and I can see her pain, and the struggle she's going through, and I know then that she really does love me, that she's torn in two. But that doesn't make it forgivable. She's hurt me, she's hurt Poppy, and now I'm going to lose both my best friend and my lover.

Just like that, my life is garbage again.

When Alice is gone, I sit there for a while, thinking of nothing, just staring. Then I look at the flip-chart again. Mutely, like a robot, I walk over and pick up the marker-pen. Because the thing I've forgotten, the final Love Secret of Don Juan, Problem X, has come back to me, and I need to add it somewhere to the list. Right at the very top.

Problem: *Women plot and women scheme. In the sex war, they are the guerrillas – cunning, fleet of foot and deadly.* **Result**: *You can't trust them.* **Solution**:

I pause. Finally the answer comes flashing up in bright cold blue neon.

Don't love them.

Never love them.
Never love them again.

Two days later, I'm sitting in the office of the marketing department of a medium-sized manufacturer of chocolate products. It's not going well.

Three men and two women are sitting in front of me, the clients. The men look uncomfortable. One of the two women, the younger one, with tightly pulled-back hair and pale pink lipstick, seems angry. The older one, who has a seen-it-all-done-it-all look on her face, seems sceptical and amused. I am standing in front of a flip-chart, having just outlined my idea of what will sell their new chocolate-and-crushed-mixed-nut product, the krusha Bar™. Lower case k. Upper case B. Cute.

The flip-chart comprises a series of diagrams, figures and strap-lines. I am looking cool and unflappable in a three-piece bespoke suit – which, I discover later, has a large egg stain on the waistcoat that Poppy made while I was wrestling her shoes on to get her to school.

There is a somewhat protracted silence as I finish my pitch. The younger woman with the scraped-back hair speaks first. Her voice is contained, but with an edge of hostility.

236

So, you genuinely think this campaign is appropriate for a middle-market, teen-to-young-adult product like krusha?

I do. This campaign says young, it says sexy. It's ironic. It confronts the problem of time famine. And it addresses the empowerment of women.

It does?

Of course. It's all about how women are strong now. How it's they who call the shots.

She nods, makes a few notes. When she speaks again, her voice is sharper, more glacial: *I don't get it.*

You don't?

The ad specifically features a woman being put into an iron maiden – a medieval torture device – and the door closing on her. Is this really the image we want for a chocolate bar? It seems more in the realm of extreme misogyny than the empowerment of women.

We're in a post-feminist era now. I think sensitivities like that are very . . . well, last-century frankly. Also, it's other women, not men, who force her into the iron maiden.

Implying that women are both torturers and victims.

I think you're overstating the political content. It's just another chocolate bar.

We see it as being rather special, actually.

Well, of course, yes, it is special – and delicious. A terrific product.

And I'm not sure that post-feminism means that we have to abandon all attempts to avoid the degradation and abuse of women on camera.

It's obviously ironic. She takes her krusha Bar^{TM} into the iron maiden, and when the spikes begin to pierce her –

One of the men coughs.

The **what***?*

237

The . . . spikes. In the iron maiden.

The younger woman takes off her spectacles, cleans them and puts them on again.

Do we actually see this penetration? It is the older woman who speaks this time.

I turn to her and become aware of a note of slight desperation in my voice. *No. Of course not. It's implied in the woman's expression. She registers pain. But the pleasure wipes out the pain. There's an obvious S and M reference, of course, but that's good, that's dangerous advertising, cutting-edge.*

Is there some reason why she needs to be naked?

Well, she doesn't **have** *to be naked. But it's more controversial that way. You said you wanted controversial.*

Another long silence. The younger woman is now tapping her pencil impatiently on the table. *And you think that this is going to deliver to us a young* **female** *market?*

I look at her face. A shrewd businesswoman, a tough cookie, someone who knows what she's doing. Why is she giving me such a hard time? Of course it will deliver a large female market. That's what all the manufacturers want. Because women just want to fucking *shop* all the time. As Marx might have been reluctant to put it, shopping is the ideological superstructure that defines the economic substructure: the spending power of women, their unique thrall to the gewgaws of twenty-first-century capitalism. Shopping: it's what they do when they're not torturing. And pretending to be victims. The whole lying, cheating, impossible, ungraspable horde of them, the whole nightmare fucking brigade of . . .

I stop. Blink. I hope the double-take I am experiencing is not transparent to my audience. The ludicrousness – the sheer *offensiveness* of what I have been presenting to these people! I want the ground to open and swallow me. I'm confusing the deployment of irony with being a complete arsehole. My throat dries. I need this gig, and unless I buck my ideas up, I'll be lucky if I don't get escorted from the premises by security guards. *Well. I . . . I . . . that is to say . . .*

I look around the room as if for help. Only five blank faces.

Well. I hear what you're saying. But on the other hand . . .

*On the other hand **what**?* says the younger woman.

***Men** are going to fucking love it.*

Not the right thing to say, it turns out. The young woman groans. The older woman, however, appears to have some sympathy for me. She smiles.

Have you brought along any alternative ideas for the campaign, Mr Savage?

I blink again. As it happens, I have. Some part of me *knew* that the iron-maiden concept was going to go down like a seven-ton boulder off the North Face of the Eiger. *Of course. OK, how about this?*

I turn the pages of the flip-chart a few times. *So, the protagonist in **this** concept is a young woman, fashionable but not too much so. The coolest girl in a not very cool school, perhaps. She's clever, knowing, grown-up. Now, she has a boyfriend but he's really not a grown-up at all. He's more like a kid. And he wants his krusha Bar™, and he wants it NOW. When she says, 'No,' he gradually morphs into a screaming **baby**. So she puts him over her knee . . .*

The exposition comes out simple, powerful, clichéd. Clever strong woman, helpless man-baby. I look at the five faces and they've changed. They're warm, interested, engaged. It's in the bag.

So the 'If You Want Him To Hush-a Give Him A krush-a' entered into the lexicon of confectionery history. Sales went up by ten per cent. Of course. Of course they did.

10

Natasha Bliss. Natasha, Natasha, Natasha. Bliss, Bliss, Bliss. If you wanted someone diametrically different from Kelly Cornelius, Natasha was your woman. I bumped into her at the agency two weeks after Kelly abandoned me for Hugo Bunce. She was an accounts director, ambitious, sexy, modern.

This was the late eighties and Natasha was of a new breed, an *über*-woman, at least in my hitherto circumscribed sexual universe. She was absolutely terrific; she was the second great woman of my life. Sexually upfront, funny, tough, fully made up and totally into fashion, but also totally into power and living it large. She didn't appear to need a man.

Why was she attracted to me? Who can say? As I've already mentioned, love isn't *personal*. It's about the strangest of needs and hidden desires. Perhaps like an old-style Alpha male needed a passive partner, an Alpha woman like Natasha needed a passive man. The débâcle with Kelly had left me heartbroken, lost. I tried to hide it, but my vulnerability was sometimes difficult to conceal.

Natasha first noticed me when I burst into tears during a

meeting she was attending. I tried to pass it off as a cough-
ing fit, covered my face with a handkerchief, made my
excuses and headed for the water-cooler. I was just damp-
ening my handkerchief with some Mountain Cool spring
water to wash off the tearstains, when I saw Natasha
approach, a concerned expression on her face. Such a
display of empathy was unusual for her: normally, she
seemed to think that to show compassion demonstrated a
softness that women in the career jungle couldn't afford. I
felt humiliated. Men still feel ashamed to cry. At that point
in history it felt like an agonizing loss of face.

Are you all right, Danny?

A touch of hay fever is all. I'll be fine.

I didn't sound fine. My voice was breaking, croaky,
hoarse. I swabbed my face with the handkerchief before
looking up at her. Christ, she was sexy – groomed, scarlet
lipstick, power-dressed, but not in that researched and
marketed way of the New York robo-chick: there was soul
in it somewhere. She was tall, willowy, with (of course) pale
yellowy hair that kinked about half-way down into tiny
spirals. I couldn't imagine that she would *ever* be interested
in someone like me, and certainly not this particular me in
this particular state.

But I was wrong. Unfortunately for us both.

In October? You're not fine, are you?

I looked up at her. She put her hand on my arm.

I'm having a bit of a tough time at the moment.

Women problems?

I nodded. Her hand was still on my arm. *How did you
know?*

*Men don't deal with relationship break-ups very well, do
they?*

242

How do you know I've had a 'relationship break-up'? I was getting hold of myself now, growing curious.

You hear things. Kelly — that was her name, wasn't it? She's shacked up with . . .

Hugo Bunce. That's right. I'll get over it.

She looked at me carefully, as if assessing my sincerity. A woman who looks like Natasha Bliss probably has to listen to a lot of nonsense. It was written all over her face, the way she carried herself — not unfriendly, but a distance, a soft sheath of haughtiness. Look — don't touch. The sort of woman I'd always thought was out of my league. It was perhaps because of this that she took to me — that I was not flirting with her, had never flirted with her: I'd considered it a waste of time, like betting on a 100–1 outsider in the Grand National.

Then, 100–1 outsiders sometimes come in.

She offered to cover for me in the meeting, and I accepted. When she took her hand away she seemed to do it slowly, almost as if it was a caress.

Nothing happened for another month. We bumped into each other at meetings, we had brief, meaningless chats at the water-cooler. I was powerfully attracted to her, but I thought I had no chance. Also, I was still in love with Kelly and hoping to win her back.

Kelly was wavering a bit over Hugo. I had had one or two letters from her expressing doubts about what she was doing, hoping that I might not 'write us off just yet'.

She was just trying to keep her options open, trying to do to me what I had tried to do with Helen. Doubtless she missed me, but primarily I was an insurance policy in case she'd made a wrong call with Hugo. I still hadn't grasped that to hold on to an old relationship is paying unnecessary

243

interest on an overdraft of pain. I plotted to win her back. My sexual fantasies about Natasha came a poor second to my romantic fantasies about the only kind of true love – the unrequited kind.

So, it was a huge surprise to me that at the office Christmas party, at Beaufoy's wine bar, Waterloo, Natasha, in a backless and virtually frontless skin-tight silver dress, walked up to me while I was standing alone, pushed me against a wall and began to kiss me. I allowed the sheer improbability of it all to register, then kissed her back.

It was heaven. Not only was Natasha kissing me, she was kissing me in front of every other man in the office, and they had all dreamed of just such a moment as this. My imaginative horizons expanded as did my unimaginative cock. Natasha Bliss was kissing *me*.

The rest of that evening came and went in a perfect blur of libidinous happiness. I vaguely remember asking her if she was doing this because (a) she was pissed and (b) she was sorry for me. She whispered in my ear that it was both of these things to some extent but mainly because she wanted to go to bed with me. I nodded sagely as if she had asked for a cup of tea, then carried on kissing her. We ended up at my place.

Even knowing Natasha's reputation, even guessing from her body language and demeanour that she was unlikely to be uncertain of herself in bed, I was taken aback. I was fully aware that women were capable of intense sexual desire. I had known that ever since Helen. But, even so, they remained pink-tinted, soft-focused in my imagination. Most of the women I had been out with still wanted to be seduced, toyed with and teased into arousal, wanted some remnant of the ancient courtly love play to be re-enacted.

There was a sense that they were giving, the man was taking. However enthusiastic a woman might have been, she had always tended towards the responsive.

Natasha knew what she wanted and she took it. She didn't make love to me, she didn't consent to have sex with me. She fucked me. In that sense, she was a male fantasy. She liked big mirrors and hard-core porn. She was Samantha from *Sex and the City* years before anyone had thought of *Sex and the City*. She was fantastic, a revelation.

And she scared me.

All the time sex was taking place – and it seemed to go on for a *long* time – part of me was standing back, split from my sweating, arching body, watching all this go on, and some unreconstructed primitive caveman part of me was thinking . . .

This *can't* be right.

After generations of the myth of the passive woman, an encounter with the next evolutionary step was seismic. I did everything I was meant to do, and Natasha seemed pretty satisfied. But I hadn't been that involved. Some part of me was still in shock.

A still larger part was wishing she was Kelly.

Once again, had I known what I know now, I would have told Natasha I wasn't ready for this, I wasn't ready for anything like her power and passion, I wasn't ready for *life*. But I was broken-hearted, and I was looking for a salve.

When I woke up the next morning, I half expected to find Natasha gone, that I would turn up in the office in the new year, and that she would pretend nothing had happened. But she was still there. Not only was she still there, but she was looking at me with eyes that were quite different from the eyes she used in the office. A haze around the cornea; soft, I suppose. Smiling, even.

In this way at least, Natasha wasn't as evolved – if evolved is the right word and I'm not sure it is – as Samantha from *Sex and the City*. She hadn't learned to strip the emotion out of sex.

Over that Christmas period we saw each other five or six times. It emerged that Natasha's reputation at the office as a man-eater, a bit of a slag, to use the schoolboy vernacular – and you're never that far from the playground when you're in an office – was wildly inaccurate. That was just men's fantasy. It was no different from what the boys used to imagine about Sharon Smith when I was thirteen.

It turned out that, at the age of thirty, Natasha had had only two proper relationships, and a couple of casual ones. The last serious relationship had ended six months earlier. It had been her identification with my distress that had attracted her to me. Over the last few days, though, we'd discovered we had a lot more in common.

We both came from similar backgrounds – her father was an electrician – and we both resented the Hugos of both sexes who populated the advertising world. We covertly held in contempt what we did for a living and harboured secret, vaguely shameful ambitions of writing the great novel. Despite her focus in the office, she had a sharp sense of the ridiculous, and deftly satirized everything that she also took very seriously. She allowed people to laugh at her, at their projects and goals – and this, paradoxically, secured her their loyalty and increased their productivity.

Amazingly, by the time we got back to the office in the new year, I sensed that Natasha was falling in love with me. It was absurd, it was insane, but there it was.

Thus my fear redoubled. Love is about timing, readiness, blind luck. I was still in love with Kelly. Natasha had passions, desires and emotions that were powerful, primal, yet evolved to a level that no woman I had known before had reached. I was enfeebled, drained. Certainly, I carried off a decent enough act with her over Christmas – I could joke the jokes, laugh the laughs, deconstruct the constructions – but I kept thinking of Kelly.

It was then that I confronted for the first time what I would later christen Martin's Law. The more indifferent you are towards a woman – particularly a sexy, attractive, smart woman whom any of a thousand men would dream of taking out – the more they want you. So long as the indifference is genuine.

Unlike Martin, I didn't treasure my indifference. Natasha was fantastic, and I wanted to fall in love with her, and at any other time in my life I would have fallen in love with her – maybe I *did* fall in love with her a little, but not the complete giving up of myself that you need to deliver for a woman like her. She would expect everything, and would give everything in return. I had so little to give.

Nevertheless, the relationship wore on towards the spring. I think it was about mid-March when Natasha told me she loved me. I told her I loved her too. And I sort of did or, at least, I loved the *idea* of her, her vibrancy, intelligence, beauty, strength. In truth, I had not got over Kelly. I wanted Kelly, and for all Natasha's remarkable physical, sexual and psychological attractions, she lacked the most important one: she wasn't Kelly. I even used Natasha to try to get Kelly back. But although Kelly was jealous, and although she was angry (angry – the injustice of it!) she stuck with Hugo. She wasn't about to let that one out of her grip. Certainly, she was disappointed that her insurance policy looked like it was expiring. But she'd just about reached the point now that she could live without it.

Meanwhile, I don't think Natasha had a clue about my confusion. I was on auto-pilot. Anyway, what was I going to say – *Forgive me, Natasha, but I'm still in love with Kelly*? There are times when it is right to speak the truth, and there are times to be silent – hoping in this case that it won't be the truth for much longer. But it stayed the truth. On some level Natasha sensed my indifference, which made her love grow, and sealed my indifference and fear. It was a mutually cancelling set of circumstances.

It wasn't until we went on holiday together that the truth could no longer be avoided. We went to California. I was hoping that the combination of sunshine, sea and being away from England would do the trick. Because Natasha, I knew, was probably the best woman I was ever going to meet, and if I could just stop being so . . . *messed up*, I would be the luckiest man in the world.

It didn't turn out that way. Somehow the intimacy and sheer weight of free time that holidays invariably involve threw the differences between us into sharp relief. Under the holiday pressure to have a 'good time', the space between us gaped. I retreated into myself, confused by my own emotions – or lack of them. Natasha became alternately tearful and aggressive. An incantation sprang up: *What's wrong*? *What's the matter with you*?

I couldn't tell her, because I still felt, in my dumb, male way, that sheer force of will could make me fall in love with her. But Kelly was just too close. In the end, half-way through the holiday, her beautiful face turned to me, she said, in a cold, dry voice, *You're going to leave me when we get home, aren't you?*

Feeling like the biggest fraud, idiot and loser ever born, I turned to her and gave a single, desolate nod.

We flew home separately. She took the next flight that afternoon, I came back a day later. When I returned to the office, Natasha wasn't there. It turned out she had been head-hunted some time ago, had turned the job down, but on her return had rung up the agency and the job was still there. I knew that she had gone because of me, and I thought what a mess I had made of this woman's life, and of my own, and I sat down and cried for Natasha, and I cried for Kelly, but most of all I cried for me, self-pitying, egotistical, cruel, exploitative prick that I was.

I didn't go out with another woman after that until two years later, and that woman was Beth – my ex-wife-to-be.

At least I've still got Carol Moon. The Great Carol, unflagging with her intelligence, loyalty, support and kindness. Thank God there are women like her in the world.

It's three months since Alice went back to Martin. I hear of them occasionally, but nothing as bad as I'd like. It sounds like it might be working out, after all. Isn't that great? I want to wish them happiness, but I hope they strangle each other, or die in a car crash. Carbon-monoxide poisoning also would be good.

I miss both of them like crazy.

Is life all loss? I say to Carol.

We're at the paddling-pool with Poppy, who's in her Hello Kitty swimming costume, looking unbearably cute. I smile. She makes it all worthwhile. Lately, she's calmed down a lot, now that Beth and I don't have anything left to fight about. She's almost like she was before we separated – sweet-natured, well-behaved, thoughtful and kind. People heal.

Carol's Marmite-coloured hair is natural again, and a few streaks of grey have started to show at the crown. It looks great. Some people have to grow into their natural age, and Carol was middle-aged when she was thirteen. She turns to me and purses her pale lips. *Stop being such a maudlin, self-pitying toad*, she replies, quite without malice.

Honesty is annoying, not to mention impolite. I've fired Terence now, so I don't have so much of it to put up with. He told me I still had a lot of 'issues with anger'. I politely disagreed, then I told him to fuck off and take his fucking introspection with him. Then I told him that, based on the lack of success of my treatment, I wouldn't be settling his final account. Upon which it turned out that Terence had some issues with anger too.

I can't fire Carol, though, and she's more annoyingly honest than Terence ever was.

Fair point. Well aimed. Taken.

I don't think Daddy looks like a toad.

Neither of us had noticed Poppy come up behind us from the paddling-pool, dripping and wriggling. I hand her a towel, which she wraps around her shoulders. She hops on to Carol's lap.

He does look a bit like a frog, though, says Carol.

Poppy giggles and cuddles up to her. *Why don't you and Auntie Carol get married?*

Would you like that, poppet?

*I love Auntie Carol. She's the **best** fun. Why don't you live with her like you used to with Mummy?*

Because we're just friends, darling. Wipe your nose.

Do you have sex with her?

Poppy!

Carol laughs her donkey laugh, half through her nose. Her shoulders shake as she tries to keep it in, knowing that Poppy might think she's making fun of her. But Poppy seems unoffended.

No, Poppy. I don't have sex with her.

Why? Don't you think she's pretty?

Of course I think she's pretty.

Don't you think she's nice?

Yes.

Is she married?

No. Not any more.

Then why won't you have sex with her?

Because it would ruin everything.

Why?

Because – oh, for God's sake, Poppy. You shouldn't even know what sex is at your age.

Carol has stopped laughing now, gives Poppy a friendly pat on the bum, then hands her a pound coin. *Why don't you go and get yourself an ice lolly?*

OK, she says cheerfully.

I look at Carol and we hold each other's gaze for a moment, then turn away.

Carol comes with me when I drop off Poppy. Beth's not in, just Oliver, of whom I've grown quite fond now that the jealousy has subsided, now we both have it clear that Poppy's only ever going to have one father. He invites us both in for a cup of tea, but we're going to a movie and I've booked a table for dinner afterwards.

Poppy throws her arms around Carol's neck and gives her an enormous kiss. *I love you, Auntie Carol.*

I love you too, Poppy.

Then she runs into the house and out of sight. The door closes. Carol and I make our way back to my car.

Do you really love Poppy, Carol?

Of course, she says, blithely. *I love both of you.*

And do you really think I look like a frog?

Yes. But I've seen worse-looking frogs.

Still, I'm a frog.

It's better than a toad.

We drive back towards Acton, so that I can change my clothes. We're going to a smart new Russian restaurant round the corner from my flat that specializes in different types of vodka, and before that, some arthouse Japanese film, *Audition*. I'm anticipating a hangover tomorrow, but looking forward to the night ahead. I haven't seen much of Carol over the last month or two: she's been working hard and, as usual, her personal life has been a disaster area. The married man she's been seeing left his wife for about a week, then went back to her. Carol's single again, but seems reconciled to it. Being alone seems to be doing her good: she's looking relaxed, tanned and slim – attractive.

When we get back to my place Carol helps herself to a cup of coffee, puts her feet up on the sofa and switches on the television. She's so at home here. There's no need to talk to fill up empty spaces as I would if she was a male friend. She kicks off her shoes. Her dress has ridden up her thighs.

I pick up a couple of letters from this morning and absent-mindedly tear them open while I go into the bathroom and fumble in the cupboard for some aftershave. I find the bottle, but leave it where it stands.

I remove the letter from the envelope. It is printed on what looks like a piece of cheap A4 paper. It is the flimsiness of the envelope that catches me off-guard. I would have thought something like this would come in vellum, with copperplate, handwritten script.

Certificate of making Decree Nisi Absolute (Divorce)
In the High Court of Justice Principal Registry Family Division
Between
Daniel Patrick Savage
and
Bethany Louise Collins

I drop the paper, a white angel wing falling to earth.

My marriage is over.

I feel the wrench inside, a jump of joy, followed by the kidney-punch of sadness. All gone. The ten years of waking up together, the years and Poppy – God, the joy of Poppy – our home together, our life together, our dreams and memories, our hopes, our fights. Our kisses. Legally null and void.

Come on, Spike. We're going to be late.

What?

It's nearly six thirty. The film starts in fifteen minutes.

OK. Coming.

I stand and stare at my face in the mirror for a few seconds. Old. Old. Then I turn, generate a convincing smile, and walk back to where Carol is waiting for me.

The movie makes me feel sick. It starts with what seems to be an innocent search for love by a Japanese man whose wife has died in a tragic accident, and ends up with him finding a new girlfriend who turns out to be a complete psycho-bitch. At the end, she shoots him full of a paralysing drug, so he remains fully conscious but incapable of movement, then gets a quiver full of acupuncture needles and inserts them in the most painful points she can find. In the eyes, the chest, the groin. As she inflicts excruciating pain on her hapless victim she laughs. It's unbelievably repulsive – yet it seems depressingly accurate as a metaphor for marriage.

When the film finishes, I'm borderline traumatized – not just by the film but by the decree absolute, which is stuffed into my pocket. I look at Carol, who seems fine.

You've gone grey, Spike.

Sick bitch. It turned my stomach.

I thought it was quite funny. And sexy.

You know why? You know what that woman represented? The universal female unconscious.

This therapy business is going to your head.

That's what it's meant to do.

'The universal female unconscious'. What nonsense. It was an S and M movie. Pleasure and pain. She was wearing a rubber dress, for God's sake.

He didn't seem to be getting much pleasure out of it.

Well, it turned me on.

*Then **you're** a sick bitch.*

No use trying to keep secrets from you, is it, Spiky? she says, laughing, her crimson mouth parting wide.

Why is Carol looking sexy tonight, when I don't find her sexy? That's why we've stayed friends for so long. I feel the paper in my pocket. Why is my heart breaking over a letter I've longed to receive?

I should tell Carol about the decree absolute, but she thinks I'm a self-pitying creep as it is. I'm just going to have to fake it through the evening. This is going to be impossible without support from my old ally, the bottle.

The restaurant has a menu of thirty-five different-flavoured vodkas. I don't think I'll be able to get through them all but, then, maybe I'll surprise myself. We drink vodka flavoured with beetroot, cherry, cabbage, horseradish – and after that I forget.

Carol keeps up with me. She's always been able to hold her drink. Her face is blurring, as if someone has spread Vaseline on it. Why have I never noticed before how sexy she is?

Goodbye, Beth. Goodbye, my dear wife.

Another vodka.

I wonder what happened to that Sharon Smith? The first time we met?

My voice, I am capable of registering, is remarkably unslurred. I've always been good at concealing intoxication – I've sat through dozens of high-level marketing meetings completely trashed. No one seemed to notice.

It wasn't the first time we met. I was the Belly-flopper, remember? At the swimming club.

The first time we spoke, then.

I heard that she emigrated to South Africa. Something to do with ecology.

She must have left a few broken hearts.

Were you in love with her, like all the other boys?

It was purely physical.

I was jealous.

You were jealous? You're having a laugh.

You were dead cute.

Come on. I'm a frog, remember?

255

Frogs can turn into princes.

I take a sip of the what tastes like cough-drop vodka. Is Carol *flirting* with me? Or trying to support me?

You'll find someone else, Spike. You just have to get clear of the wreckage of your marriage.

It follows me about. It's **possessed** wreckage.

So what happened to you and Beth in the end? What did you learn from it? What did you write in the . . . What's it called?

The Love Secrets of Don Juan.

What did you write in The Love Secrets of Don Juan about it? What was the lesson?

Skol!

Skol!

We toss back another glass.

I learned that when it comes to love, people get what they need. Will do anything to get what they need.

Is that peculiar to women?

No. I went after Alice, even though she was my best friend's ex-girl. I knew what I was doing. I sold out Martin. Because it was what I needed. Then Martin did whatever he had to to get her back – because it was what he needed. Alice went back to him – because that's what she'd planned in the first place. Three examples of an immutable law. Morals count for nothing when it comes to love. The stakes are too high.

Carol nods. For once, she hasn't got a snappy comeback. *Your theory about the three great women. Was Beth one of them?*

Sort of.

What do you mean?

I thought she was the third great woman a lot of the time

we were married. But when you stay with someone that long, you start to strip away their layers. You find out what they're really made of. I thought at the time that Beth was one of the great women, but now I think she wasn't. I expect Kelly and Natasha wouldn't have stayed great women if I'd married them. Life corrodes everything. You don't know what people are like until life puts you to the test. Always, there are tests. Then, in a moment, all the things that you thought were true about someone are wiped out. A moment of decision, a moment that requires courage, or dignity or even self-sacrifice. Beth isn't who I thought she was. Not that she was lousy to get married to, but she was really, really lousy to get divorced from.

I liked Beth.

You know, Carol, I want to tell you something. Something important.

What, Spike?

I'm utterly pissed.

I thought you were going to say something profound for a moment there.

I was. Oh. What was it? Yes. When I started dating women . . . I used to think women were good. I used to think they were **better** than me. People to look up to, almost.

Women have changed. 'Being good' was just code for 'being exploited'.

Maybe they've changed. Or maybe they've just come out of the closet. Either way, where are we now? All in the swill together.

Carol laughs, a big fruity laugh. She toys with her vodka glass. *Am I one of the three great women, Danny?*

I shake my head, pick at a dollop of sour cream on the

257

side of my blinis. *You have to sleep with them to qualify. That's when the wrapping comes off, see?*

So all you've ever seen is my wrapping?

Outstandingly choice wrapping it is too. What happened with you and that married ponce by the way? Howard, or whatever his name was.

He was a lying, duplicitous, scheming bastard.

Sounds familiar. I bet you love him for it, though.

Carol looks thoughtful. *I don't, actually. I think I'm finally waking up to the fact that unpleasant men are really what they appear to be. Unpleasant. They're not waiting for some woman to come and save them, change them, reform and redeem them. They're just wankers. Full-time. Unredeemable. I'm not interested in Howard any more. I'm not interested in any of the Howards out there any more. They can all get stuffed.*

Good for you, Belly-flopper.

I'm going to find myself a good man. A man like you, Danny.

She looks at me. Is this a come-on? After all these years? After our relationship has been codified and concretized into what it is?

There's no such thing. No good men, and no good women. Just people doing what they must.

People can surprise you.

They certainly can.

By the time we make it back to my flat, I'm convinced. I worked my way down to strawberry on the vodka menu, so perhaps I'm not thinking straight. I'm certainly not *walking* straight. Carol has to support me. It's the way she holds my arm, the way she keeps her face pressed close to mine. Some-

258

thing's happened. More than thirty years of resisting my charms has proved too much for her.

I still feel sick with sadness at the decree absolute, but the vodka and Carol have taken the edge off. She's laughing as she propels me up the stairs. Christ, what a great woman! Why *shouldn't* we sleep together? It's only natural. Amazing that it hasn't happened before. She looks good tonight. *I was jealous. Frogs can turn into princes.* She wants me. And why not? We're both alone, we both like one another, both *love* one another. The most natural thing in the world.

She's cautious, obviously. She needs a little help, a little encouragement. She needs me to show her what she wants. *People say no when they mean yes.* We've both been saying no all these years. But what we mean is yes.

God, I'm lonely. Lonely and sick. Ten years together, fallen to dust.

Come on, Spike. Up those stairs, you reprobate.
Want a coffee?
*I'd better make **you** one.*

She's coming up for a coffee. That *confirms* it. I need someone to hold tonight. But what will it do to our friendship? I'm too far gone to *care* about our friendship.

Carol drags me on to the sofa. I flop back on the cushion. The room is spinning. Carol tries to pull me upright so that she can feed me a cup of coffee. I gather myself, raise my back towards her. She has her hand at the back of my neck, and she's slightly off-balance.

She held my gaze at the paddling-pool. Her skirt rode up her thighs. She loves Poppy. She loves me. A frog can turn into a prince.

Suddenly, I have my hands round the back of her head and I'm pulling her towards me. Before she has a chance to resist, my lips are against hers, my tongue seeking a space. In my drunken, desolate mind, the logic seems perfect, the signs are clear.

Carol pulls back. She tries to laugh it off. *Come on, Spiky. What are you doing, you drunken nutter?*

I pull her down. This time she loses her balance and falls on top of me. For a moment her weight is full on me, her breasts on my chest. I put my arms around her back, start kissing her neck.

Now Carol isn't laughing. *Spike! What are you . . . No!*

You have to show them what they want. You have to let them slip responsibility. I run my fingers up the inside of her thigh. I want to find what I found with Sharon Smith. That portal. In a moment, my finger has found the gap between her knickers and her inner thigh. She pulls back, but I hold her tight with my other arm. Then, suddenly, I feel Carol's other arm reaching over my head, and I feel it brush my hair and I know she is letting go, she is finding out that she wants what she didn't even know she wanted.

Then I feel boiling liquid, down my shirt, my face, my trousers. The coffee is all over me – scalding. I am yelling: *What the fuck did you do that for?*

Seizing her chance, Carol jumps off the sofa, as I stand there drenched. She is shaking, pale. *You IDIOT, Danny. You stupid, pathetic . . . What did you . . .*

I stare up at her, a chill working its way to my heart. My head is clearing and I recognize the awfulness of what I have done. *Carol. I'm sorry. I didn't mean to . . . you know. I thought you . . . Don't be angry.*

She's crying now, and grabbing for her coat. *Carol, I'll call you a cab. I'm so sorry. It was a stupid . . . Don't hate me*. But I'm talking to her back. She's walking towards the door.

She's gone. Gone to join Beth, and Alice, and Martin, in the house of nowhere.

11

People can surprise you. Not when there's pain and
need and the dog-fight that is human mating they can't. Not
when there's loss and anger, pride and revenge. Even I don't
surprise me. It was horribly predictable that I would do
something so fucking idiotic. Why? Because I'm a fucking
idiot – and that's what they do.

I've blown it all. All my attempts to heal my life have
come to this. I've lost my marriage, Martin, Alice, and now
Carol. What more destructive force is there in this universe
than the search for love? The earth is scorched.

It's a week since I made my ludicrous, doomed pass at
Carol. My date-rape, my date-grope, my single act of
carnality in over thirty years of knowing her, and it's
enough to smash our friendship to pieces.

I've called her repeatedly. The answering-machine every
time. It's a grey day, and my tiny flat is cramped and untidy.
A free Smurf from McDonald's is wedged between the sofa
cushions. I drag a razor across my face, cutting myself in
three places, then make a cup of coffee, put on Radio Four

and stare out of the window. I've got work to do on the krusha Bar™ campaign today. I've got maintenance to pay, recompense to make for sins deep and numberless.

I stare out of the window until I hear the mail arrive. I'm a great window-starer. Staring at nothing – a fence, a bird, a piece of sky – my mind as blank as air. Then sometimes the knowledge that it's all pointless, all meaningless hits me, and I rush to make myself busy to blot out the truth. But today all I have is a melancholy calm.

I rouse myself, still in my dressing-gown, and make my way to the doormat. One letter. At least it doesn't appear to be a bill. I pick it up and inspect it. My heart sinks. I've been hoping for a letter from Carol, but it's from Beth.

Beth only sends me letters (1) when she wants something and (2) when what she wants is so outrageous that she doesn't want to be around me when I find out what it is.

I toy with the idea of sending it back unopened, but curiosity, I know, will get the better of me. I feel particularly piqued because we're divorced now, for fuck's sake. Why can't she just leave me *alone*? Is this going to go on for ever? Am I going to be haunted and mugged like this for the rest of my life?

I take another slug of the coffee, put it on the cluttered table where the remnants of last night's chill-cook meal lie. My bedsit is a mess. Indifference to life produces only chaos.

Slowly, reluctantly, I tear open the letter. I can see at once that it is much longer than usual. As a rule, letters are short, angry and to the point: little paper daggers. I take a deep breath, brace myself, and start to read.

Dear Danny,

A few days ago I received our decree absolute through the post. I suppose you must have had the same by now. I don't know what it did to you. Delighted, I expect. I suppose you hate me nowdays.

Beth's always had a bit of trouble with spelling – dyslexic she claims. I mentally insert the *a* in 'nowadays' – habit from when I used to proof-read.

I've hated you too, Danny, over the last – oh, I don't know how long. Since all this blew up. But I just wanted to say that when that letter came through the post, it was one of the saddest days of my life.

Oh, Danny, what happened to us? We have a daughter, Danny. We loved each other, Danny. And now we can't even speak to each other, now we can't even be in the same room as each other. It's all so insayne.

I pick up a pencil, put a little mark through the y in 'insayne'.

The other day when you accidentally called me darling, when you were picking up Poppy – after I closed the door I just burst into tears. I cried for – I don't know how long. An hour. All you saw was my smile. Perhaps that is the secret behind the failure of everything.

I don't know how to show you who I am.

I know you think I'm a bitch, and I suppose I have been sometimes, because I've just been so hurt. You didn't want me any more – or, anyway, you weren't prepared to keep on fighting for our marriage any more. I know it wasn't working out very well, and I have to take some of the blame for that. I wish I could go back and . . .

But I can't, can I? We can't. We had ten year's together,
Danny. It's a big piece of someone's life. We have a
daughter. Oh, I've said that already, havent I?

I cross a pencil through the apostrophe in 'year's' and insert
one in 'havent'.

I don't know. Don't know anything any more. How does
life do this to people? How do things get so twisted up? I
don't wish you any harm. For God sake, your my husband!

I put down the pencil now, let the mistakes stand.

Sorry, your not are you? Not any more. It's going to take a
bit of getting used to. You made me happy sometimes,
Danny. You remember that holiday we had in Devon? When
Poppy took her first steps? I'll never forget.

My tears are falling on the page now in large, uneven
drops, smudging the ink. Page one is finished. I turn to page
two.

I don't know what I'm going to do any more. I know you
think I've tried to use Poppy against you, but I would never
never never never try and keep her away from you Danny. I
would never do that. She loves you so much. She misses you
so much.

I want to say sorry, sorry for everything. I don't know
what I did, I don't know what you did. But I'm sorry. For
the bit that was my fault, whatever that bit was, I'm sorry.
I'm crap sometimes, I know. But I tried, really I tried.

It's so hard being a single mum, you know, Danny. I
know you think I've just gone after the money, but the
money doesn't matter to me, it really doesn't, it's just that
I'm scared, and I'm angry, and now it's all over and I'm not

angry any more I'm just scared and sad and wondering what's happened. I'd give the money back if we could just be a family again. I'd put the money on a bonfire if I thought it would mean that Poppy could wake up every morning and see her mummy and daddy together again.

But she never will, will she, Danny? I guess we just messed up too much.

OK, well, I'm going on a bit now I suppose. I just want you to know that, well, I don't suppose that maybe one day we can be friends can we? It would mean so much to Poppy. And to me Danny. But maybe it's all gone too far.

Whatever happens, please believe this. I know how hard you want to be good, I know how much it matters to you, although I think you'll never feel good enough to please your mother, and anyway I'm not your mother and that's one of the ways it all went wrong. But I don't want to get into that now, what I want to say is that you are a good man. I wish you well Danny and I truly, truly hope you'll find happiness somewhere. I miss you. I miss us.

Goodbye, Pookie. I guess I can't call you that any more, can I, but just this last time doesn't matter really. Take care of Poppy when you're with her. Love her like only her father can.

That's it.

Your (ex) wife.

Beth

People can surprise you.

I sit there, turn the letter over and over in my hand and consider this proposition: maybe she really was one of the three great women, after all.

*

266

I met Beth two years after splitting up with Natasha Bliss, when I was in my early thirties. Something had happened when I hit thirty: I don't know if it was the thickening waist-line, the receding hairline, a progressive sense of panic because all my friends were getting hitched and I was still on my own, but things between me and women were on the downslide.

After I'd split up with Helen, I'd felt sad, but there was another world, a world of casual sex and conquest, parties and drugs.

But by this point in my life two important things were drying up. First, the supply of women. The hard fact of relationships is that if you haven't got yourself sorted by your early thirties most of the best women have been taken. The occasional young one might want a father figure, but have you ever been out with someone who's ten years younger than you when you're, say, thirty-one? I have. Think of the most boring thing you've ever done, and double it, then extend it over a whole evening in a pub or at a club. There's nothing *there*. They're blank, unleavened. They talk about school like it was yesterday – and it was! There might be some interesting sexual experiences to be had at the end of the (interminable) evening, but they will be of the most perfunctory and unsatisfying variety imaginable, whatever enthusiasm and technical skill goes into it. You're trying to connect with thin air, and that's OK when you're thin air too, when you're twenty-one, because it's all part of . . . thickening yourself. Of learning how not to be thin air.

The other thing that was faltering, along with the supply of women, was desire. Desire in the sense of good, positive desire, desire fuelled by myth, the myth that a relationship can make everything all right, can complete your world and heal your wound. This myth is crucial.

When you have to live in a world in which all the myths have been punctured, when you realize that all that's out there is life itself, neutral, unvarnished, imperfect, random, blissless, blissful, pain-edged, then something of your energy in pursuing certain goals evaporates. More and more positive pursuit of joy is replaced by negative flight from solitude – since what the world tells you is going to deliver joy rarely does. Joy, it turns out, is a less active or potent force in the world than misery.

This change in perception shows in you: women can see it and men can see it in women. Suddenly you've had one relationship too many, you want another relationship a little too much. At the same time, simultaneously and paradoxically, you don't really believe in the whole package any more. That shows too.

So. The pond is depleted. Your rod is broken. You've gone off fish anyway.

But you're hungry.

It was in this context that I met Beth who also had a broken fishing-rod, a depleted pool and an empty stomach. In short, we were attracted to each other's damage and we were in a hurry.

This isn't to say that the love we quickly discovered wasn't genuine – at least, it felt genuine on my side. But who can be sure that what they're experiencing isn't illusion, isn't a highly variegated form of wishful thinking? Sometimes people manufacture their emotions because they need them. Born-again Christians manufacture certainty out of nothing. Those who have lost someone they love manufacture a sense of purpose out of nothing – a new campaign, fund-raising, reform. We call into existence those emotions we require.

When I met her she was a nurse. I was at some media party, full of ad executives, journalists and TV hustlers, and I was bored and wanted to go home. I had no interest in these people, and they had no interest in me. I hated advertising, I had decided. I wanted to write, I wanted something real. And I wanted *someone* real.

When I overheard this very tall, slightly overweight blonde woman (blonde again – yes, Terence, I *know*) talking about the day she'd just spent in the intensive-care ward, and how she'd lost a patient, and how she was fed up because she also seemed to spend half of her day wiping old men's behinds when she was a highly qualified medical professional, I immediately took an interest. I sidled – I did, I sidled.

Hello, I said, when I found a gap in the conversation, and she seemed at a sufficiently loose end.

Hello, she said, glancing at me momentarily.

My name's Spike.

Right.

This was clearly going to be hard work. Something, however, made me continue: *What's your name?*

Are you trying to chat me up?

Not yet, no. I'm just asking your name.

Now she let her eyes rest on me a little longer. She took another swig of her drink. *I'm sorry. My name's Bethany. I'm afraid I'm a bit down on men at the moment. I'm on the point of giving up on them altogether, to tell you the truth.*

Hello, Bethany. Oh, we're not so bad. We're like cigarettes. You always go back. Anyway, you apologized. I like that in a woman. Very rare quality.

Well, I didn't really mean it.

269

I know.

Because men are pathetic.

Is that right?

Yes. They don't . . . they're not . . . human.

She said this, not in an angry way but in a disappointed sad way that stopped me in my tracks. She looked as if she was about to burst into tears in front of me, a complete stranger. She finished her drink.

If you're accepting them from non-humans, I'd like to fetch you a drink.

She looked at me with these tired, yet sexy eyes, and I saw a phrase in those eyes, a lament buried in the weariness. I know because the same phrase was in mine, and I suspected she could read mine as well as I could read hers. The phrase was 'Here we go again'. Then she said, *Sure. Why not?*

So she told me her hard-luck story, about what bastards men could be, and I went along with it, because I knew it wasn't in the rules for me to talk about what bastards women could be, and after a while we struck up a working rapport based on the general non-legitimacy of men. I would, of course, disavow most of my opinions later, but since we were in the theatrical stage of our embryonic relationship, the acting and role-playing stage, I was ready to speak my lines. It did the trick.

I found out more about her. She was thirty-two, and had recently been abandoned by her boyfriend for no reason that she could fathom. She was on the rebound, and was cautious and edgy, but was also, I could tell, keenly aware, like me, of having depleted value in the unregulated free market that is urban love. She couldn't face going to another salsa class, she told me. She was sick of Marks & Spencer's meals for one. If I'd been someone else, at a different time of my life, I'd have said she probably told me too much, that she revealed too much need. But I was me, and I was at the same imaginative place in my life as she was. So need was OK with me. Need was valid.

When it came to the end of the evening we exchanged telephone numbers, almost wearily. Both of us were in the later stages of young-adult courting life – searching for sanctuary rather than a ride on the roller-coaster. We'd had enough of hunting in bars, ritualized conversations, 'getting to know' new people. We both wanted it to end. We were perfect for each other. We were the right-enough people at the right-enough time.

We started dating the next week, slept together the time after that, then fell into an accustomed and comfortable groove that had been, as it were, waiting for us. We went on holiday together. We told each other we loved each other, and we meant it, we really meant it, but perhaps that was partly because we were so *ready* to mean it. It was fine, it was lovely, I guess – but there was something perfunctory about it, as if we were filling in the time before I asked her to marry me.

This was what the relationship was about. Fate had it in for us, it was our destiny – I think we both sensed that, and neither of us was prepared to resist. We were both too long in the tooth to fail to register each other's flaws – I could be lazy, distanced, patronizing, she could be bitchy, fickle, anally retentive and obsessive. But we chose to ignore them, dressing up denial as mature tolerance. Disillusioned idealists, we had decided to opt for a practical sort of love.

We *did* fit together well. We shared interests – books, fashion, soft drugs, politics. We were attracted to each other. We rubbed along – we had the average number of arguments about the average number of things, we had the average number of hand-holding moonlit walks on the average number of deserted tropical beaches. We were old enough to understand that love was not the proverbial bowl of cherries.

Perhaps that was the problem. We were both too ready, too grown-up, too clear-eyed to believe in the myth any more. You need to believe in your product before you start counting up its virtues and failings. The brand outranks the product every time.

We moved in together a year after starting to date. We tried for a child almost straight away, but in fact it was a few years before anything happened. When at last she got pregnant, I was happy. She was happy. We were happy. Inasmuch as we believed in happiness. All we really knew was that we weren't hurting like we used to hurt. We had each other, and although we weren't one of the century's great love stories, we rubbed along OK. Our respective friends liked each other. It was enough, especially after Poppy was born.

That was our happiest time although it was also our unhappiest time. Now we had something that transcended our lives, which truly bound us together. Yet the practical, commonsensical, fatalistic approach we had taken, which had always worked, began to come unstuck. It was as if bringing something this special into the world *deserved* more passion, more blind love between its parents – or, at least, that was how I saw it. We had taken the biggest step a couple could take, and I was fine with it. But only fine. Fine wasn't enough.

Two other things happened that, looking back on it, sowed the seeds of our future destruction. First, Beth found out that she couldn't have any more children – some problem during Poppy's birth had damaged her uterus, and she was now effectively barren. Our commonsensical arrangement was being unpicked by the God that didn't exist: we had both wanted at least three children, and that mutual desire was one of the things keeping our marriage afloat.

The grief and bitterness that Beth felt at her inability to have more children started to impinge on her thinking. She blamed me, because she needed to blame someone. It's female, the proposition that disaster calls for a sinner. It's religious – the product of the metaphoric mind.

Beth became obsessed with Poppy, pouring not only her love but, dangerously, her hopes, dreams and ambitions into her, fantasizing that she might become a ballerina, a great concert pianist, a poet.

This drove a wedge between us, because I felt that what Poppy chose to be was *her* business. I disliked the idea of parents projecting too powerfully their wishes and needs on to their children, using them as puppets, a dumb-show for their frustrated desires. But Beth was determined.

Which made my decision to give up advertising peculiarly significant. For Beth, if Poppy was going to be the great Renaissance woman of the twenty-first century, we needed money. Beth had already given up nursing, tired of the oceans of bodily waste. She'd decided she wanted to work in public relations, because it sounded good and she'd heard it paid good money. She was only kept back from this ambition, she decided, by having to look after Poppy all the time.

When she managed to snatch some time away from motherhood, Beth worked at Miranda Green's PR company, MG Media. I last saw Miranda in the back garden of the house, blandly watching her son, Caleb, torture worms. Beth made phone calls, licked stamps and filed files. This kept her illusions alive – that she was more than 'just' a mother. Paid work, Beth had come to believe, made a person's life meaningful.

At the same time, I was reaching the opposite conclusion. I was in the process of deciding that work was a Trojan horse, full not of warriors but of emptiness. That the whole nineties idea (our marriage occupied most of the 1990s) that the way to Valhalla was through how many hours you could put in at the office, or how much income you could generate, was a con, another illusion in a life that was a parade of competing illusions. Life was life: not work, or your 'relationship', or your struggle. Life was only what it was.

So I decided I was going to abandon the nine-to-five, Freddy's Fifteen Fruit Flavours and Yogi's Yoghurt Fizz, and instead of writing clichés, I would live one. Like many in advertising before me, I was going to write the great existential novel. I was going to abandon pseudo-creativity for the real thing. For art.

This would mean we would have to move to a smaller house, cut corners, and even stint on some of Poppy's precious school fund.

Two years of the hell that is writing a novel ensued. I never had a *clue*, how difficult it would be. I thought you just sat down, waited for inspiration, then wrote. It would be fun, and fulfilling, and at the end of it, you would have something immortal and someone would buy it, and if it didn't sell many copies it didn't matter. You had expressed yourself. You had done your bit. You had paid your talent a bit more respect than writing cheery jingles and constructing breezy strap-lines for pointless products all day long.

It wasn't like that. Number one: money worries. Number two: relationship problems. Try telling your wife, who's at the end of her tether with your infant child, that you need the space to be left alone and possibly just stare out of the window – for, believe it or not, and partners never *do* believe it, an essential part of writing is just loafing about doing what looks like nothing.

Number three: writing is a nightmare. You sit at your word-processor writing words that mean nothing to you, that stare back at you with no ring of truth, no wit, no life, no nothing, and without even much hope of publication, while your child is crying, and your wife is sick to death of it, and you think you're probably hopeless anyway. It stinks.

But I did it. I wrote *The Sandstone Ghost*, 400 pp, 110,000 words, a tragedy in the Greek style about a man who is swept away by the winds of fate, who is not up to the demands made of him. It's set in a fast-food outlet in Dalston and it's post-modern, witty and knowing (lots of not very omniscient narrators, lots of plots within plots, characters announcing themselves as characters, blind alleys and red herrings) but finally it was about irresistible fate. After two years, I proudly printed it out, and even more proudly gave it to Beth. She read it that same day. You know what she said? She said, *I thought it wasn't meant to be autobiographical*.

That was just about all I got out of her on the subject. I still don't know what she meant. It *isn't* autobiographical. It's about a man who pushes Pukka Pies and gets drawn into a doomed bank heist. It's about identity and meaning and the search for truth. It's about failure and the limits of life. It's not about *me*.

Bloody Philistine.

Beth's critical assessment of my book, such as it was, did not do much to help our marriage either, particularly since it seemed to fare no better with the thirty or so publishers and agents to whom I posted it. Every one of those rejection slips was a piece of shrapnel in the heart. I wasn't the sort of person who was going to keep writing novels that nobody liked or wanted. I'd had my go at Art, and that was that. Nobody would go near *The Sandstone Ghost*. It's still in my bottom drawer, where it will doubtless stay.

I went back to work at the agency and the money started coming in again, but it wasn't the same. Beth and I were now both living with punctured dreams – for me the book, for her the big family, for both of us the relationship – and that was like trying to run the London Marathon with a punctured lung.

I knew the game was up when we started having arguments over my dreams.

Towards the end I had the same dream again and again – or, rather, slightly different dreams with a connecting theme. They always featured buildings of some sort – buildings that were apparently small, with cramped rooms and tiny corridors. Sometimes my old girlfriends would live in them, in inaccessible basements and crannies. But I could never quite find them, only hear their voices. Beth rarely featured. The girlfriends came and went, or were absent. The buildings changed location and shape. Yet all the dreams had one thing in common. At some point, I would discover that the buildings were much bigger than I had previously realized. I would come through a familiar door, and suddenly see that the house I was living in, which I had lived in for years, had a whole section that I hadn't found before. Parts of it were full of light and air, with great vaulted roofs, and huge open spaces and my heart would fill with light and hope.

After I'd had this dream two or three times, I made the mistake of telling Beth. She looked at me with fury in her eyes. *It's only a dream*, I said.

Beth knew better. She withdrew further into herself, and my dreams multiplied in frequency and intensity. She knew what the house represented. She knew what the spaces I longed for would cost us both.

What is more sour, what stinks worse, what is in more bad faith than a marriage in decline? I don't really want to record it all because declining marriages are boring – they're similar to what Terence would call a 'stuck state'. They're just a series of set, monotonous patterns out of which no one can break, because there's too much invested in the rigidity. Every argument is the same argument reinflected, every dispute is drawn from the same stagnant pool. Neither of you believes in the marriage enough any more to put in the effort needed for any kind of progress, change or resolution. Both of you have been too disappointed too often to have that kind of faith.

What's left is just a practical arrangement, a series of well-rehearsed moves, both in bed and in the house, in which you decide that the person you're with is the only person in the world safe enough to unload your pain and disappointment on. You can't unload those things on to your friends, because your friends would dump you. You can't unload them on to your child, because she's your child. That left her and me to use each other as punch-bags.

It was an impossible situation. You've never experienced pain, you've never known anger until you've been in a marriage break-up where there's a child involved. The regret, the guilt, the anger, the blame, the fear. When the only dreams you have left are those of hidden spaces in dark buildings, the end is upon you. After my book failed, after her womb failed, we failed.

I moved out; Beth called her lawyer. Then the trouble really started.

I've been expecting to hear from Carol for a long time. Now an envelope has arrived, but it contains no letter, not even a note. I hold the contents in my hand – a piece of cheap jewellery. I turn it over and over between my fingers.

What's that, Daddy?
Just a toy. From long ago.
Let me see. I want to see.

I hand her the tiny golden heart, still untarnished, set in the 'broken' position. Hard to believe that Carol kept it all these years, since I gave it to her on the night of Sharon Smith's party, more than thirty years ago. No need for a note.

You can't start over. No second chances.

It's nice. Can I have it?
Of course you can. It's a present from Auntie Carol.
When are we going to see her again?
I don't know, poppet. She's gone away for a while.
I love Auntie Carol.
Me too.

Poppy pulls the heart open and closed. Then she pins it on to her T-shirt. *Does it look nice?*

Very pretty.
Are you going to wear it?
It's not really for boys.
Unless they're sissies.

278

That's right. Boys don't have broken hearts.

Are they better, then? Because a bit of them isn't broke? Because I think girls are better.

Do you, sweetheart? Why?

Because everybody says so.

Well, everybody may be right.

Do you really think so, Daddy?

No. Maybe. I don't know.

Tell me.

I can't.

Tell me. Who's the best?

Shall I tell you a secret about grown-ups?

I like secrets.

You might not like this one.

What is it?

We don't know what we're doing. We don't know where we're going. And we don't know what we think.

Daddy, are you ever going to get another girlfriend?

I don't know, sweet-pea. I'm trying my best not to.

I wish you did have a girlfriend. Are you sad?

I'm not sad really, popsicle. I'm just . . . fallow.

What's that?

It's when a field grows lots of things one time, and it's fertile, and then it gets exhausted and you have to let it rest for a while until it can grow things again.

How long does it last?

I don't know. Maybe I'm not fallow. Maybe I'm tundra.

What's tundra?

Frozen. Like in Siberia. Dead. Unthawable.

I don't understand.

Don't worry. I'm sure I'm not tundra. I'm fallow, all right. You'll see. There'll be green shoots one day.

279

But are you going to get a girlfriend? Are you?
I don't know.
Are you going to marry Mummy again?
No, darling. No, I'm not.
Ohhh. What about Auntie Carol?
No.

Poppy sighs. She seems disappointed but not distraught by this revelation. The waters close over everything so quickly when you're a child. For adults, the recent past is so much more persistent. The powers of recovery decay.

Poppy takes a lollipop out of her pocket and begins thoughtfully to suck it. *What happened to Alice?*
I don't know.
Can we go and see her?
No.
Why can't we?
Because she's gone away.
To the same place as Auntie Carol?
Sort of. Yes.

A year has passed now since Alice went back to Martin. She sent me a letter once: I returned it unopened. I've learned that much at least. The one Love Secret that still holds true. Be ruthless at the end. The weak torture the weak.

I've never found myself in this state of mind before – having given up completely . . . in, I think, a good way. I've always invested too much hope in relationships. It's one of the reasons Martin always said I was too much like a woman. But I don't want it any more. I'm beyond it. There's Poppy and me and work, and that's enough. I don't want the struggle any more. It's not worth the prize. It is for some people, I know, but not for me. I'm not cut out for it. Love, for me, is not just more pain than it's worth – it's *far* more pain, it's an utterly unbalanced equation, a lousy over-investment for an imaginary return.

I see Poppy more often now that Beth's been made a partner in Miranda Green's PR firm. I have her for four or five nights a fortnight, and she's everything to me, the last arena in which I still have feelings that operate.

I've put my bedsit on the market. By working every hour that God sends I've been able to raise enough money to buy a two-bedroom flat, so there'll be enough room for Poppy when she comes round. Beth and I have stopped fighting. Nothing to fight about any more, I suppose. Also, her letter changed me, changed the shape of the past once again. Words are so powerful. We should learn to use the right ones more often. She and Oliver are getting along well. He's a lovely guy. I wish her well. I wish him well. I wish everybody well.

God, I'm such a nice guy. Except that I'm a nightmare, and I tried to grope Carol and I ripped off Martin's ex, and I dropped a condom on Juliet Fry's lap, and I told an eight-year-old boy to fuck off, and informed my infant daughter that I hated her. Of course I'm a nightmare, otherwise my life wouldn't be such a disaster. But I'm not sure, other than those few isolated specifics, *how* I'm a nightmare. What links it all together? What's the *subtext*?

If I could work out what it was, I could solve this thing. I could get another life. Then again, I'm not sure I want one. There's something comforting about being fallow. Or, if it's Siberia, if it's really tundra, that's fine too. I don't want women any more. I haven't got enough left to give. I can't go over the top one more time. Call it war psychosis, call it shell-shock, whatever you want, but I'm on permanent furlough. I'm going to be an eccentric, solitary old bachelor. It's enough. No pain any more. Nothing much, except for the ring of Poppy's laugh and the feel of her arms round my neck. I've lost all feeling, which means, at least, that I'm not angry any more. It takes too much energy out of you. I'm fallow. I'm a fallow fellow.

Today I've got a presentation to make to Probe, Willis and Cooper, Britain's leading manufacturer of plastic dish-towel holders. I've got a good chance of clinching it. See, it starts with this fumbling, incompetent man trying to get a dishtowel into the dishtowel holder and . . . You get the gist. I may not be able to write the great existential post-modern novel, I may not be able to maintain a functional relation-ship with a woman but I can still write a trite, meaningless, superficially attractive, misandrist catchline. No one can say my life has been in vain.

I check my watch. Late. I grab my folder, rush out of the front door and begin the three-hundred-yard sprint to the tube station. I'm nearly there when I see her. Her hair is shorter, she looks paler, and I am not at all sure it is her at first, because it's too downright improbable. She doesn't even live in London any more, from what I've heard. Why would she happen to be walking down my street? In the direction of my bedsit, too.

My determination to breeze past her without a glance or a word is undermined by the fact that, at that exact moment, with my eyes fixed straight ahead, I trip over a carelessly discarded 1.5-litre bottle of G-Wiz, fall flat on my face and send my folder flying into the gutter, where it opens and scat-ters the papers for my presentation into the road.

Furious, bewildered, and with what smells like cat-shit on my lapel, I pick myself up, grab the folder and stuff what paper I can find back into it. She bends down and retrieves a crucial document. She holds it out to me. I snatch it from her without a word, put it away, then fumble with the zip of the folder so I can be on my way.

Hello, Spike.

I take a step towards the tube station. She moves across the pavement to block my path.

Don't go, Danny. Give me a chance to say what I've got to say.

I pause, stand there on that street corner. *I'm late for an important meeting.*

I've left Martin.

Is that so? I think I'm going to faint with surprise.

I left him two months ago. Ever since, I've been trying to pluck up courage to . . . do this.

That's very touching. Can I go to my meeting now?

Inside, two feelings are competing. First *fury*: for what she did to me, to Poppy, to us. *Fury* at her sheer arrogance in daring to show herself to me again. The other feeling is equally strong – but I can't identify it. Whatever it is, it's making my heart hammer. Maybe that's a by-product of the fury. I turn back towards the somehow much safer emotion and try to push past her, but she grabs my sleeve. I shake off her hand, and walk away from her. She follows, talking quickly but clearly. People stare at us as we walk past, her in my wake, me trying to accelerate without the indignity of running.

*Danny, I know I messed up. You were right. Martin only wanted me because you had me. I mean, he **did** love me only not in the right way. But I'd loved him for so long, and I'd wanted him for so long. I'd only been out of the relationship with him a couple of months, just like you'd only been out*

of your marriage . . . well, not long enough. I didn't understand what was happening. It was so fast. I was torn. I
didn't know what to do.

Why are you telling me this?

I'm still walking. I can't bring myself to look back at
her.

*I just thought . . . maybe . . . what we had . . . it might
have been good. This Martin thing – it's out of my system
now.*

*Out of your system? That's great. Terrific. Goody goody
gumdrops from the gumdrop tree.*

I risk a glance at her. She's trembling, seems smaller than
I remember her.

*I just . . . I know I should say sorry for what I've done,
and I am, I'm dreadfully sorry for causing you such pain.
But it hurt me too. I missed you so much. And I **had** to do it.
I **had** to live it out, to know that it wouldn't work, before I
could be free. Now I have. I have lived it out.*

I stop, turn, regard her coolly. *I apologize for repeating
myself, but why are you telling me this?*

Now she stares at the ground. Her voice is quiet. I have to
strain to hear.

*I just thought there might be a chance that we could give
it another go.*

*What? Until Martin whistles for you again, you mean?
Trying to make him jealous again, are you?*

Alice doesn't say anything, just stares at the pavement.

*I hope you're not going to have the gall to tell me that
you love me.*

*No. No, I'm not. I don't know, Danny. I don't know
what I feel. But I know what I felt when we were together.
And it was real, and it was something. For all that's gone*

before – maybe there's a chance. Maybe it's worth a try. If you haven't killed your feelings for me completely.

I've still got feelings for you, Alice. Of course I have.

She looks up at me, a look of surprise, of hope in her eyes. *Have you?*

Yes, I have. First, contempt. Second, disdain. Third, anger. Fourth, complete indifference. Fifth, contempt. Oh, I've said that before, haven't I? Sixth, amazement that you've got the sheer fucking nerve even to show me your face.

Now her eyes flash defiance. *Don't lay all the blame on me, Danny. It was you who slept with your best friend's girl-friend.*

Ex-girlfriend.

That doesn't stop it being a shitty thing to do.

Well, I guess we're equal, then.

Alice sighs. *What do you want to do, then?* she asks, sadly.

What do I want to do? I want to tell you in the plainest, most unequivocal terms to fuck off and die.

There are only two Love Secrets that have turned out to be true. Don't Trust Them. And: Be Ruthless. These are all I have to cling to, the last truths I have left, my final defences in the face of an incomprehensible, hostile life. I *have* to stand by them. What I need to do now is walk proudly away into the sunset, my dignity intact, my pride shining, leaving me with a fantasy of Alice as a reduced, regretful wreck.

Only I am unable to move. Meanwhile, Alice just stands there, seemingly having run out of things to say. *Perhaps we could go and have a cup of coffee?* she says, in a slightly more confident voice.

I don't see the point.

I've come all the way from Brighton. Couldn't you just spare me a few minutes to talk it through?

There's nothing to talk about.

But if there's nothing to talk about, why am I still talking? A cab approaches with its yellow light shining. All I have to do is put up my hand. There's no way back for us now – not after what she did to me, what she did to Poppy, what I did to Martin, what Martin did to me. Too much damage. Too much history. The weak torture the weak. It's another disaster waiting to happen.

Do you still love me, Danny?

Don't you dare. Don't you fucking dare.

But do you? Do you still love me?

You haven't got the right to ask that.

Just tell me you don't, Danny, and I'll go away and never bother you again. Truly I will. Just say the words.

A bus goes past, pumping out fumes. The taxi drives past, unhailed. The taste of lead in my mouth. A child pushes past on one of those new metal scooters, whooping with joy. For some reason I notice the sky. Changing, shifting, re-forming itself every second of every day.

Of course I love you, Alice. When you truly love someone, you never stop loving them, not in your whole life. The truth is, I still love Kelly, still wake at two a.m. with a dream of her gentle face fading inside the darkened room. I still love Natasha Bliss, although I could never show her I did at the time. And I still love Beth, still see her face when I look at the pillow on the bed. And I still love Alice, and I always will, whatever happens. The four great women. That movie was wrong about there only being three. Maybe the writer wasn't old enough to know.

I still love her. Worse luck. Because it's stupid, and

shallow and immature, and guilty of the worst kind of wishful thinking. Because it goes against the only remaining truths in this life that I know for sure. Because my belief in the myth is dead, and yet here I am saying, slowly, regretfully, as if delivering bad news to a distant relative, *I don't see any harm in a cup of coffee, I suppose.*

That afternoon, I'm ashamed to admit, we ended up in bed. Then cautiously, tentatively, incredibly, given what had gone before, we began picking up where we had left off. Over the following days and weeks we somehow kept it together. You could even say that we edged our way towards a place from which we could move forward.

It was all kid gloves at first, all circling round each other. The anger, resentment and scepticism that I undeniably felt pressed and bothered at every weak spot when we were together. At first Alice was scrupulously apologetic, then, deciding that she couldn't spend the rest of her life being sorry, eventually became defiant.

Why do you never bring Poppy round when I'm here?
You must be joking. So she can be hurt all over again?
We've been with each other two months now.
I don't trust you. How can you expect me to trust you?
You have to trust me. There isn't any choice. Even though I don't know how it's going to turn out. Even though I can't make you any promises. You have to trust me.
I don't think that Poppy would understand the sophistication of that particular thought.
I think Poppy has a right to know what's going on in your life.
I don't want you anywhere near her. That's a giant step. To show you to her means you're going to be around. That

you're a fixture. I can't break her heart a third time. Or is it a fourth? I've lost count.

She's going to have to take her chances like everyone else on the planet. You can't carry on like this.

No. You messed up my life. No.

Long pause. I feel the knot of anger in my throat tighten. In order to calm down, I go to the bathroom, wash my face. When I come out, Alice is holding a wad of A4 paper. I recognize the coffee stain on the first page. *Please put that back where you found it.*

The Sandstone Ghost.

I wouldn't waste your time on it.

I already have.

So there's a few hours of your life you'll never get back. Has this got something to do with the subject currently under discussion? Give it to me, please.

She hands it over.

It's no good, says Alice.

*I **know** it's no good. But, at the risk of repeating myself, what's that got to do with anything?*

I'm still angry, still hurting, still bewildered. I want an argument, not a discussion about my lack of literary talent.

But do you know **why** it's no good?

It's no good because I can't write.

No. You can write very well. It's only no good because it's not true. It's all about what you want people to be, it's all about what you want **you** to be, and what you think you might be. You can definitely write. You just don't know how to be honest.

Thanks for the input. Really. It gives me fresh hope.

You know what I thought when I read this book? You know what I think it should be called?

288

Is there anything I could say that would prevent you telling me?

It should be called The Victim. *Because that's what it's all about. About poor little Danny Savage. About all that you haven't got and all you should have. It's dressed up as some version of a Greek tragedy, but really it's a novel about self-pity. It's about not accepting what life serves you up.*

You haven't got the faintest idea what you're –

I stop. I am suddenly aware that what Alice has said has set off a long-neglected series of connections in my synapses. Electrical impulses pulse. Gears mesh. Keys turn locks. The only sign of this from Alice's point of view apparently is a series of rapid blinks. She says, *Have you got something in your eye?*

I may be self-deluding, I may be vain. However, I've learned the truth about truth – that it's intuitive. That sometimes you just know it when you hear it. I shake my head as if the clarity is like a blow. *I'm not sure what you mean.*

It's all about there being no God, isn't it? No one to sort things out for you.

I look at her. Synapses connect with other synapses. The whole network lights up. **I'm** *the martyr.* **That's** *how I'm a nightmare.*

What?

Never mind. Carry on, carry on.

Where were we?

No God.

That's it. You need to come to terms with something you must have always known.

I know.

Things aren't fair, Danny. You haven't accepted it.

I know.

You haven't accepted randomness. Yes, there's no God.
And there's no Mum and no Dad there to make it all right.
There's no partner who will stand in for your mum and dad
who are in turn standing in for God and making it all right.
We're all on our own. Once you've accepted that, we can
start being together.

You're right.

*So. Do you **forgive** me?*

Long, long pause.

Do I forgive you? Is that what this is about?

That's exactly what this is about. Because whatever I did,
and however rotten it looked to you, it was just the way
things were. I was doing the best I could, I was trying to
survive. I didn't mean to love you, I didn't mean for you to
love me. I just thought we could comfort each other, and
that perhaps if it got Martin back a bit for what he did to
me that would be OK, and if it brought him running back
again, that would be even better. Only of course it wasn't
because you were right, because it was never going to work
between him and me then. Because the improbable
happened, as it does. You and I fell in love. So I screwed up.
Totally. But to tell the truth, in the same circumstances, I'd
do it again. You have to make mistakes, your own special
mistakes. Mistakes are life's roughage. They're good for
you. Loss and folly, they're the only way you learn, the only
way you grow. And no one can save you. Because . . .

Because there's no God.

So you can spend the next Christ only knows how long
hating me for what I did if you want, and I can spend the
next God knows how long apologizing to you for what I
did, and hating you for having to apologize, but that's not
a relationship, that's a . . . that's a . . . mutual crucifixion.

*That's S and M. You have to forgive me, and you have to forgive me even if you think I don't think I did anything wrong. And I **don't**. It was just life, but even without blame life demands forgiveness. The world seizes up without it.*

You're not responsible for anything. That lets you off the hook nicely – doesn't it?

*I'm not being moral – just practical. We have to put it behind us. We **have** to. I have to have the licence occasionally to be an unreasonable bitch without you saying, 'But you did that terrible thing.' And you have to be able to be an insensitive arsehole towards me from time to time without me automatically thinking, He's punishing me again.*

That's a very romantic way of looking at it. So we can be bitches and arseholes.

It's the way it is. Forgive me. Do you forgive me?

*Let me get this straight. You want me to forgive you for something you think you haven't even done **wrong**?*

*Yes. And then I want you to forgive me for **thinking** that I haven't done wrong as well. Then maybe we can move forward.*

I'll think about it.

You should. Because we can't go on like this.

Some weeks later, I enter my flat to see something standing in the middle of the floor that I haven't seen for a long time. My flip-chart. Alice has taken it out of the cupboard I had stored it in. She's left it in the middle of the room and taken Poppy to the swings. Poppy was overjoyed to see her again. She trusts Alice. And, against all the wisdom of my life to date, so do I.

There's a Post-it note on the front of the flip-chart, which says: 'Read me.'

I lift the top flap. All my pages of reflections and analyses and comments and annotations have been erased. In their place, in Alice's small, precise handwriting, are four words: *Nothing can be done.*

The eraser isn't very good. The grey shadows of my ten precious Love Secrets are still just about legible. I followed all the rules, learned every lesson. None of it stopped Alice leaving me for Martin. Then Alice returned – and I, weak, foolish and ridiculous, took her back. As a result of this insane act of folly, I am completely happy.

Nothing can be done. We are helpless. All the words add up to zero. Life is what happened to happen. Some lessons we learn and some we don't, and thinking or not thinking doesn't seem to have much to do with it.

Nothing can be done. In place of beliefs, which are impossible, there is only faith. Although I've had the dream and lost it time and time again, I know I can make it work this time. Because I love Alice. I love her more than any woman I've ever been with. The person I was before she came back to me, washed-out, resigned, cynical, has disintegrated. What is this if not evidence of faith – or blind foolishness? Perhaps they are the same thing.

Nothing can be done. Everything that's real is an illusion. Everything that's true is untrue. Paradox reigns supreme. In this there is hope.

Nothing can be done. I have no insights, only happiness. It came out of nowhere, with no explanations. I did no work for it. I applied no philosophies. It adhered to no rules of justice or karma.

Women didn't put me here. Men didn't put me here. I didn't put me here. I'm just here.

I close the flip-chart, and sit down. *The Sandstone Ghost*

is still sitting on the shelf under the table where Alice left it. I take it out and flick through it, then stare at the flip-chart. I know I'm going to write another book. This time it's going to be a book all about men and women and how they mess up and how they hurt each other as they try to understand each other, and how they blow up their lives to escape them when their lives are all they've got.

It's not going to be like *The Sandstone Ghost* or anything literary or post-modern or existential. None of those things allow for happy endings. But happy endings *do* happen. Call me Robin Williams, if you like, but they do. It's just as real as giving everybody cancer, or having your main character commit suicide in the face of eternal nothingness, which is what happened to the gloomy protagonist in my first book.

Happy endings are real. I'm going to make them happen. Why not? I'm the omniscient narrator, goddamn it. I can do what I like.

There *is* a God. And it's me.

postscript

Helen Palmer is now professor of Women's Studies at Warwick University. She is the author of several books including *The Case for Castration: A Radical Solution to Male Violence*, *Wanting It All, Having It All, Losing It All, Getting It All Back Again* and *The Beauty Virus*. She has been married twice, but is currently 'successfully single'.

Kelly Cornelius is happily married with three children. She has yet to sell a painting, and is shortly to make a shift to conceptual art making use of recycled nappies and vulcanized bottle teats. She lives in a large house in Holland Park with **Hugo Bunce**, who has become a leading adviser to the Blair administration. He visits Anya, a Russian prostitute, in Shepherd's Market once a fortnight.

Natasha Bliss is now the head of her own advertising agency, and features in the *Sunday Times* Rich List.

Beth Collins married **Oliver Ferris** at a register office in Hammersmith. She was recently ousted from the board of MG

Media by Miranda Green, is now training as an independent life-skills consultant.

Poppy Savage has recently achieved her Swimming Proficiency Grade 3 certificate, but has abandoned violin lessons after setting fire to her instrument. Her brand loyalty to McDonald's has switched to Pizza Hut after a free Happy Meal toy was found to be defective. She has developed a mild fear of enclosed cylindrical spaces, which makes flying problematic.

Martin Gilfeather has, for the past three weeks, been dating a seventeen-year-old MTV presenter. Her requests to cohabit are awaiting Martin's decision.

Carol Moon never contacted Danny Savage again.

Iris and Derek Savage have moved from Yiewsley to Watford. They are currently planning a new bathroom.

Terence has lost most of his clients over the last three months as a result of a protracted bout of depression that has rendered him temporarily incapable of speech. He is currently awaiting a bed at St Charles' Hospital mental health facility, North Kensington.

Daniel 'Spike' Savage and **Alice Fairfax** live happily in a terraced house in Hanwell, West London, three streets from where Daniel grew up. Daniel's début novel, *Ten Nightmare Things About Women* (Iron John Press, 266 pp, £6.99) was remaindered after five weeks. He has recently made a successful return to the world of advertising. Alice is due to give birth to their first child in the spring.